"May I see them now?"

Although Joel was asking to see the photographs, Adria knew—as well as he—that he was asking another, more important question. The two of them alone in her cabin would generate an intimacy....

He released her from his embrace, but made no effort to move away from her. His dark hair curled profusely around the face that hovered above hers. His white shirt, tucked into tight-fitting jeans, was unbuttoned part way to reveal a wedge of muscled chest covered in dark hair. If he were wearing a black patch over one eye and a small gold earring in his ear, she would have her pirate, her handsome scoundrel of the silver seas!

"I really want to see the photographs," he said, "and if anything else happens, it will be because both of us want it. Right now, I confess, I want it."

ABOUT THE AUTHOR

Having completed two successful terms as president of Romance Writers of America, Emma Merritt now devotes full time to her career as a novelist of romance fiction. She lives in San Antonio, Texas, with Paul, her husband of twenty-seven years, and her toy poodle, Joubert. She believes love is eternal and is presently working on her next novel.

Books by Emma Merritt

HARLEQUIN AMERICAN ROMANCE

276—WISH UPON A STAR
337—RETURN TO SUMMER

EMMA MERRITT

SILVER SEA

Harlequin Books

TORONTO • NEW YORK • LONDON
AMSTERDAM • PARIS • SYDNEY • HAMBURG
STOCKHOLM • ATHENS • TOKYO • MILAN

To Pat Leonard,
dear friend

Published April 1991

ISBN 0-373-16386-X

SILVER SEA

Chapter One

Standing at the window of her second-story office, Adria Gilby gazed in pride at the salvage yard below. Only hours ago it had been aflurry with activity. Now a lone employee moved through the cargo, cataloging the items of Gilby and Son's latest haul, one of the best the company had had in over a year.

Adria raised the window and called to the man, "How much longer before you're done?"

Ford Lowell finished writing, then looked around the yard at the cargo. He reached up to scratch his temple, knocking askew his sweat-stained baseball cap and giving freedom to several sprigs of thin gray hair. Finally he lifted his head. "Fifteen or thirty minutes, I'd say. If you need to go before then, that's fine with me. I'm gonna stay until I'm through, no matter how long it takes. I don't want this hanging over my head through the weekend."

"I'll be here a while longer myself. I want to finish the entries for the week. Like you, I want a worry-free weekend." *For a change,* she silently added. "Besides, my car is in the shop for a tune-up, and I'm stuck here until Uncle Solly comes to get me."

Lowering the window, Adria brushed her shoulder against a grouping of wall photographs, among them one of an older couple—Solomon and Chesna Smith. Now that Adria's parents and her brother were dead, the Smiths were like family to her. They had been a part of her life ever since she could remember, Uncle Solly working first with her father, John, then with her brother, Danny, and now with her, while Aunt Chessy kept house for the family.

After she straightened the frame, she returned to her desk and stood for a moment looking at the open ledger. She needed a computer—in fact, the company had needed one for a long time—and with what they cleared on this haul and on the next contract, she was going to buy one. But until then, the old-fashioned method of hand-posting would have to do. In another couple of hours she would close the office and enjoy a well-deserved weekend. Easing into her chair, she picked up her pencil and began to work, unconscious of the passage of time until the door opened.

"Thanks for staying late, Ford," she said, never looking up. "I really appreciate it. Give me just a minute to finish here, and I'll check the inventory with you."

"Take your time. I'm in no hurry," an unfamiliar masculine voice drawled, a hint of amusement underlying the lazy words.

Surprised, Adria looked up from her work. She stared at a stranger who lounged in the doorway. Laying her pencil on the ledger, she pushed back in the chair. Her eyes narrowed with speculative and artistic interest, as her gaze quickly but thoroughly swept over his tall, lanky frame.

Bright early evening sunlight spilled into the room, seeming to spotlight the man. Adria couldn't have planned the setting any better if she had tried. Beard stubble shadowed lean cheeks, and black unruly curls teased the collar of his blue windbreaker, beneath which he wore a white T-shirt that stretched tightly across a rather broad chest. And, Adria noticed, his faded jeans fit hips and muscled legs as snugly as the shirt fit his upper torso.

Her hands itched for her camera. She would love to photograph this man. She didn't know what kind of person he was, she really didn't care; but she was interested in him as a model. He exuded a raw sensuality that made for great photography, that made for a winning contest entry, that made for judges awarding merits. Just standing there he seemed to be manly...cool...arrogant. And that was only her initial reaction! If only she could capture all these characteristics on film. For a moment—one short moment—she wondered if, with a photograph of him, she really had a chance of winning a merit in the upcoming competition. She was only two short of being a Master Photographer.

She almost laughed aloud at her thoughts and wondered what the stranger would do if she were to blurt out, *May I take your photograph so I can enter it into a contest?*

Enough of the dreaming! She came back to earth and deliberately lifted her arm to look at her wristwatch. "It's after five. Gilby and Son Salvage is closed for the day...in fact, for the weekend. Why don't you come back on Monday after eight o'clock? We'd be happy to—"

"Since we're both here," he interrupted, "and you haven't locked up, would you be so kind as to hear me out?"

"About what?"

Ignoring her question, the man closed the door and walked farther into the office. He crammed his hands into the pockets of his windbreaker and stopped in the center of the room, his gaze sweeping around until it finally came to rest on Adria. His expression, as well as the gray eyes, was cool and emotionless, reminding her of a polished, keenly sharpened steel blade. The image of an accomplished swordsman quickly leaped to mind. Her eyes swept up and down his physique again, and she shivered at the impact of her thoughts. This man possessed an ability to slice a person through with nothing more than a stare. God forbid anyone should ever be on the wrong side of him.

Adria wasn't frightened of him, but the longer he refused to answer her question the more wary she became. Thoughts of photographs slipped from her mind. The beachfront spawned drifters and bums, and from the look of it, this man could easily fall into that category. With all those other characteristics that only moments ago had made him photogenic, he seemed to exude another which she disliked intensely—irresponsibility. And she'd had enough of that during her lifetime, first from her father, then from her brother.

She stood and said, this time her voice firm and authoritative, "Look, I really do want to finish my posting so I can close up and go home for the weekend. We've had a long, full week, and I'm tired. If you want something, let me know. If not, please leave."

"I'm Joel LeMaster. Diver."

So that was it! She breathed a sigh of relief, but at the same time she thought he didn't seem like the average diver. "We're not looking for a diver. If I'm not mistaken, Corbett's at Southport may need a fill-in, or you could try Hanson Godair down the street."

The man smiled, a slow movement that began in the depths of those steely gray eyes long before it reached his lips. "I just said I was a diver, I didn't ask for a diving job." In no apparent hurry, he ambled toward the window. Rocking back on his heels, he stared into the salvage yard. "Good haul . . . which you needed."

That the man was right did not lessen Adria's growing irritation. Also his reaction was puzzling. If he had not come for a job, why was he here? Now her artistic interest was waning and was replaced by genuine curiosity. She reached up and pushed a stray brown curl out of her face. Turning her head slightly, she felt the long, thick braid as it brushed across her shoulders.

"How would you know what I need, Mr. LeMaster?"

"Talk about town. Small towns are good for that, you know."

She couldn't see his face, but she heard a smugness she didn't appreciate.

Then he asked, "Do you just run the office, or are you a salvor, too?"

This question—no matter who posed it—always irritated Adria. During the past year, since she had taken over the running of the company, she had heard it from every corner—her friends, her competitors, her creditors. Many were of the opinion that being a salvager was dirty business, certainly no job for a woman. So Adria had her stock answer.

"Although it's none of your business, you might say I'm a jack-of-all-trades, and I wear a hat for each." She moved to the side of her desk, affected a casual stance, and crossed her arms over her breasts. "I'm the sole surviving Gilby of Gilby and Son. I own the company, run the office, do the books. I'm janitor, diver and salvor."

Joel LeMaster slowly pivoted, the turn graceful and smooth. He reminded Adria of a sleek cat who had sighted his prey and was coming in for the kill.

"With your wearing so many hats and doing so many jobs—" his courteous tone was at variance with the gleam she saw in the depths of those eyes "—do you ever have time to be a woman?"

Definitely the man's audacity eradicated manners!
When she spoke, her voice was crisp and cutting. "I'm a
woman twenty-four hours a day, three hundred sixty-five
days a year, Mr. LeMaster."

The thick, well-shaped masculine brows hiked, and he
stared at her with such intensity that she suddenly became
aware of her appearance—a blue cotton sweater and worn
jeans. She reached up again, to swat that aggravating curl
from her face. She was not the image of a businesswoman, and right now she hoped she appeared as calm,
cool and collected as the man who stood across the room
from her.

"I don't pretend to be the stereotypical southern lady,"
she said, extending her thoughts into dialogue. "I don't
have time for pretense and affectation, nor do I lay claim
to being a superwoman or business magnate."

He laughed softly and heavy lashes drooped over his
eyes. Adria felt his gaze linger on her breasts before it
flicked over her hips and slowly down her legs. Uncom-
fortably aware of the clinging sweater and tight jeans, she
nevertheless met his insolent challenge with a quiet dignity and presence it had taken her years to perfect. But
beneath that studious gaze—yes, it was studious, certainly not sensuous—her composure strained to the
breaking point.

"Neither of them is my type, but I'm not here to discuss your claim to fame or womanhood. I'm really here
to—" the paused seemed forever "—to find out if I can
interest you in a treasure hunt."

Now the cat was out of the bag! And not your common
variety, either. This was a polecat—a stinking polecat—at
that! Shaking her head, Adria exclaimed unequivocally,
"Absolutely not!"

"How can you answer so quickly? You haven't even
heard my proposal." He moved across the room with a

disturbing quietness and economy of movement that disconcerted Adria. He was tough and lean, quick and agile, and Adria knew that he would be a very difficult adversary.

"No matter what the details, the answer is the same. No."

Dear Lord, her father had almost ruined them with treasure hunts, and her brother, older and wiser in his estimation, hadn't been much better. They had always chased their dreams, hunting for the pot of gold at the end of the rainbow, never considering their family or the debts they incurred.

LeMaster walked over to a cluster of pictures that hung on the wall. "Is this your family?" he asked softly, breaking into her thoughts.

She nodded and looked at a photograph of her father, Danny and herself, the three of them laughing. LeMaster took several steps, moving to another grouping. These were older, the sepia finish faded with age. He reached out to straighten one that was slightly off-balance.

"That's my grandfather," Adria said, then pointed to another. "Next to him is my great-grandfather."

One by one, he gazed at the pictures. Finally he said, "Salvaging is in the family."

Adria walked to the refreshment table, where she unplugged the coffee maker and screwed lids onto the sugar and powdered cream jars. "Commercial cargo salvage, as you must have noticed when you surveyed my yard below."

"Your employee is staying late to finish cataloging the inventory, in case the government agent should possibly come by tomorrow to inspect and stamp the cargo."

"That's right." By sheer willpower, Adria kept herself from gaping at LeMaster. Her frustration growing by leaps and bounds, she crushed some napkins in her fist. Was there anything about her and her business this man did not know? "A cargo that is going to bring us a handsome profit." By Wednesday the latest, she thought, she would have the money in her pocket.

And next week, she reassured herself, she would be able to announce to the men that she had a new salvage contract with the government. *Dear Lord,* she silently prayed, *let it be so.* She'd been over the job with a fine-tooth comb and had cut her bid to the bare minimum. She intended to get that contract; it would not go to her competitors. There was no way Lamar Corbett could underbid her proposal without taking a loss, a heaping big loss, and even Corbett, no matter how much he wanted Gilby and Son, was a businessman first; he wouldn't undercut her at such a tremendous loss. Also it was not the kind of job old Mr. Hanson Godair handled.

She had several bids out for much smaller jobs—jobs that neither Corbett nor Hanson would ever consider bidding for—and they were almost guaranteed. Yes, things were looking up for Gilby and Son. Tonight Adria could go home with a light heart and would be able to enjoy two full carefree days with her camera.

"I understand you and Corbett are bidding against each other," said LeMaster. "What if he gets it?"

"He won't. The contract is as good as mine." Adria threw the wad of napkins into the wastepaper basket.

"Don't you ever get tired of this bread-and-butter, hand-to-hand business?"

Having finished straightening the table, Adria walked over to her desk where she picked up a sheaf of papers and thumped them a little harder than necessary before she dropped them into the top drawer.

"Tired is a mild word to describe how I feel," she said, her gaze moving to the assortment of colored pencils that lay scattered across her desk. "I get damned tired, but you said the words that pretty well sum up my feelings. Cargo salvage is what keeps bread-and-butter from becoming hand-to-mouth." Her gaze moved to her camera on top of the filing cabinet on the far side of the room. Sometimes she was more than tired; she was bitter.

"What if I could promise you caviar and champagne?"

"Never developed a taste for it," came Adria's dry retort, but she did feel a tingle of excitement skitter up her spine. "I was raised on soul food."

"What if I said about five or six hundred million, or more?"

"Caviar?" she asked, quelling the impulse to raise her head and stare at him. Dear Lord, did treasure-hunting addiction run in the family?

"Bucks," he said.

She slowly lifted her head and saw him smile. He enjoyed taunting her. Playing high stakes, she thought, and taking his time about it. She could play, too. After all, she had been groomed for this role from infancy. No one could boast better teachers than she.

"Five to six hundred million bucks." His words, like the serpent that tempted Eve, slithered across the room, to wrap themselves around her, to titillate her curiosity. She only stared.

"Or more." He waited just a tad before he added, "Have you ever heard of the *Golden Fleece?*"

"Jason and the..."

He shook his head. "No, Sir Sidney Billington and the..."

Adria shook her head.

"Well, Ms. Gilby, let's go back to Good Queen Bess of England, say several years before the sailing of the Spanish Armada, and I'll commence with my tale." He settled into the chair in front of Adria's desk, crossed one leg over the other and waved his hand through the air, motioning her toward a chair.

Something about Joel LeMaster compelled her to listen to his story. He was a man of authority, which she liked. It made him even more interesting, and whetted her desire to photograph him. At first she had only envisioned him as a beach bum, but now she was beginning to see unlimited prospects. From the way he spoke, she sensed he was educated. She could see him in a more sophisticated setting, dark-rimmed glasses in hand—an executive, perhaps, or a scholar.

When he motioned a second time for her to sit down, she did. She had nothing to lose by listening. If his story didn't interest her, she could always show him the door. Maybe while he was talking, she could figure out a way to approach him about a photograph.

"Sir Sidney Billington was the nephew of Sir Arthur Greenville," LeMaster said, "one of Elizabeth's advisors—not necessarily one of her favorites, but one of the most influential before the Armada. At Greenville's insistence, Elizabeth finally gave Billington license to sail for the crown as one of her privateers. Immediately uncle and nephew equipped a ship that they intended to christen after the queen, to show her how she had honored them by allowing them to pillage legally in the name of the Crown. Some of the names they played around with were Glorious Bess, Virginia and Virgin Queen. Whatever name Billington decided on, his ship was dubbed the *Golden Fleece*."

"Sidney Billington, a sea dog," Adria murmured. "I don't remember ever having heard about him or the *Golden Fleece*."

"You wouldn't," he explained, "unless you took a detailed course in Elizabethan history, and even then you might not have heard of him. His uncle lived long enough to win fame, glory and disgrace, but Sidney died before winning any of the three. He may yet find a prominent place in the textbooks if his ship is found and excavated."

"How?" Adria asked dryly, evincing no real interest and wondering exactly where this tall tale was going.

"Our newest and youngest sea dog made a daring raid along the coast of Mexico, filling his ship with a two-year backlog of Spanish gold and silver shipments. Enroute home, Billington was intercepted by Sir Alfred Chatworth—whom Elizabeth had sent to summon her privateers in preparation for the Armada. Chatworth recorded that he and his officers dined that evening aboard Billington's flagship."

When LeMaster paused and looked at her as if he were waiting for an inevitable response, she didn't disappoint him. Pretending a nonchalance and disinterest contrary to her true feelings, she said, "I believe the script calls for me to say, 'So the plot thickens.'"

"Right on cue." LeMaster nodded. "Chatworth was quite impressed with the exploits the young privateer professed. With relish, Chatworth recounted Billington's tale of daring plunder along the coast of New Spain. He described the treasure that Billington showed him, and recorded that Billington's *ships* were fine vessels, heavily laden with Spanish gold and silver. They were indeed the *Golden Fleece* of Britannia and were rightly christened after the queen." Again he paused and stared at her before saying, "Notice Chatworth said ships, not ship."

"How many?" Adria asked, this time her question prompted by interest.

"At least three. I don't know how many more. The records are scant at most, and the nation was in too much turmoil awaiting the imminent attack by the Spaniards to be interested in whether Billington—a virtual unknown—sailed with one or two ships, and Chatworth assumed everyone would know. If we are to believe the value of the cargo Chatworth recorded, Billington had on board his ships treasure assessed at eight or nine hundred million dollars in today's currency. On his flagship alone was reputed to be about five hundred million. Probably the rest was evenly divided between the other two ships."

The figures LeMaster quoted caught Adria's attention and set her imagination afire. In a matter of seconds she had spent a couple of million and could have spent more. "I assume *Golden Fleece* then, was the name of the fleet and not Billington's flagship?" When he nodded, she asked, "Have you learned the name of the flagship?"

"I believe it was the *Glorious Bess*."

Adria pushed back in the chair and studied the man who was staring so intently at her face. She saw the pleading in the depths of those gray eyes and had a momentary and idiotic compulsion to tell him she would go with him, but she couldn't. Her father and Danny had both been dreamers, both touched with wanderlust; all their lives they had chased the illusive dream. If they hadn't, she wouldn't be sitting here listening to this stranger spin tales of riches while she worried about getting *one measly* government contract. Her whole world wouldn't be measured in dollars and cents, wondering where the next—either dollar or cent—would come from.

"What happened to Billington and his treasure?" Adria finally asked, settling back in her chair.

"No one knows," he returned. "Each sailed away the next day, Chatworth in one direction, Billington for England. Billington and his ships were never heard from again. The only evidence we have is the skimpy account in Chatworth's log."

"Did anyone search for the ships?" Adria asked.

"No, they were too busy preparing to battle the Armada. Chatworth was killed in the battle, and afterward Greenville lost favor with the queen and was literally up to his neck in his own problems. So Sir Sidney Billington and the story of the *Golden Fleece* sank into obscurity. In the following years interest was revived once or twice, but no clues were found."

Despite herself, Adria forgot her pecuniary interest as the story itself began to excite her. "For nearly four hundred years it's lain dormant, and no one thought about it or even knew it existed. But now something has happened, or has been found, to motivate the quest for the *Golden Fleece* once again."

"Yes, it has." He stood, sinking a hand into his jacket pocket. Then standing in front of Adria, his arm extended, he opened his hand. Jewels glittered on his palm. Adria stared at a delicate crucifix, two coins and a beautiful gold ring set with three large diamonds.

"Here," he said, clasping her hand warmly, firmly in his and turning it palm-up, "hold them and look at them closely."

Adria looked first at the coins, then the crucifix. He pointed to the large emerald at the bottom.

"Seventy-five carats," he said. "There may be more. The Spaniards had a reputation for smuggling large shipments of uncut stones on their ships."

The gold cross set with eight large emeralds was magnificent, but the ring fascinated Adria more. It was small and delicately crafted; it had to be a woman's ring.

"Spanish coins—a two-*reales* and a four-*reales* piece—but an English ring," he told her, as if he understood her fascination. He picked up the two coins and the crucifix and dropped them into his jacket pocket. "Hold it against the light," he instructed.

Moving closer to the window, Adria did and noticed an inscription. Silently she read: *My love is forever.* LeMaster, moving to stand beside her, caught her hand in his again, took the ring from her and slipped it onto the third finger of her left hand.

"A wedding ring, no doubt. In no period of history have rings been so popular as during the sixteenth century, when Spain was the ruling power. They were associated with love and marriage." He twisted it so that the diamonds were atop, then lightly brushed the sleeve of his jacket over the jewels to buff and polish them. His voice soft, almost seductive, his touch on her hand almost a caress, he murmured, "My love is forever."

Adria experienced a breathless moment of silent wonder; a poignant moment of gentleness. His touch sent a rush of tenderness through her, and she felt as if he had uttered a declaration of love rather than reading the inscription on the ring. A romantic herself, she lifted her head, expecting to meet soft gray eyes, but she was disappointed. His eyes were deep pools of pewter, not sharp and cutting as they had been when he was assessing her, but not comforting, either. Certainly not romantic. But then...she had not attributed that characteristic to him from the beginning. Had she only imagined the moment of softening? she wondered. She lowered her head, pulling her hand from his and looking at the ring again.

"It's beautiful, isn't it?" he asked softly.

"Yes."

This time Adria didn't look up, because she knew his face would be empty and void and she didn't want to see the stark coldness. Slowly she lifted her other hand and pulled off the ring. Sparing it one last look, she dropped it into his palm.

"Where did you find it?" she asked.

"Surprisingly close to home," he evaded, his hand closing around the gold band.

Adria smiled to herself. LeMaster knew psychology—she had to give him credit—but so did she. She had often wondered if the weakness for wanderlust and treasure hunting was inherent in her family, and fearing it was, she had resolved to be on guard for any symptoms. She recognized them, and as long as she did, she was safe. Admittedly she was a romantic and an adventurer, but she would not allow herself to get caught up in the romance of the past. In fact, she wasn't going to get caught up in daring adventures with this man, period.

She was not a treasure-hunting addict. In that respect she was not like John or Daniel Gilby at all. She would admit she was rather sentimental when it came to keeping her home, Avalon, in the family, but she felt she had a legitimate right to these feelings. After all, five generations of Gilbys had lived there and had owned Gilby and Son Salvage Company. Sentiment had nothing to do with her saving the business and the family home. But she was stronger than her father and brother, her goals firmly in place. She was a level-headed businesswoman, and that's exactly what she wanted to remain.

"I'm sure, Mr. LeMaster, with these you'll find someone who will help you with your treasure hunt."

"But not you?"

"No." When he only stared at her with pleading eyes, Adria felt compelled to add, "Please understand, Mr. LeMaster, treasure hunting is not good for me, and I wouldn't be a good partner for you. I'm sure you can appreciate that, in the long run, I'm doing you a favor."

He laughed, the sound devoid of humor. "How many times have I heard that worn-out cliché?"

"Not knowing you, I have no idea. In this instance, it's the truth. I appreciate your inviting me to be a part of your adventure." She walked to the door and opened it. Smiling to take the sting out of her refusal and staunchly refusing to think about the emerald cross or those pleading gray eyes, she said, "I hope you can appreciate the honesty of my answer. I wish you well in finding someone to go treasure hunting with you."

Chapter Two

Adria Gilby waited at the opened door, ready to sweep him out as if he were unwanted dust. "I'm sure either Lamar Corbett or Hanson Godair would be interested in your story, Mr. LeMaster."

Still Joel did not move. One step in the direction of that door meant defeat. Reaching up, he rubbed his cheek with his palm. Although he had been told Adria Gilby would not go on treasure hunts, her refusal was like a slap across the face. In fact, he could have accepted a slap much better than rejection. He had not realized until now how much he was counting on circumstances to press her into participation. During the past two weeks, since he had arrived in Freeport, he had learned a great deal about Ms. Adria Gilby. For one, she owned and operated Gilby and Son by herself and was in a financial strait. He had thought this, coupled with his persuasive story, would compel her to join him.

Evidently he thought wrong! Either her financial problems were not dire enough or he was not persuasive enough. In all honesty, he admitted it was probably the latter reason.

"Have you thought about approaching either one of them?" she asked.

He shook his head. "I don't trust Corbett, and although I think Godair is an all-right fellow, he's not the right one for this job."

"But I am?"

"Yes—" Joel hoped he saw a tiny ray of hope glimmering over the horizon "—you are. You'll look after your salvage rights but will also respect the historical treasure we uncover."

Her eyes narrowed. "How well do you think you know me, Mr. LeMaster?"

He thought of several glib answers, but uttered none of them. Nothing had gone according to plan since he had walked into Adria's office earlier. He had expected the woman to be tough and hardened and older. She was tough; she could possibly be hardened, but she definitely was not older. He could have dealt with the situation much better if she were. He was not prepared for the youthful softness or aura of innocence that surrounded Adria Gilby.

He decided honesty was the best tactic with her. "I did quite a bit of research before I came here, and I'm also a good judge of people. I trust you. If I didn't, I wouldn't have shared even this tiny bit of information with you about my find."

Despite her reaction and her refusal, Joel knew Adria was intrigued by his story. He knew people well enough to know when they were genuinely interested in a subject; he also knew she appreciated the honesty of his answer. But to get her to accept his proposal she had to be more than interested; she had to be more than appreciative. She had to be as caught up and committed to salvaging the *Golden Fleece* as he was. Therein lay the problem. Wondering what he could say or do to convince her, Joel lifted a hand and raked it through his hair. He knew he must persuade her tonight, because he wouldn't get another chance. She was still standing at the door smiling. He would have given his weight in gold to know what she was thinking.

"I've been searching for the right person for a long time," he said, "and I finally found her."

"No, Mr. LeMaster, you haven't found *her*. If anything, your research should have revealed that Adria Gilby does not, and I repeat emphatically, does not under any circumstances go treasure hunting."

"But you are interested in Billington and his *Golden Fleece?*" Joel pressed, glad that Adria wasn't a treasure diver. Although he had long ago thrown his lot in with commercial salvagers, they could be shortsighted when it came to the preservation of historical data and artifacts.

"I enjoy history lessons."

"Will you listen to the rest of my story? The information is interesting, and it's certainly historic." She said nothing, and that was encouraging. At least she didn't turn him down outright. Feeling as if he had gained a little ground, he pressed, "All I'm asking is that you let me tell you the rest of the story."

Her expression never changed, but her eyes seemed to soften. He was confident of his ability to sway the staunchest of opponents, if given time; he only hoped he was reading her body language correctly.

As Joel waited for Adria's answer, he realized that silence had never seemed so loud or lasted so long. As she had done when he first entered the office, she looked at her watch; then her gaze returned to him.

"You have until my ride arrives to take me home," she announced and closed the door.

Emitting a sigh of relief, Joel dropped the ring into his windbreaker pocket. "About five years ago, when I was on a dive, I located the remains of a wreck—after months of careful and painstaking research, I discovered it was the

San Pablo, a Spanish merchant ship that had sunk in 1596.''

''The *San Pablo,*'' Adria murmured, her brow creasing as she looked at him. ''Wasn't there a write-up about it in the *National Geographic?*''

Joel paused, wishing there had been a mere ''write-up'' of the excavation, but it had been more than that. He and the inquest had been front-page news nation wide for several months. But strictly speaking, no article about him or the *San Pablo* had been in the *National Geographic.* Deciding now was not the time to confess past transgressions, real or imagined, or to quibble over inferred or literal honesty, he used the name of the magazine for the basis of his answer.

''There was some media coverage.'' What an understatement! ''But *National Geographic* didn't cover it.''

''I'll remember where I read about it, given time,'' Adria said. ''Generally when I read something about an extraordinary excavation, I don't forget it.''

He didn't doubt that, and only hoped she didn't remember before he had a chance to tell her about his proposal. If she did, it could throw a kink in the works. Hoping to divert her, he launched into his story.

''It was while I was doing research at the Library of Congress on the *San Pablo* that I discovered a valuable document. At first it was just a piece of interesting research, but it led from one document to another—one discovery to another—one country to another.''

As he talked, Adria moved to the refreshment table to remove the filter and lift the pot from the coffee maker. When she passed in front of him on the way to the tiny kitchen adjacent to her office, he drew in a deep breath, inhaling her perfume—a light fragrance that reminded him of springtime. For someone as tall and slender as she was, she was also curvaceous, he thought. She moved with dignity and grace.

Talking loudly enough so that she could hear him in the other room, he said, "The author of the document I was just talking about was a wealthy lord, a high-ranking government official whom, for the sake of this conversation, we shall call Don Juan. Don Juan, returning to Spain from Mexico, was aboard one of the ships of the *Tierra Firme Flota* when she rescued a survivor who was floating on a piece of ship wreckage."

Adria reentered the room, and plugged in the refilled coffee maker. Returning to her desk, she sat down. Joel wished she would quit fiddling with things and listen to him. He wanted her full attention, and so far he had not received it.

"Because Don Juan was the only man aboard who spoke English, he had to interrogate the prisoner and file a report. He recorded that the Englishman was delirious when they rescued him and regained consciousness only once before he died. Therefore, Don Juan had been unable to learn anything of significance. According to him the man kept muttering the Scriptures and was apparently wanting to confess his sins. Don Juan jotted down some of the key words that the Englishman kept repeating: *the moon, and sheep, and the angry seas hurling ships together*."

Joel paused in his narration and turned to look at Adria. He wondered if his words were having an effect on her at all. He couldn't judge. She seemed to be listening, but he still felt as if he had not gained her full attention. Before his story was over, he promised himself, he would have her on the edge of her chair with curiosity, or he was not Joel LeMaster.

"Don Juan also wrote in his report," he went on, "that he was pleased to announce the Englishman was not a heretic. His last words were quite coherent, and he talked about Christ calming the angry seas and died with the name of the Blessed Virgin Mary on his lips. I began to do research on the particular ship that Don Juan had sailed on, and I located about twelve thousand pages of documents. I also located three charts that pinpointed the site where the survivor had been found, but it took me a long time to piece the puzzle together."

The coffee perked, Adria poured two cups, handing one to him. He took his and walked to the window. Once again she sat behind the desk, and sipped her coffee. He had to make her understand the importance of this find, the importance of this particular hunt.

"I knew that an English ship had sunk where the sailor was rescued, but I didn't know which one. So I did some preliminary work in England. Since this was the era of the English privateers, the Committee of Nautical Archaeology gave me an exhaustive list of those who had been in Elizabeth's service. I also contacted the corporation of Lloyd's, but their records on shipwrecks go back for only two hundred years. And there were other sources that I checked, but since these listed only sixteenth-century wrecks, they didn't help me."

When Adria lifted an eyebrow quizzically, he explained. "Only shipwrecks were recorded, and no one had any record of Billington's ship having sunk—it simply disappeared. So I had no recourse left but to dive. A fellow diver and I went to work, using the charts to pinpoint our area."

"And you came up with—"

Setting the empty cup on the small table beside the coffee maker, Joel returned to the chair and sat down. For the first time since he had begun his story, he felt as if he was making headway. Adria was really beginning to get interested. He couldn't tell it from the tone of her voice or her facial expression, but he could feel it.

Encouraged, he said, "After months of diving we came up with artifacts, which made us think we had located another sunken Spanish galleon. Of course, I was happy with my find, but I was also disappointed. I wanted to locate the English ship. Then I found the ring, but that didn't really prove anything. The Spanish and the English were stealing from each other at every available opportunity during those years."

He paused, remembering the day he had located the artifacts, and his mixed feelings of happiness and disappointment.

"Six more days of diving, and nothing. Then on the seventh day, our last day, we found a rusting bulkhead with part of a ship's plaque affixed to it."

"The *Golden Fleece*," Adria cried. He stared into her face, which was now a reflection of undiluted interest. Her blue eyes were glowing and her voice quivered with excitement. She was really pretty. The thought gave him a jolt. He had been so focused on his reason for coming to see Adria, that only now had he really noticed her.

"One part of the *Golden Fleece*, I believe," Joel said, and smiled. He had scored a victory on this one. Now he knew he had Adria's full interest. "All that is left is a part with the letters *E-S-S*." He could hardly contain the satisfaction that raced through his body; he leaned forward. "Remember what Don Juan wrote in his report after interrogating the prisoner?"

Adria thought a moment, then murmured, "He died with the Virgin Mother's name on his lips." The words were no sooner out of her mouth, then her eyes lit up and she exclaimed, "Yes, but how does all of this fit in? The Spaniard wouldn't have thought Bess was the same word for the Holy Mother."

"What if in his rambling, the sailor referred to his ship as the Virgin Queen herself? The Spaniard didn't understand English well enough to know that the sailor wasn't talking about the Virgin Mary."

Adria thought a minute and shrugged her shoulders. "Sounds reasonable to me."

"The hurricane season started, and I had to stop diving. I returned to England, researching the list of privateers the CNA had given me. Because the list was alphabetical, I discovered the Chatworth papers first. After I read his log book, I knew I had found my ship. Piece by piece I reconstructed the story. Billington's ship was the *Glorious Bess*—another name for Elizabeth."

He leaned forward. "I know for sure a ship is there, Adria, and everything inside me tells me that it's Billington's flagship with treasure worth perhaps about five hundred million dollars aboard it."

"But you can't be sure," she reminded him, and he heard the doubt in her voice.

"I also have a hunch we're going to find Billington's second ship," he said softly.

Adria stared at him.

"Remember, Don Juan recorded that the sailor quoted the Scriptures during his last hours. What if it was not the Scriptures but the events that had taken place during the past days? The angry seas would denote a storm."

"Of course." Adria sat back down. "He said the ships were hurled together. You think that during a storm Billington's two ships collided with each other and wrecked?"

"I think so. If they did, Adria—" he stared into two blue eyes that sparkled with life "—this will be one of the most valuable finds speaking archaelogically and numismatically. Wouldn't you like to be a part of it?''

She pushed out of her chair and walked around the office. Deep in thought, she lifted her hand and brushed it through the loose curls around her face. Elation rushed through Joel's veins. Adria was fighting with herself.

''I would and I wouldn't,'' she replied slowly, looking at him, then adding quickly, ''but the I-wouldn't feeling is much greater than the I-would.''

''I've obtained an exploration lease covering a fifty-mile stretch of water,'' he said, his heartbeat slowing as he recognized the resolve in her voice; still he determined to press his point. ''Also I've pinpointed exclusive salvage leases on the ship that I've discovered and explored.''

Returning to the desk, Adria ran the tip of her index finger around the rim of the cup. Without looking at him, she said, ''And now you need to form a team to assist you in salvaging the wreck?''

Joel didn't immediately answer, and when he did speak he chose his words carefully. ''No, not really. I will need some experienced divers, but this is such a delicate mission I'll select them myself. All I want from you is a ship, diving tenders and deckhands.''

Adria folded her arms across her chest and raised her face to gaze at him through narrowed eyes. ''My diving tenders, my deckhands, my ship...but not my divers. Why me? Why my ship?''

A good question, Joel thought, and one he really would rather avoid, since the answer would only raise her dander even more. Personally he had no confidence in most treasure divers, but he certainly wasn't going to make that confession to her. It really didn't concern this expedition because he intended to choose his own divers. Returning her measured gaze, he shoved his hands into his jacket pockets and decided to tell the truth. She deserved it.

"For one thing, I chose you because of your reputation." Her expression said she didn't believe him and dared him to convince her. "I chose you because everyone knows you're adamantly opposed to treasure hunting. They also know you're into government contracts for iron salvage. On the side you do some construction, but not too much— because you're too small. You'd do more towing, but you don't have the vessels. Because of your attitude and former experience, no one would suspect you and your crew of embarking on a treasure hunt."

"Certainly not." She tossed her head, the blue eyes flashing, the thick brown braid swinging across her back. The way the sun shone on her hair, it appeared to be streaked with copper.

Joel had expected opposition; everyone had warned him that Adria was stubborn. That hadn't bothered him; the *Golden Fleece* was worth whatever price he had to pay to get her to throw in with him. But he was unprepared for such vehemence. Still he had to persuade her. She was his best chance. At the most, she was his only chance of getting to the *Golden Fleece* first.

"Second, I selected you because I want a small company. With a large company, the finder has a tendency to be swallowed and eventually lost." He paused and plunged into revealing more of the truth. "I want *absolute command* of the entire operation."

She gave him a brittle smile. "That's why you were baiting me earlier. You had done enough research to know that I never went on treasure hunts, but you pushed just the same to see how strong I was."

Joel winced as she hit home with a truth.

"You were testing my mettle," she continued. "Well, Mr. LeMaster, I have plenty. And I'm intelligent enough to know what you're up to. You're hiring me for a smoke screen. You're not hiring me because of my experience or expertise in the field. You're hiring me for what I'm not—I'm not reputed to be a treasure salvor and I'm not a big company. And could it also be that you're wanting to hire me because I'm not a man?" But she didn't wait for him to reply. "Do you think that just because I'm a woman I'm going to hand my ship over to you, lock, stock and barrel?"

"That's ridiculous," Joel snapped. He did not like her uncanny ability to hit the nail square on the head, especially when he was the nail. "Your being a woman has nothing to do with this operation. I want absolute command because this is my find and because it's extremely important. I don't trust—" He stopped. In his desire to persuade her, he had almost erred. He began again. "I don't trust divers I don't know. And it shouldn't matter to you. You'll be amply compensated."

"I'm sure I will." The words were loaded with sarcasm.

"Percentage of the find."

"After the government gets its share."

Joel nodded. "Twenty-five percent of the value of the recovered goods or twenty-five percent of the items themselves, or a combination of both at the option of the government."

"That leaves us with seventy-five percent to divide how?" Adria lifted a brow as she shot the question.

"Eighty for me, twenty for the crew and you." He deliberately excluded her from the diving group. He would never again assume responsibility for a beautiful woman—any woman—diving on a salvage hunt, not again. If she didn't accept his proposition, there was no need to get into an unnecessary argument.

"What if there is no treasure?"

"We have the salvage value of at least one ship."

"Which may not be so great," Adria pointed out. "You're just guessing these are Billington's ships."

"This is more than a hypothesis." He was tired; he had given it his best shot and still she was not convinced. "It's closer to being a theory. Even if it's not the *Glorious Bess* or a part of the *Golden Fleece,* even if there is no treasure, and even if there isn't another English ship in the same general area, you can make money off this."

"How?"

"You can have exclusive rights to the sale of the story, as long as you give me credit for the find."

Adria smiled, but the gesture was only lip service. "Thank you kindly, Mr. LeMaster, but no, thank you. I'll let someone else have the honor of writing that story."

"You can't mean that!" Joel exclaimed, disappointment making him forget caution. "You'd be a fool to bypass this chance."

She glared at him. "I'd be a fool to take it. As you well know, and have already said, I don't have the vessels necessary to keep my business going, much less one for your treasure hunt. I have only one ship large enough to handle an operation of this size."

The truth of her words made him feel guilty. How well he knew she had only one large ship. She had been forced to sell the other two. Her financial statements were as weak as a frayed rope. She desperately needed three ships, and he had counted on that need to motivate her to join him in the venture.

"If that one ship is tied up on a treasure hunt," she continued, "I have no way to work, and salvaging is what brings in the money to pay my creditors. I couldn't market the story of our excavation until it's over, and for it to be a big story, we have to uncover a lot of treasure which would be of unique interest to the public. Even so, I can't wait that long for money."

The door opened and the man who had been working in the salvage yard poked his head through the crack. "Hey, boss, Solly's here and he's ready to go home."

"Tell him to leave without her," Joel said. "We're not through talking." He had to persuade Adria. She was the one person whom he had found who answered all his needs. If she walked out on him now, he didn't stand a chance of getting her cooperation.

"Well, doc, I reckon that's up to Miss Adria." The man dropped his hands into the plackets on each side of the faded overalls and stared at him for a second. Then he looked at Adria, grinned, and pushed the sweat-stained baseball cap farther back on his head. Joel followed the direction of the older man's gaze. Adria reddened, and Joel knew immediately he had made a mistake.

"You're wrong again, Mr. LeMaster. We are through," she said and glared at the employee, who seemed to be enjoying the scene. "Tell Uncle Solly I'll be right out."

Softly chuckling, Ford nodded and closed the door. Adria moved to the file cabinet and pulled open one of the drawers, taking out her purse. Before she could sling it over her shoulder, however, Joel walked across the room and laid his hand on her lower arm.

"I'm sorry," he said.

She jerked her arm away. "No one speaks to me or about me like that, or in that tone of voice. No one orders me around."

"I didn't mean to," he said, deliberately speaking in a gentler tone. For all the anger in her voice, the blue eyes looked as if they were dark with pain. "Please don't go, Adria."

"My ride's waiting."

"You can't just walk out on this. If we find both ships and the entire treasure, our share would be five to six hundred million. Your share would be above two million." He paused, daring her to visualize the sums he had just mentioned. "Think about it. Just imagine what you can do with that money. You can buy the third ship you need. New sonar equipment. You can update your office. I noticed you don't have a computer. You could buy one, to take some of the clerical load from your shoulders."

"Talk is an empty purse. It doesn't feed you, nor does it clothe you." She sighed, her face growing hard and closed. "It's the purse my father and my—my brother carried around with them for many years because they played their hunches." She shook her head. "Your story sounds great, but Daddy and Danny heard some that sounded even better than yours. No, thank you, I can't afford your scheme."

She started to move toward the door, but Joel blocked her. His arms lifted, his fingers closed around each of her forearms and he pulled her toward him until his face was inches from hers. "You can't afford not to."

A car horn honked several times, but Joel didn't turn her loose. She was his last chance; he couldn't let her go. "This isn't a hunch. Well, it is, but it's the kind of hunch that has its basis in truth. It's backed up by research. I know what I'm talking about. It's ours for the taking. It's never been touched."

"I'm not interested." Her tentative half whisper coursed through the small office.

"Then you should be." His words were as soft as Adria's. "I know that you're headed for a fall. You're barely making ends meet."

"How dare you!" The color drained from Adria's face.

Before either could say more, the door opened, and a grizzle-haired man wearing dark blue bibbed overalls walked into the room, his towering frame totally dwarfing the small office. Large hands, tough and callused, landed on his hips, and his legs were astraddle. His brown eyes rested on Joel's fingers which still curved around Adria's arms. As if the big man had issued a command, Joel dropped his hands and stepped back.

"I'm Joel LeMaster," he said cautiously, moving toward Solly, extending his hand.

"Solomon Smith." The older man's hand firmly clasped the younger man's. He slowly looked Joel over before he glanced over Joel's shoulder to Adria, as if to make sure she was all right.

"It's okay, Uncle Solly," she assure him. "He's a diver."

"We don't need no diver." The voice was deep and musical. "Get your stuff together, honey. Your Aunt Chessy is gonna be madder than a wet hen if we're late to supper tonight."

"He didn't want to hire out as a diver," Adria informed Solly. "He wanted to entice me on a treasure hunt."

Grinning, Solly cocked his eyebrows in interest and fastened a steady, curious gaze on Joel. Joel nodded his head, but offered no explanation. Rather he spoke to Adria.

"I'll let you think this over before I take my idea to someone else. My plan is to be underway by the fifteenth of May, but absolutely no later than the first of June, so I have no time to spare. I want an answer by Friday, a week from today. If you decide to throw in with me, we'll be cutting it right on schedule.'' He stepped closer to her desk and picked up a pencil. As he wrote on her scratch pad, he said, "Here's a number where you can reach me. If I'm not there, leave a message. I'll get back to you.'' He threw the pencil down, and it rolled across the desk. At the door, he said, "If I don't hear from you by Friday, I'll have to get someone else.''

Looking at the pencil that teetered to a halt at the edge of the desk, Adria said, "You're that sure of yourself.''

"That sure of myself. That sure of my find.'' *Hoping that you're desperate enough to contact me.* He looked at her for a moment longer, then turned away from her and from the guilty knowledge that he had used her financial need to fire the fantasy of all salvagers. A fantasy that could make her rich or destroy her dreams. He hadn't figured it would bother him, but it did. Smiling sardonically at his own discomfort, he walked out of the office.

The slamming of the door reverberated through the silent room, punctuating Joel's departure. Solly slowly turned so that he was looking directly at Adria, but he didn't move from his position beside the desk. Adria continued to stand at the window, watching Joel walk across the yard to the gate.

"I feel like I ought to know him, Uncle Solly," she finally murmured. "But I can't place him or the name. Do you know him?''

"Heard of 'im," Solly replied. "Good diver. Generally right about his finds. I'm mighty interested in his offer. Guess I'll hear about it on the way home?''

Adria turned. "Knowing you, Solomon Smith, you won't give up until you do.''

A big grin on his face, he said, "Guess we better go. Your Aunt Chessy is about as adamant on her due dates as this Joel LeMaster is, and you've already stretched her patience to the limit by staying so late tonight. If we don't get a move on, your Aunt Chessy's going to be—''

"Madder than a wet hen,'' Adria finished. "I know your wife almost as well as you do.'' The two of them walked out of the room laughing together.

As they drove across Freeport, Adria repeated to Solly all that Joel had told her, including details of his offer. Solly listened, periodically stopping her to ask questions and make comments. When he braked to a jarring halt at the side of the white colonial three-story frame house badly in need of repair, he asked, "What's your feeling on the subject?''

Adria jumped out and grabbed two bags of groceries from the bed of the pickup. "You know how I feel about treasure hunts, Uncle Solly. But even if we were to consider LeMaster's offer, we would have little time to get ready. This is the first week of May, and he wants to sail by the fifteenth. That would give us little time.''

"Don't think that would bother the crew,'' Solly answered, slamming his door and moving to the other side of the truck. "We done things in a shorter time than that.''

"I know, and look where it's landed us—deeper in debt.''

"Don't make a hasty decision,'' he admonished, neither acknowledging or disagreeing with her. "Think about it some, and we'll talk later.''

Adria sighed. "There's nothing to talk about.''

"It sounds like a money-making proposition to me. He's found one ship, whether it's part of that *Golden Fleece* or not. That's money, Adria. It's not as thin as some of the stories that got your Daddy and Danny all fired up.''

"It sounds like a harebrained scheme to me," Adria replied flatly, her tone clearly closing the conversation. She walked across the flagstones to the back porch.

As her foot hit the bottom step, Solly called softly, "You've got to talk it over with the crew, Adria. They've got a right to some say in this. After all, we've been together for a mighty long time now. And remember, your daddy, and then Danny always let us have our say." Solly's arms circled two bags of groceries.

"Solomon Smith," Adria cried, exasperated. "There's absolutely nothing to discuss with the crew. I'm not Daddy or Danny. I'm the head of the company, and I've made an executive decision."

"Humph!" he snorted. "You made a decision all right, but I don't know if it's executive or not. It sounds rather shortsighted to me."

"Whatever. It's the end of the subject."

"What are you two arguing about?"

Both Adria and Solly turned to look at Chessy Smith, who stood on the edge of a porch that spanned the entire width of the house. She wore a yellow shirtwaist dress, and her short black hair was combed back from her face in deep waves; her full lips, softly tinted with color, curved into a welcoming smile.

"To have created all this silence," Chessy said, "it's definitely something we need to discuss."

As Adria passed the older woman, she landed a kiss somewhere in the vicinity of Chessy's cheek. "We were just discussing business. Nothing that would interest you."

"You'd be surprised to learn how diversified my interests are, young lady," Chessy declared, following Adria into the kitchen. After Adria set the groceries on the counter, Chessy delved into the shopping bags, pulling out the groceries. "I declare," she cried when the bag was empty. "What am I going to do with you, Solomon Smith?"

"I'd tell you," Solly replied, pulling on the screen door with the tips of his fingers, "but you never want to listen to me. You keep saying we're too old for things like that."

"Solly," Chessy exclaimed, balling her hands into fists and clamping them on her hips, "will you get serious?"

He chuckled. "I'm trying, Chess. Really, I am."

Chessy's lips twitched into a winsome smile, and she asked, "Why didn't you get me that gravy mix I wanted? That was the main reason for your having gone to the store. I wanted to add that to my roast drippings, so's we could have some real good gravy to go with the biscuits."

"Yes ma'am," Solly replied, winking at Adria as he moved to the counter, "I did get that gravy mix, 'cause I knew you were going to fix me a pan of them homemade biscuits. It's in this bag." Chessy reached for it, but Solomon swung the groceries out of her reach. "Un...uh. Before you get it, woman, you got to give me a little loving. Got to apologize for speaking so unkindly about your ol' man."

Chessy's brown eyes twinkled, and she giggled, pushing her hands through her hair. "Pshaw, Solly. I got to get supper on the table. We don't have time for games. Besides Adria's here."

"Ain't no game, and Adria don't mind you and me having a kiss or two," Solly told her, setting the bags down and taking her into his arms. "This is a way of life, baby. And the way I figure, it'll soon be thirty-six wonderful years."

Chessy locked her arms around Solly's neck. Her smile was gentle and sweet; her eyes glistened with love. "That's right, Solomon Smith. It'll soon be thirty-six wonderful years." She stood on tiptoe and gave him a smacking kiss.

"Now what were you and Adria arguing about when you got out of the truck?"

"We weren't arguing," Solly answered. "We were discussing a prospective contract."

"Contract, my foot," Adria howled indignantly, placing the last can in the pantry. As she washed and dried her hands and set the table, she once again repeated in minute detail—Solly interrupting frequently to add his comments—all that Joel LeMaster had told her. With each telling she found herself more interested in the treasure hunt and in Joel LeMaster.

"You're not going to do it!" Chessy exclaimed, when Adria finished.

"I would, if it was left up to me."

Chessy wheeled around to glare at her husband, who sat at the head of the table reading the paper.

"That's a right good share of money," he added placidly, never looking up from the page he was scanning. "But I've had my say, the decision is Adria's. As she informed me on the way home today, she has the right to make the executive decisions—even if they're not the smartest ones."

Adria giggled, but Chessy exclaimed, "Sakes alive, Solly. Can't you remember how it was when John and Danny were out chasing treasures? Times was mighty lean."

"But we made it," Solly calmly retorted, totally undaunted by the argument. "An' we enjoyed it."

"We barely made it," Chessy uttered, setting the gravy bowl down with a thud. "An' you and the Gilbys enjoyed it more than I did. Remember, Adria and I were the ones left home to face the creditors, when we couldn't pay the bills." The table fully set, she stopped her tirade. "Now put that paper down and let's eat."

But the discussion was hardly over; Solly really hadn't had all his say. While they ate, the conversation continued, getting even more heated as Chessy sided with Adria, adamantly opposing their joining Joel in a treasure hunt. Still both of the Smiths concluded by telling Adria the final decision belonged to her. Whatever she decided they would accept, and they were sure the rest of the crew would feel the same way.

For a long time after Adria went to her upstairs bedroom she attempted to read a novel, but it failed to keep her attention. Her mind was a jumble of thoughts about Joel LeMaster and his *Golden Fleece*. Finally she showered and went to bed but couldn't sleep. Burdened with the responsibility of making a serious decision, she knew the scales were unjustly tipped against her. Uncle Solly wanted to take the chance with Joel, and deep down she knew the crew would share the same sentiment. She almost felt betrayed.

She had worked so hard during the past year since Danny had died and she had taken over the company. She had paid off most of the outstanding debts. All that remained were the first mortgage on the company and the house, and the notes for the equipment. Lamar Corbett had offered to buy Gilby and Son from her, and with that money Adria could pay off the debts and the mortgage on the house. But she would have nothing left for the renovations. Everything she had spent the past year working for, everything Daddy and Danny worked all their lives for, would all belong to Corbett. Adria could not—would not—turn Gilby and Son loose until she had made a success of it, until she had enough money to pay off the mortgage on Avalon and to completely renovate it.

Avalon belonged to the Gilbys. In a way it *was* the Gilbys. Five generations of them had lived in Freeport at

Avalon and working as salvagers, her father and Danny the last. Now it was up to her to carry on the tradition, although she still could not bring herself to change the name of the company.

How was she going to carry on the tradition? she wondered. Corbett was getting all the big contracts, and Hanson Godair, all the smaller ones. Even if she did get a bid, she didn't have the ships or the equipment to handle the job.

After turning and twisting for what seemed like hours, she sat up in the bed and switched on the lamp, the light spilling over the small group of photographs clustered on the nightstand. Reaching out, she touched an older one— one of her and her mother, taken when Adria was six years old. It was the last photograph taken of Adriana Gilby prior to her death in an automobile accident a few months later.

Then Adria's gaze moved to another photograph of her father, Danny and herself. She was standing in the middle, her arms wrapped around the two men. People had always commented on how much alike she and Danny looked, yet Adria had never been able to see the similarity.

Despite the seven-year age difference between them, their mother's death had brought them closer together as their father had withdrawn, throwing his life into the company and spending more time chasing dreams than salvaging. Then when he had died five years ago of a heart attack, Danny had taken over the reins of the company and she entered the University of North Carolina, Wilmington to earn a degree in photography.

The business had been too much for Danny. In fact, Adria thought with a sigh, life in general had been too much for him. He never learned to shoulder responsibility and resorted to alcohol as a crutch. As the business continued to fail, money became scarce, and she left school to take a full-time job as a classified-ad telephone clerk for the *Carolina Gazette,* a daily newspaper in Wilmington. After Danny died in the diving accident a little over a year ago, she had given up her job and returned to Freeport to take over the faltering company, despite the mountain of debts Danny had left behind.

Adria's attention now went to her parents' wedding photograph. She had been lonely since her mother died, but somehow she felt lonelier tonight than ever before. If only Mama were here for her to talk to!

Slipping into her robe but not taking the time to put on her slippers, she fled down the stairs into the den. Chessy sat in the large oak chair, gently rocking back and forth as she crocheted. Her glasses rested on the tip of her nose.

"Couldn't sleep?" the older woman asked, never looking up or missing a stitch.

"No, I have a lot on my mind."

"Making decisions is the tough part of life, hon'," Chessy said. She laid her crocheting in her lap and pulled off her glasses. "Once they're made, whether for better or worse, we somehow deal with the consequences. If it's a good decision, we accept the praise for it. If it's a bad one, we find someone else to blame."

Adria sat down at Chessy's feet, her favorite position, and laid her head against the older woman's knees. "I don't know what to do. I'm frightened of taking risks. Daddy and Danny took them all their lives, and we almost lost the company."

Gentle fingers firmly massaged Adria's scalp. "I know, hon'. I've been sitting here thinking ever since Solly went to bed. What it comes down to is that you've got to make the best decision for you and the company, something you can live with now and later on down the road.''

Adria and Chessy continued to talk for another hour, not really introducing any new subjects into the conversation, mostly mulling aloud all that had already been said. Finally Adria kissed Chessy good-night and returned to her room. She was glad she had talked with her foster aunt, but her heart was still heavy. She missed her mother; no one, no matter how wonderful and loving, could ever take her place.

Turning off the light, in a way hoping it would turn off the flow of sad memories, Adria slipped out of bed and walked to the bay window. Sitting on the faded rose cushion, she drew her knees to her chest, circled her legs with her arms and watched the moonbeams as they danced through the large trees that surrounded the house.

A part of Adria wanted to take Uncle Solly's advice about the treasure hunt. He liked Joel LeMaster and was fascinated by the story of the *Golden Fleece*. But she was intrigued by the man. She couldn't put Joel LeMaster out of her mind. The gray eyes, the black curls that seemed to soften the harsh visage were indelibly imprinted in her memory. Everything he had told her kept spinning around in her mind. Sir Sidney Billington. The *Glorious Bess*. Another unnamed ship. The *Golden Fleece*. The *San Pablo*.

The *San Pablo!* Adria bolted upright. She remembered! There had been articles about it. Not in the *National Geographic* but in the newspapers. The *San Pablo* had made headlines! *Mass-media headlines, for that matter!* That's why Joel LeMaster was so familiar. Vaguely Adria remembered photographs of a beautiful female diver who died during the expedition; she remembered the interviews that had followed the tragedy, but could not recall any of the specific details.

Sleep eluded her, as bits and pieces of information leaped around in her mind, none fitting together. She could hardly wait for morning, to go to the library to find out what it was that bothered her about Joel LeMaster and about the woman's drowning. She didn't drown. She was murdered.

Chapter Three

Adria pushed on the door and walked into the small, smoke-hazed cocktail lounge. Although it was already dark outside, she stood for a moment, listening to the noise and blinking as her eyes grew accustomed to the dim interior lights; then her gaze swept around the room. So this was the Beachcomber, and Joel's answering service! At least it was in keeping with the kind of person she had initially pegged him as, a description that seemed to be substantiated by the newspaper accounts she had read the previous Monday. She looked around the room several times, but did not see him.

She moved to the bar and spoke to the bartender, a huge man with a flowing carrot-red beard that clashed horribly with his red shirt and wide purple suspenders. Faded jeans hung beneath a large paunch.

"Is Joel LeMaster here?"

"Nope, sure ain't. Want me to take a message?" Never missing a lick on the glass he was polishing, he turned his head and nodded toward a stack of papers near a black telephone at the end of the bar. "Don't be bashful. He's got a lot of 'em."

"I know. I'm one of them. I've been calling since Friday."

"Three days. That's not bad. Some people have to call for weeks before he answers. You one of Joel's women?"

"Absolutely not!" Adria felt the heat rising to her face.

The man threw back his head and laughed, and although the sound was loud, it was warm and friendly. "Don't take offense, miss. Just plain ol' curiosity on my part. I don't mind taking his messages for him. Kinda nice to see one of the faces, for a change." He winked. "And it does my old heart good to see that Joel knows some decent women. I'm kinda fond of the kid myself."

Hardly a kid! And what kind of women did Joel hang around with? "Do you have any idea when he'll be in?" she asked, ready for this conversation to end. The bartender was friendly, but much too nosy.

"Not really. If you'll have a seat, little lady, I'll check with the boss." He set the glass on a tray on the counter behind him and threw the dish towel over his shoulder. "Can I get you anything to drink while you're waiting? On the house, of course."

"Diet 7-Up, please."

"Coming right up."

Once the bartender had served her drink, he whistled and waved his hand. A young man came running from the other side of the room. "Take over for me, Tommy. I'll be right back."

"Will do, Charlie."

Sipping on her drink, Adria pondered the circumstances that brought her to the Beachcomber this Sunday evening. She still found it hard to believe that one week and two days had passed since she had first met Joel LeMaster. So much had happened, it seemed as if she had lived an entire lifetime.

She had no idea what she would do if Joel LeMaster had already found someone else to help him with his treasure

hunt. He had said contact him by Friday, at the latest. She
had no greater love or respect for treasure hunting today
than she had that Friday when he first entered her office,
but she was closer to being bankrupt today than she had
been then. Lamar Corbett had seen to that. Bitterness left
an acid taste in her mouth. Of course, there was the money
she made from the photographs and articles she sold, but
that had already been invested in new equipment for her
smaller ship, the *Silver Colt*.

Monday morning when she returned to work after a
glorious weekend of photographing, her world had turned
upside down and had not yet righted itself. Corbett had
underbid her, causing her to lose the big government contract she had worked on so meticulously. She could believe Corbett capable of undercutting her, but she still
couldn't believe he would take such a loss.

She had other bids out, but no better hopes for them.
She was just too small to compete, especially with Corbett
willing to lose money in order to undercut her. He was determined to force her out of business, and if she were a
pessimist, she would say he was succeeding. But Adria
didn't give up that easily. She believed in fighting for what
she wanted. Hadn't she been doing that for the past year?

At first she had thought Corbett wanted only Gilby and
Son, but last Monday when he came by the office to gloat
over having secured the bid, he made it clear he wanted
Avalon as much, if not more than the company. He wanted
the home that had been in the Gilby family for five generations, the home that started out as a grand plantation
and now was an old decrepit house, sitting alone on five
acres of land. A latecomer to Freeport, Corbett had the
erroneous idea that owning the house would provide him
roots and a place in southern society. Adria had a surprise

for him. About all he would get at this point, if he were to get Avalon, was a pain in the neck and lots of expense.

For herself Adria didn't mind the pain or the expense. Avalon was hers, and she loved it. It was the last she had of the Gilbys and she meant to hang on to it, even if it meant throwing her lot in with Joel LeMaster and the search for the *Golden Fleece*. Besides, she thought, her employees were quite happy with the idea of a treasure hunt.

Friday night after she had remembered some of the incidents concerning the *San Pablo* excavation, she promised herself she would go to the library the following morning and do a thorough research. By Saturday morning, however, she had decided against the treasure hunt, and her drive to learn about Joel LeMaster has lessened. She spent the entire weekend taking photographs.

But on Monday, after hearing the devastating news of Corbett's underbid, she knew what she had to do. As soon as she got off work, she went to the library, hoping the media cast Joel LeMaster in a better light than she remembered. Not so. She spent the entire evening photocopying articles about him and the *San Pablo*. After a restless and sleepless night, she left for the yard early Tuesday morning and called the crew together, outlining Joel's proposition for the quest of the *Golden Fleece*.

Not wanting their decision to be based on her needs alone, but respecting the family policy of openness and honesty, she told them about losing the bids. They had to know where they stood financially with Gilby and Son. She showed them the news articles and allowed them to read about Joel LeMaster, the *San Pablo* and the investigation into the death of one of the divers, his fiancée, Vanessa Langston.

It was described as a needless death that many of the *San Pablo* crew had blamed on LeMaster's neglect. Now, Adria announced, the choice was theirs: they could throw in with her and go treasure hunting or look for a job elsewhere. Uncle Solly and the crew dismissed the news accounts and welcomed the idea of the treasure hunt. So here she was.

"Care for another drink, ma'am?" the young man named Tommy asked, breaking into her reverie.

Adria shook her head. "Do you know Joel LeMaster?"

Nodding, he swiped the bar with a white towel several times. "Sort of. He's been in a couple of times when I was working. Most of the time he's with Miss Rose."

"Whiskey," a man called down the bar, and Tommy quickly disappeared before Adria could find out who Miss Rose was. And she had no doubt she would learn.

Then, as the minutes ticked by, her thoughts returned to Joel. Somehow from what the garishly dressed bartender had said about Joel, Adria inferred that he had many women in his life. Why should that tidbit of information stick in her mind? His love interests certainly weren't any of her business.

Her thoughts once again returned to the treasure hunt and to her present financial predicament. Although Joel LeMaster had looked more like a beach bum when he walked into her office than a knight in shining armor, she wanted him to prove her wrong. At this moment in her life, she needed what Joel LeMaster promised. She needed the pot of gold at the end of the rainbow; she needed the *Golden Fleece.*

"So you're looking for Joel?" A woman behind Adria spoke.

"Yes, I am." She turned to see a waitress pushing up to the bar.

The red-bearded bartender had returned and lumbered down the counter to where Adria sat. "There you are, Rose. I've been looking all over for you. This here young lady is looking for Joel. Her name is—" he began as the brassy blonde slid onto the stool next to Adria. He grinned and looked from the waitress to Adria. "Sorry, but I don't even know."

Grinning back at him, she said, "Adria Gilby."

He extended a huge hand over the bar to engulf hers. "I'm Charlie Weston, and—" he nodded toward the waitress "—this is Rose Red."

"Hello, Rose," Adria said and turned to look at the woman, more specifically at the heavy makeup she wore: bright red lipstick; equally red rouge; black artificial eyelashes; and iridescent blue mascara. Adria thought she might be wearing a wig. Surely even out of a bottle no one could get hair that color! Rose Red. The name was quite appropriate. Adria caught a whiff of her perfume—the odor distinctively unusual—distinctively Rose Red.

The blonde smiled at Adria. "Really it's Rosanne Redding, but the guys have nicknamed me Rose Red, and I don't mind. I think people really like you when they find a pet name for you."

The soft, cultured voice was so at odds with Rose's appearance that Adria was momentarily disconcerted. She was glad when Charlie spoke.

"Have any idea where Joel is or when he's going to be back, Rose?"

The woman nodded. "He's been gone for the past few days, but I think he's home now. At least, he told me he'd be home before Monday." Her eyes twinkling, she said, "And tonight is Sunday."

"Do you have his phone number?" Adria asked.

Rose grinned and pointed to the instrument behind the counter. The long fingernail was as red as the lipstick and rouge. At least she matched her cosmetics. "That's it. He refuses to have one installed in his bungalow. Likes his privacy."

Adria sighed. There was only one other alternative. She was prepared to go the limit to find Joel LeMaster and talk with him. That much she had promised herself and the crew. "Can you tell me how to get to his place?"

"Sure can." Rose pointed. "It's the white house about a half mile up the beach. If he's home, you'll see a red Jeep parked next to it."

"Thanks." Adria slid off the stool and made her way to the door. She was glad for the cool evening air that touched her flushed face and drove away the cigarette smoke and Rose Red's heavy perfume. Once Adria's feet hit the wooden planks of the pier she looked at her car, fondly named Goldie because it was a bright yellow Mercury Topaz. She would love to slip behind the wheel and head toward home, but she had to face the crew tomorrow and let them know about her visit with Joel.

Then Adria turned her head and looked at the line of bungalows decorating the beach. As much as she wanted to distance herself from Joel LeMaster and his treasure-hunting scheme, she could not. In fact, she had been praying fervently that he really did know what he was talking about—and he should. After all, he was a marine archaeologist of great renown. Perhaps the words "great renown" were stretching the truth somewhat, but he was quite well known. Perhaps *infamous* was the right adjective.

But, she repeated to herself for about the hundredth time, whether he was renowned or infamous, she needed

Joel LeMaster and his *Golden Fleece*. If she was to save the company, she had to have the money his find promised.

She began to walk up the beach toward Joel's bungalow, appreciating the moonlit night and listening to the ocean as it swelled in and out, its sound soft and soothing. Wondering what he would say when he saw her, she finally stopped. She turned to stare across the silvery waves that dashed the sandy bank. After a while she closed her eyes and breathed deeply, crossing her arms over her chest. The wind, like a gentle caress, moistly touched her face and brushed strands of hair against her cheeks.

"Hi."

Her heart thumping wildly in her chest, Adria opened her eyes and spun around to see Joel standing there. His windbreaker was hitched over his shoulder on a thumb, a blue T-shirt stretched tautly across a chest that seemed to be broader than it was the first time she had seen him. The moonlight touched his face to reveal a lazy smile.

"Just the person I wanted to see," he said.

"I'm glad." Surprise caused her to sound breathless. Or was it surprise? "I thought perhaps you didn't, since you haven't returned any of my calls during the past week."

"I've been out of town," he answered.

"So I was told."

He hiked a brow in question. "Charlie?"

"And Rose Red."

Joel chuckled softly. "May I presume from the direction you're strolling on the beach you were headed for my bungalow?"

"You may."

"I just arrived home from Charleston and was on my way to get my messages. Do you mind returning to the Beachcomber with me?" After she shook her head, he said, "May I also presume that your being here indicates your interest in my proposition?"

"It does, but there are a few details we need to work out before I make a final commitment."

"All right. Let's pick up my messages, then we'll go to my place, so I can put all your fears to rest."

"I wish you had the power to do that," Adria said, an eerie feeling running up her spine when she recalled her earlier thoughts about the knight in shining armor.

"Don't sell me short, Ms. Gilby. Maybe I do."

He cupped a hand under her elbow, and they silently walked along the beach. Feeling at ease with him, Adria glanced up and noticed he was several inches taller than she. At the same time, he looked down and they smiled at each other. If Adria had not known better, she would have thought they were out for the evening, strolling along the beach after a dinner date or a movie. At the Beachcomber, he opened the door for her and guided her to a corner table.

"It might take me a few minutes," he explained. "No one will bother you here. I not only have to get my messages, I—"

"You have to call from here, too, because you don't have a phone at the bungalow."

A black brow hiked. "You've learned quite a lot about me, Adria."

She grinned. "I've done my research."

The gray eyes studied her face, and the answer was grave. "I'm sure you have." Then: "Can I get you something to drink?"

"A Diet 7-Up." Adria sat in the chair he pulled from the table.

After he slung his jacket over the back of the opposite chair, he threaded his way to the bar and was soon in conversation with Charlie. He took a handful of messages and quickly sorted through, then stuffed them into one of his front pockets. After he made a couple of calls, he paid for the soft drink and a beer. On his way back to the table he put a coin in the jukebox and country-western music swelled through the room.

Placing the drinks on the table, Joel sat across from Adria. "Well, Adria, what brought about the change of heart?"

"Change of mind, not change of heart," she corrected, wanting them to get off on the right foot. "I took your proposal to the crew, and they voted to go on the treasure hunt."

Joel lifted the bottle to his mouth and took a long drink. Swallowing, he leaned back; his gray eyes stared directly into hers. "Corbett undercut you."

"He did," Adria answered, her eyes never wavering from his. "But I have other bids out, which I'm sure I'll get."

"No, you're not—otherwise, you wouldn't have taken it to the crew. The only way you could save face and come to me was to have your crew override your veto." He took another swallow of beer.

"Are you always this assuming?"

"No, but I'm an excellent judge of character, and I know, for a fact, that you're not sold on the *Golden Fleece* yourself."

"I'm sure you're concerned only about our partnership—not about my opinion, one way or the other." She lowered her head and stirred her drink with the straw.

"I am," he answered quietly, and she looked up. "I'm damned interested in what you think, since it appears that you and I are going to be business associates and our lives will depend on one another."

Not that it should, but for some reason his answer disappointed Adria. As much as she had wanted to get him out of her thoughts, she had not been able to. Even with all she had read about Joel LeMaster, she was intrigued by him. At the oddest moments during the past week she found herself thinking about him—the way he walked, the way he smiled, the way his brow furrowed when he was deep in thought. Yet he seemed to be concerned only with business.

Then with that uncanny knack he had, the knack that made her wonder if he could read minds, or if she was simply that transparent, he smiled. He really smiled—a smile that began in his eyes and slowly spread across his face, smoothing out the craggy roughness.

"Fact of the matter is, Adria, I've thought about you a great deal during the past week."

"Me or my ships?"

"Both," he answered, and Adria appreciated his honesty.

Saying nothing else, they stared at each other. The silence was broken only by the sultry voice of the female country-western singer warbling through the room. After a while, Joel's chair grated against the floor as he stood. His fingers tightened around Adria's hand, and he tugged.

"Let's dance."

"I really don't have much time," she said. "I would rather we talk about the *Golden Fleece.*"

"We'll talk while we dance." Joel pulled her to her feet. A craggy brow cocked its challenge and his smile, though faint now, played around his lips. His eyes, however, positively danced with devilish delight. Then the music stopped, and Adria smiled. Fate seemed to be on her side tonight.

"Another time, perhaps," she said.

"Another time is right now, Adria." He slipped a hand into his front pocket and pulled out a coin which he held up. His other hand catching hers, he began to sing softly, "I'll put another nickel in . . ."

"Mr. LeMaster—"

"Joel. Since I have a feeling that we're going to be business associates, why not call me Joel? And I'll call you Adria."

"You already call me by my first name."

He grinned. "So I do. Well, I'll continue to call you Adria, if you'll call me Joel."

"If I promise to use your first name, can we talk about the *Golden Fleece?*"

"We sure will, but first let's dance. I really enjoy dancing. Do you?"

The man and his gray eyes were persuasive, but it was the music and the idea of dancing that beckoned to her. It had been a long time since she had enjoyed an evening out, and dancing was one of her favorite forms of recreation. Without answering the question, she said "All right," and followed him to the jukebox.

When a male vocalist began to sing, Joel swung her onto the small dance area, and she was entranced by the magic of the music and the dance. His movements were graceful and flowing, reminding her of the pleasure she had denied herself since she'd taken on Gilby and Son. *He dances as smoothly as he walks and talks,* she thought dreamily, her feet following his, her body moving to his every command. For a long time they said nothing, simply enjoyed dancing with each other, their bodies swaying together in synchronized movement. When his hand pressed into her back and he nudged her closer, she complied, resting her cheek against his shoulder, letting her feet glide with his.

"You dance beautifully," he finally said, resting his cheek on the top of her head. "You enjoy it?"

"Um-hum." She truly relaxed for one of the few times during the past year and let the music flow through her. "But it's been a long time."

"Why?"

"First one thing, then another."

"First work, then work," he murmured.

"Something like that."

"You need to take some time out of that busy schedule of yours for relaxation and fun."

His concern touched Adria. "Since my brother died, I've had to work overtime to keep the company going."

"How long's that been?"

"A little over a year." She took a deep breath. He smelled good—spicy, clean and masculine.

"Have you been an iron salvor all your life?"

She pulled back to look up at him. "You make it sound like one of the Seven Deadly Sins."

"May not be a sin, but it could be 'deadly' if you don't take some time out for playing."

He pressed her cheek against his chest once again and she was content to say nothing, just listen to the music and to dance.

"What did you do before you took over the business?"

"Right after graduation from high school I enrolled at the University of North Carolina, Wilmington working for two years toward a degree in photography," she answered. "Then—what with one thing and another I had to give up college and get a full-time job working for the *Carolina Gazette* in Wilmington."

"Enjoy it?"

"Um-hum." She swung around with him, her feet nimbly following his. "But giving it up to come back home wasn't the biggest sacrifice I've ever made." Again she pulled away from him, this time as far as the circle of his arms would allow, and smiled into his face. "Much to everyone's horror, salvaging's in my blood. I'm an iron salvor's daughter, and I'm proud of my heritage."

"Your father was also a treasure hunter, but you're not proud of that."

"Yes, he was, and no, I'm not," Adria admitted. "That's one of the reasons why I'm here."

"You resent me and my proposal," Joel said.

"No," Adria confessed, "I resent being in a predicament that forces me to resort to treasure hunting and dream chasing."

"Would it lessen your resentment any to think of this as an archaeological excavation rather than a treasure hunt?"

"I wish I could," Adria answered, "but I know my primary interest is not the preservation of historical artifacts and heritage. I'd be doing it for the money."

After a few minutes he asked, "Are you always brutally honest?"

She looked up at him. "I'm always honest. I didn't know I was being brutal."

As the music stopped, the bartender's voice echoed through the small building. "Hey, Joel! Phone call. Want to take it or not?"

He hesitated fractionally before he said, "Yeah, I'll take it."

About that time a group of men, looking to be in their early twenties, walked into the lounge. The tallest waved and called, "Hey, Joel, come join us. We found some artifacts when we were diving today and wondered if we were on to something big."

Joel smiled and waved. "Later, Chad. I'm busy right now."

"It won't take long," the man named Chad replied. "We'll be sitting in our regular place. You and your date can join us. We'll buy you a beer. We'll order for her, too. Just tell us what."

"Not tonight, Chad."

"If you don't mind," Adria said, "I'll get your windbreaker and meet you at the door. It's time for us to go. It's evident we're not going to get much business accomplished here."

Joel nodded and moved toward the bar, saying over his shoulder, "We'll leave as soon as I'm finished with this call."

Adria slowly made her way to the table where she picked up the jacket and by the time she was at the door so was Joel. He pushed open the door, and they exited from the Beachcomber to stand on the deck in the bright illumination of exterior neon lights.

"And now, Adria," he announced, flipping his jacket over his shoulder, "it's time for you and me to go."

His gaze caught and held hers. She had been aware of his eyes from the minute she looked up to see him lounging in the door of Gilby and Son, and the longer she knew him, the more fascinated with them she became. Although they were gray, they changed in shade and intensity as frequently as did his moods. She had seen them cold and sharp as a stiletto's blade; she had seen them look like deep pools of pewter. Now they were a soft gray—full of laughter. She was captivated by the magic of his eyes.

"I'll take you to my castle, even if it be ever so humble."

How odd that he should refer to his home as a castle, Adria thought, remembering the earlier image she had of the shining knight coming to the rescue. Immediately Adria caught herself and broke out of the spell he seemed to have cast over her. How easily one could be mesmerized by those eyes, she thought.

"Your castle, humble or not," she said, "will be better for our discussion than the Beachcomber."

Once her feet hit the wooden planks of the deck, Adria lifted her face and inhaled deeply, once more welcoming the clean spring breeze that blew off the ocean. Glad to have escaped the intimacy of the Beachcomber, and the physical closeness of Joel LeMaster, she gazed at the millions of stars twinkling in the night blue sky. It was beautiful, and she never tired of looking at it. Lapsing into a companionable silence, they strolled down the beach. Finally Joel stopped and turned to look at Adria. A lazy smile touched his lips.

"Let's go swimming."

Adria laughed. "Are you always so impulsive?"

Joel shrugged. "In some things." He squatted and picked up a shell. Lifting it to his mouth, he blew off the sand. "You're never impulsive?"

"Sometimes," Adria reluctantly admitted, glad he was looking at the shell rather than her. "Generally I study situations carefully before I make decisions."

"That's a good rule of thumb," he said, "but I don't think one should observe it too rigidly. Otherwise, he...or she...will miss out on a lot of the small blessings of life."

"Perhaps you're right."

Dropping his jacket, Joel sat down and shucked shoes and socks. Then he rolled up his jeans. "If you don't care for an evening swim, how about wading with me?"

His grin was as infectious as his invitation was welcome. Adria sat down, quickly shedding her shoes and socks. After she rolled up her slacks, Joel sprang to his feet and held out a hand, helping her up. Hand in hand they ran to the beach's edge, and she gasped as the cool water lapped at her feet. They laughed together as they walked.

When the wind blew her hair, it brushed against his arm. She hastily reached out to retrieve it, but he was quicker. Holding it, he asked, "Do you always wear your hair in a braid?"

"Most of the time. Otherwise, my hair gets in the way. When I'm swimming I pin it up and tuck it securely beneath my cap. I've thought about cutting it, but—"

"No," he said, "it's much too pretty to cut."

"Thank you," she said.

"I'd like to see it hanging free sometime."

Now was her chance. "I'd like to take some photographs of you."

"I don't know why you'd want to."

"Because you're an interesting subject."

As he stared at her, she once again studied his face and wished she could see the color of his eyes. Truly they fascinated her.

"We could trade off," he said.

"We could," she murmured. Although the words in themselves were innocent, they were suggestive. What could he want in exchange? she wondered.

Before she could pose her question, he said, "I'll never forget the first time I saw you. I was prepared for a much older woman, and there you sat in your sweater and jeans and your braid. Before you looked up, I thought you were a little girl."

"Hardly! I'm twenty-six." The moment was past, the opportunity for her to ask what he wanted in exchange for posing gone.

"A real old woman," he teased. "Do you cover the gray?"

"Only my beautician knows," she countered, wondering if she had indulged in a wild flight of imagination. If so, she was glad the conversation had taken a turn. "How old are you?"

"Thirty-three."

Moving away from him, Adria took several steps and stared across the silver water. "Had Danny, my brother, lived, he would have been your age. From the minute you walked into the office, you reminded me of him."

"Is that good or bad?" he asked, and from the casual tone of his voice Adria knew that he was expressing mere curiosity, nothing more. When she turned to look up into his face, he wasn't even looking at her. He was gazing at some distant point on the darkened horizon.

"Neither, I suppose." She lowered her head and watched her toes as they dug into the soothing, damp sand.

"Earlier when I asked you if you resented me, you said no. You only resent the predicament that you're in, but I have the feeling, Adria, that you do resent me."

Deciding that truth would serve better than diplomacy, Adria said, "I don't resent you. I'm just not sure I trust you."

Now Joel turned to look at her. "There's not much in this world that I do swear on, Adria, but this one thing I promise you. I am trustworthy."

"I went to the library and researched the *San Pablo*."

"And?"

"Is it true?" she asked.

He turned and took several steps. "Is what true?"

He was making it hard on her, but she was determined to hear his side of the story. She followed him. "Vanessa Langston?"

Joel suddenly stopped, and Adria collided into his chest and stumbled. His voice was harsh when he spoke. "Are you asking me if I'm a murderer?"

Chapter Four

"I haven't said anything about murder!" Adria exclaimed as Joel caught her upper arms to keep her from falling.

"You certainly implied it."

She pulled her arms from his clasp and stepped away; his hands fell to his side. "Your imagination is running wild. I simply wanted to hear your side of the story. I know how biased the media can be."

"I'll be the first to admit they were biased, but to give the press their due, they were fairly accurate in their description of Vanessa's death," he replied tightly and stared at her for a long time before he turned and walked to where he had taken off his shoes and jacket. He tucked his shoes and socks into his jacket pockets and slung the jacket over his shoulder. "If you want to hear my side of the story, Ms. Gilby, then you shall. But I'm not going to tell it out here. Let's go to the house, where we can be comfortable."

Adria quickly grabbed her shoes, and the two of them crossed the distance to his house, a white bungalow with a deck completely surrounding it. The Jeep was parked to the side. Joel sprinted up the steps; she followed more leisurely, gazing with fascination at the nautical fixtures that had been converted into deck furniture. He unlocked the patio doors to his bungalow and slid one side open, reaching in to switch on the overhead light in the living room. The drapes were open, and a soft glow spread across the deck. Adria walked to the large table—a converted pilot's wheel—and sat down in the deck chair.

Joel dropped his jacket and shoes on the floor inside the house and leaned against the doorjamb, bending his leg and hiking one foot up, resting his sole on the frame.

"I like your house," she said.

"Thanks. It's comfortable. Would you like something to eat or drink?" When she shook her head, he said, "I guess you're ready for the nitty-gritty?"

"If you mean your side of the *San Pablo* excavation, yes."

He pushed away from the doorjamb and walked to the edge of the deck, running the tips of his fingers over the railing and looking into the distance. "I dislike talking about it," he said, "because it resurrects old memories that are better left alone. And through the years I've learned that people would rather believe the worst about someone than the truth."

"I'm not like that," said Adria, "and I'm not asking for myself. I have an obligation to my crew. If I sign the contract, I'll be giving you control of my vessel and my men."

His back to her, he nodded. "You have a right to know. I should have told you that night in your office, but I didn't figure it was in my best interests at the time. You were already prejudiced against treasure hunts, and I didn't want another strike against me before you heard me out."

"Evidently your game plan was successful," Adria said lightly. "Here I am."

He turned, but he was standing outside the arc of light and she couldn't see his expression. She heard his sigh of resignation, and saw his body relax. He leaned back against the railing, crossing his arms over his chest.

"At the time of the discovery of the *San Pablo,* I was a professor at a small university in Florida and I was a member of the American Nautical Archaeology Foundation." He laughed bitterly. "I presented my find to them, dedicated marine archaeologist that I was, and we went after the prize. Since I was an idealist and looked at the world through rose-colored glasses, I never imagined what was in store for me."

Rising, Adria walked to the other side of Joel and leaned over the banister to watch the ocean as she listened. Although he spoke in a monotone, she sensed that he was struggling within himself to describe the events that led to Vanessa Langston's death on the *San Pablo* expedition.

The evening breeze touching her clammy skin was cool and refreshing. She reached up to run her hand around the collar of her shirt, brushing strands of hair into her braid.

"Woodrow Westbrook and I were the two archaeologists assigned to the find," Joel eventually said, "and since he had more tenure, he assumed the position of archaeological director. And that didn't really bother me, because titles have never meant much to me." He paused. "There were the deckhands and the diving tenders."

After a long silence, Adria said, "And there was Vanessa Langston."

Joel nodded. "She was an inexperienced diver who shouldn't have been allowed to go. I told her no. Then she went to her father, who tried to persuade me to take her. Baxter Langston, the institution's most wealthy financial backer and the one who pressed them into searching for the *San Pablo,* thought his word was law. In the past whenever he demanded something, he received it. But this was his daughter! I explained to him the danger involved, but he wouldn't listen. I had the feeling that he didn't love Vanessa as much as he tolerated her and would do anything to shut her up and get her out of his hair. He was as determined to get her on the excavation as she was."

Joel shrugged. "That's only my opinion about Baxter Langston, and it's not for the record. When I refused to give my permission for her to accompany us Baxter went to Woody, who gave in without hesitation. He knew as well as I did that Vanessa was too inexperienced to be signed on as one of our divers. The one consistent characteristic of Woodrow Westbrook is his lack of self-esteem. He can always be bought for nothing and almost always is."

"Was she your fiancée?"

He dropped his head. "I guess you can say we were engaged. I had proposed, and we were living together."

When he said nothing else for a long time, Adria finally ventured, "According to the newspapers, she broke the engagement soon after you sailed?"

Joel nodded. "At times she could behave like a spoiled brat, and she was steamed at me because I had refused to allow her to come on the find. Breaking our engagement was her way of getting back at me, her way of letting me know how insignificant I really was to her."

"I'm sorry," Adria apologized, somehow feeling as if she was intruding on his privacy.

"Thanks." He was quiet for a long while, then he said, "Vanessa and I were underwater at about thirty-six feet using the airlift, next to a massive coral ridge. We dug at the base of the coral formation and uncovered a large wooden box that contained what looked like several thousand clay pipes. We dug deeper and found a copper teapot and a slate and stylus that were probably used by the ship's navigator in plotting the ship's position. I'd had finds like this before, so it was nothing new to me. It was

Vanessa's first significant find and she was really excited. I knew exactly what she was feeling."

Joel turned around to face the ocean and laid his palms on the banister. "Something was wrong. I sensed it. Then the tremors started. I knew we had little time. I grabbed Vanessa, trying to pull her to safety. She—"

His voice trailed into silence, and he shook his head as if he still had difficulty believing the events he was describing. "She disregarded the basic rudiment of diving and paid me no attention. She swam away and made a lunge for the slate and stylus."

Joel doubled his fist and slammed it against the railing. "A damned slate and stylus! She was too young and too inexperienced to know the signs, but even worse, she was just plain too hardheaded to obey orders. She was still angry at me and failed to understand it was the experienced diver/archaeologist speaking, not the heartbroken ex-fiancé. The piece of coral—God, it must have weighed at least a ton. It toppled into the hole on top of her."

Rubbing his nape, he moved over to the table and into the full illumination of the porch light. Adria saw the pain that wracked his face, and she felt his grief. His cool demeanor was but a facade for deep remorse. Then he returned to the railing and for a long while they stood quietly, only the swell of the ocean breaking the silence.

"I'm—I'm sorry," she finally said, knowing the words were inadequate, but feeling she had to touch him somehow. She had to console him. Right now, he looked vulnerable and in need of a friend.

"I am, too." After a long pause, he said, "Woody testified that I gave Vanessa permission to dive, but I didn't. Explaining the hazardous conditions under which I was diving, I advised her against coming. In fact, I insisted that she stay topside, but as usual she made her own decision, listening to no one's advice. And there was no papa to stop her—if he would have. Woody never tried to stop her."

"You could have delayed diving," Adria pointed out softly.

"I could have," he admitted, "but I didn't. Right then, time was of the essence, and I never really expected her to react like she did. I don't know—" He broke off, his voice thick.

Adria remembered the newspaper article. "You had only a few days before the hurricane season would come in, and you wanted to find the ... the treasure." She tried to understand the complex man who stood so close yet so far away from her.

"I wasn't interested in the treasure as *the treasure,*" Joel returned tightly. "I was interested in my find. If I hadn't pushed, the *San Pablo* might have eluded us for several more centuries."

He took a step in her direction, still in enough light to illuminate his face. He looked directly into her eyes. "Vanessa was an adult, Adria, a woman who could make up her own mind. Although she was an inexperienced diver, she was a diver and understood the odds. It was her decision to make, not mine. For the record, I wish I could change it—but I can't. You don't know how many times in the past I wanted to go back and have a second chance. But that's one of the opportunities life doesn't grant us, Adria. I can't go back and change the past. Neither will I whip myself for the rest of my life for something that was not my fault."

Their gazes locked, and Adria nodded her understanding. Then to break from their cocoon of intimacy, she pushed away from the railing and moved to the table to sit down.

Joel spoke again, his voice low and bitter. "In an effort to keep suspicion away from him because of his irresponsibility and neglect, Woody tried to heap the guilt on me. His testimony was so sanctimonious. He stated that since I was in the throes of emotional trauma because of my broken engagement, he advised me to voluntarily disqualify myself from the excavation. He promised that I would get the credit I deserved for the find."

"Was he right?" Adria asked.

"Hell, no! Woody would have loved nothing better than to get me out of the picture so he could take full credit for the find. As for being emotional—yes, I was. Vanessa Langston was the first woman I had truly loved. I suffered many emotions when she broke the engagement, among them hurt, disappointment and anger, but I was not negligent or incapable of making sound judgments when it came to my work. Woody was negligent when he signed her on as a diver, but in the end it was Vanessa who killed herself. I did everything I could to save her."

He walked to the table to stand behind one of the vacant chairs. "Since I haven't allowed myself to go on a guilt trip because of Vanessa's death, a lot of people seem to be upset. I'm sorry she died, but I'm tired of being on the defensive because I'm alive and she's dead. All along I knew Vanessa would never marry me. Even though we were engaged, I was an interlude and I knew that. So I enjoyed what we had together, taking it a day at a time. I suppose deep down I hoped our living together would make a difference. I was hurt when she broke the engagement—ego, I suppose. But I'm a trained diver and marine archaeologist, not the kind of man who allows his emotions to get in the way of his work or anyone else's safety."

He walked toward the door. "I'll readily admit, Ms. Gilby, I'm not the stuff a hero is made of. I'm a man, all man—flesh and blood. I have my good points. I have my bad. Most people contend that the bad outweighs the good. I'm not sure, and I'm not sure that I care. I promise you I didn't murder Vanessa. I was not, I *am* not guilty of accidental, deliberate or negligent homicide.''

''If you feel no guilt, why did you give up on life?''

''What?'' He whipped around and glared at her.

Adria had hit a tender cord. ''Resigning your positions at the university and at the foundation, drowning your sorrow in the bottle, living out here like a beach bum.''

''You read all the articles, I see—even the smut tabloids that branded me an alcoholic recluse.''

''Well, you must admit the evidence does appear to substantiate the assertion. You don't have a telephone, and your answering service is a bar. You hang around the beach all the time, with no visible means of livelihood.''

''And you, Ms. Gilby, are merely repeating what others have written. You have no idea what you're talking about.'' He moved across the deck and knelt in front of her, placing a hand on each knee. ''Let me tell you why I quit, my innocent. Let me tell you why I suddenly declared, 'Have tank, will dive—if the price is right.'

''Even after I was acquitted, I wasn't absolved of the blame for Vanessa's death. No one else was blamed. Just me. Not Dr. Woodrow Westbrook, the senior archaeologist, the archaeological director, who insisted on bringing her in the first place, and who had the authority to stop her from diving. Every chance he got he proclaimed my guilt to the world, especially to the academic world. No one blamed Vanessa Langston, and it was she who insisted on diving under any conditions. On Westbrook's recommendation, the foundation advised me that it would be better if I resigned. I was attracting too much unfavorable publicity, and as long as I remained on staff they wouldn't receive any grants from the wealthy and influential Langstons. I was asked to resign from my teaching position at the university because I was considered to be immoral. A professor living with a student.''

His fingers bit into the tender flesh of Adria's legs. ''Not too immoral. Her father knew about it all along. He had even given his blessing on the engagement. Ironically, he had told me earlier he thought I was a good influence on Vanessa. But when she died, the story changed.''

He sprang to his feet. ''Absolved of all guilt, yet I was judged guilty of everything. With the shadow of the *San Pablo* forever following me, I couldn't get another *decent* job. That's why I became an adventure diver, Adria, no risk too great if the price was high enough. And that's why I have had to go to such lengths to get a ship and crew. Who wants to go out with a diver who has the shadow of murder hanging over his head? So I relax every once in a while with a bottle of beer or a drink. I'm not an alcoholic, and I don't let it interfere with my work.''

Adria watched him walk into the house, but she didn't immediately follow. Rather she pondered his confession. Maybe she was grasping for straws, but it sounded like the truth to her. *Come on, admit it, Adria,* she said to herself, *you want to believe him because his treasure hunt is all you have left.*

Inside, the refrigerator door opened; ice cubes tinkled in a glass; then she heard the tab hiss on a can. Standing and picking up her shoes, she entered the bungalow, blinking as her eyes grew accustomed to the bright light. She was taken aback. Rather than being unkempt and cluttered, as she had imagined, the house was almost spotless. Surprisingly, the bright, airy colors and the contemporary furniture blended well with the antique artifacts, showing them off to a great advantage.

"I don't have any Diet 7-Up." Turning from the refrigerator, he set an opened can of beer on the table. "Will a Pepsi do?"

"Yes."

He moved back to the breakfast bar, where he set the soda next to an open bag of potato chips. Leaving her shoes at the door, Adria moved into the house and poured the cola into a glass. Leaning against the kitchen counter, Joel took several long swallows of beer. Then he picked up the bag of chips and after setting it on the coffee table in the living room, he shuffled through the scattered mail. As he read through the stack, Adria sipped her drink and wandered around the room, finally coming to a stop in front of a large glass showcase.

Hearing Joel's low growl of irritation, she looked up. "Bad news?"

"Just the usual," he returned, carelessly dropping the letter on the table. "Soon a person won't be able to afford to pay his utility bills."

When he walked to where she stood, she pointed to the collection of pewter tankards. "From one of your finds?"

He nodded. "They were being transported from Holland to Port Royal."

In a soft voice, mellow with nostalgia and with a love for his work, Joel told Adria about the excavation that yielded the tankards. When his story ended, he was sitting in the chair across from her. She was curled up in the corner of the large soft-cushioned sofa, her interest having strayed from the artifacts on display in the showcase to the collection of photographs on an end table, several of which she figured were his family. On the other table was a lone photograph of a beautiful woman with dark, exotic features, which caught Adria's attention.

"Adria, where are you?"

The question seemed to come from afar. She lifted her gaze to see him smiling at her. "What?"

"What are you thinking so deeply about?"

"About the excavation you were describing," she murmured, her eyes darting back to the photograph of the woman. "It's very interesting."

Joel lifted his thick brows. He was laughing at her, but she didn't mind.

"The story or the photograph of Tassja?"

"Both, to be truthful," Adria replied, giving vent to her curiosity. "She's beautiful. Who is she?"

"Nastassja Zeeman, but she goes by the nickname of Tassja," Joel answered, gulping the beer. His gaze traveled to the photograph and smiled. "One of the two women who are consistently in my life...perhaps the only one who really understands and accepts me as I am."

"Pretty serious?" she asked.

"Longtime friend and business acquaintance." He picked up the picture and held it closer. "We work well together. She's as dedicated an archaeologist as I am."

Although Joel's explanation left Adria still curious about who Tassja Zeeman really was and her role in Joel's life, she asked no more questions; it was, after all, none of her business. She was glad, however, when Joel admitted to being a dedicated archaeologist. His admission was reassuring to her.

She glanced at the other grouping of photographs. "Who's the other woman?"

Joel returned the picture to the table. "Rose."

"Rose!" Adria's eyes opened wide, and her gaze swung to Joel. Her curiosity about the other photographs was immediately forgotten. "Rose Red. The woman at the Beachcomber!"

He laughed. "Rose hasn't worked at the Beachcomber all her life. She attended the university in Florida for two years, and was one of the students who accompanied Westbrook and me on the *San Pablo* find. Rose happened to be one of the few who believed in me."

"She came to North Carolina with you?"

"Not exactly with me," Joel replied. "I was working with a group of treasure divers who needed a cataloger, and I recommended Rose. After the job was completed, the two of us ended up in North Carolina, but each of us goes his separate way."

"With her college education, I'm surprised Rose continues to work in a place like the Beachcomber," Adria said.

"She owns it," Joel said.

So she was definitely a part of Joel's life—his answering service to be sure, but what else? Did she and Tassja know about one another?

"Are you bored by the small details of my life?"

"No," Adria answered. "I—I find them...fascinating."

"I'm glad. I had the impression last Friday that you found nothing about me or treasure hunting fascinating."

Adria mulled her answer, finally saying, "Earlier I said you reminded me of my brother."

Joel nodded.

"He was addicted to treasure hunting. He spent every dime he could rake together to support his hobby. He mortgaged everything he owned for his last great venture, and when that ended in disaster, he drank himself into oblivion. His drinking resulted in his death." She paused for a second before she said, "Because of his irresponsibility we almost lost our business. It's taken me all the money I can scrape together, and the last year of my life, to keep my head above water."

"And now Corbett seems determined to drive you out of business."

"He intends to buy me out—lock, stock and barrel." She grinned. "Desperate times call for desperate measures. Thus, my fascination with your treasure hunt."

He smiled. "Now that you've heard my side of the *San Pablo* story, are you satisfied?"

"Yes."

"Then I trust we're ready to discuss the *Golden Fleece?*"

"I'm ready to start negotiating."

Joel shook his head. "No negotiating. I made that clear Friday. I set up the terms."

"No good!" Adria pushed herself up on the sofa and reached for a chip, which she promptly popped into her mouth and munched.

"Have you forgotten that your crew wants you to go on the hunt for the *Golden Fleece?*"

She washed the chip down with a swallow of Pepsi. "I haven't, but you seem to have forgotten that I own the ships, and I'm the one who negotiates the deal."

Joel finished off the beer and tossed the can into a nearby wastepaper basket. "Out for a bigger percentage, Ms. Gilby?"

Adria noticed that every time he was a little irritated with her this evening he had called her Ms. Gilby. "No, the percentage is reasonable, Mr. LeMaster," she returned, adding, "that is, if we find a treasure. If your theory proves to be correct, and we find both of Billington's ships and salvage them, I'm happy with the percentage we've already discussed."

"What then?"

"No alcoholic beverages will be consumed aboard the *Black Beauty* or during work hours." Joel simply stared at Adria. His silence embarrassed her and put her on the defensive. "I won't have the lives of my crew endangered. Nor will I have my equipment or ship abused."

"I can live with that. What's next, boss lady?"

"You will use my divers as divers, not diver tenders."

He thought a long time before he said, "Only if they pass a test that I'll administer."

"They're all certified."

He shook his head. "I'm glad they are, but I still want to test them myself."

Despite all Joel had said, Adria realized that he did carry the burden for Vanessa's death; otherwise, he wouldn't be so adamant about administering a diving test to certified and experienced divers. She waited a moment before she said, "Agreed."

"Next point, Ms. Gilby."

"I will be signed on as a diver." His gaze was hostile, but she refused to cower. With a sense of bravado, she reached for another potato chip and tossed it into her mouth.

"No!" Joel rose and began to pace.

The impact of the word unnerved Adria, and she almost choked as she swallowed.

"And I don't care that you're certified and have a hundred years' experience."

"Only ninety-nine," Adria said, sounding more composed than she felt. "If I'm not allowed to dive, our negotiations are ended."

He stopped in front of her, his hands in his hip pockets. "Adria, please understand—"

She looked up at him. "I will dive. There's no negotiating this. If you want the anonymity my company will provide, you have no option but to hire me as one of your divers. While underwater photography is my special diving interest, I'm also good at commercial diving, light salvage, wreck exploring and search-and-recovery—all of which will be most beneficial on an excavation, *Mr.* LeMaster.''

Joel's face tightened with anger, and he stared at her long and hard before he finally said, ''You'll have the opportunity to take my test, but you'll have to pass it to be one of my divers.''

''I accept,'' Adria answered. She'd show him. No test could be more exacting than the one she had taken to receive her diving certification. She reached out, picked up another crisp golden potato chip and happily crunched away.

''Anything else?'' Joel asked.

''Oh, yes,'' she mumbled as she chewed. ''If we re-locate the *Glorious Bess* or any other ship and find no information to substantiate your theory that it or they are a part of the *Golden Fleece,* I have the salvage rights, in addition to exclusive rights on photographs and on the selling of the story—as long as I give credit to you for the excavation.''

Joel's eyes narrowed, and his pause was long. Finally he said, ''All right.''

''And last, we will stipulate a deadline. If we find no ships or treasure within the agreed-upon time span, you will give me a lump sum for rental of ship, employees and equipment, to be paid at the end of the search.''

''You're driving a hard bargain.''

''Be glad I'm driving a bargain at all,'' she said, finishing off her soft drink. ''I'd feel a lot more comfortable with government contracts.''

''But you won't be getting too many more contracts, if any,'' Joel said. ''You don't have the equipment, the ships, or the crew to handle the work. You're constantly being underbid by Corbett and other salvors.''

Adria winced at the truth of Joel's statement, but said only, "I've laid out my deal. Take it or leave it."

"What if I said I'd leave it?"

"You won't," Adria countered. "You want Gilby and Son, and the obscurity my company can give you. Can you come up with the money?"

Joel folded his arms across his chest and rocked back on his heels. "I think I see the picture, Ms. Gilby."

He was irritated again.

"You couldn't persuade your crew to your viewpoint, so you agreed to come talk with me. But you designed changes in the contract which you thought I wouldn't—" His voice trailed into silence and he looked at her warily, rubbing his hand under his chin. "Or perhaps they were conditions which you thought I couldn't meet. Maybe I appeared too overeager for your services. Well, Ms. Gilby, I agree to your conditions. All of them."

Adria eyed him suspiciously. "I must be sure that you have the money before we leave. I want you to draw a cashier's check, give it to me and have the money transferred to a special account." She hesitated, letting her words sink in. Her eyes inadvertently darted to and lingered on the mail that was scattered on the coffee table.

Joel followed Adria's gaze. As if he divined her thoughts, his eyes narrowed to silver slits. "Rest assured, I can pay my bills, but I've exhausted all the cash I can get my hands on presently, to finance the research and the filing of the leases. But I promise you, Adria, if we don't find the treasure of the *Golden Fleece,* I'll pay you the sum you're asking for."

Adria shook her head. "No good, Joel. Maybe you can pay your bills, but promises won't pay mine. I want the guarantee before we begin."

Joel looked long and hard at Adria, but she didn't quail. Finally he asked, "Haven't you ever learned that you don't judge a person by his appearance?" He walked to the bookcase next to the wall and pulled out several magazines. "You didn't do your homework all that well, Ms. Gilby." As he talked, he threw them on the coffee table and flipped through the pages. "All you were interested in was the sordid story in the newspapers. You didn't read the other articles about me and my work."

He thumped his finger on the opened book. "Here, for example. The *Nuestra Señora de la Santa Maria y la Fontana* off the Mexican coast." He opened the other magazines and cited his finds. "I'm not a wealthy man, by any means, Adria, but I have enough in investments to cover the amount you're asking for. However, it'll take too much time to convert my holdings into cash. So you can take my promise or leave it. It's your decision."

With that cat-like grace that Adria admired, he spun around and walked to the counter that separated the living area from the kitchen. Propped on one elbow, he leaned against the bar and silently watched her, his eyes full of mockery.

Dumbfounded by the turn of events, she turned the pages of the magazines and skimmed the articles. Then she lifted her head and returned the stare. Joel LeMaster had adroitly outmaneuvered and outwitted her. He knew, and was gloating about it. His entire carriage blatantly assumed the conqueror's stance; his eyes glinted victory.

"Well, Adria?"

Adria wished she could throw Joel's proposal into his face and walk out, but she couldn't. Neither would she back down in her demands. "My way or nothing," she said.

Joel was silent for a long time before he nodded.

"We'll have my lawyer draw up a contract," she said. "Meet me at the office in the morning, at eight o'clock sharp."

"I can't have the money by then," Joel said, "you'll have to give me some time."

"All right," Adria replied.

"When are you going to make the announcement to your crew?"

"After we sign all the papers," Adria replied. "I suppose you're eager to see the ship and our equipment."

Joel nodded. "Am I hoping for too much to hope for sonar equipment?"

Not putting his mind at ease, Adria said, "It didn't seem to matter enough for you to make it a condition of acceptance. In fact, if you remember, Mr. LeMaster, you said that with the money I earned on the treasure hunt, I could have sonar equipment installed in my ships."

"I believe, I said *new* sonar equipment."

Adria shrugged. "Whatever. I do assure you the *Black Beauty* has deep-water diving and heavy-salvaging gear."

"Is she that outdated?" Joel asked, his brow furrowing in consternation.

After a few more minutes of teasing him, Adria shook her head. "We have some of the most advanced sonar equipment aboard. How quickly you've forgotten my father and brother were ocean-floor dream chasers."

"Thank God for small miracles." Moving into the kitchen, he returned in a few minutes with two glasses and a bottle of champagne. "Shall we drink to our new partnership?" he asked as he filled the glasses, handing one to her.

The tinkle of crystal echoed through the silent house, as they touched glasses and toasted the *Golden Fleece*.

After taking a sip of the wine, Adria lowered her glass and said, "Have you thought about resuming your career at a university, Joel? I hate to see you—anyone—wasting his life...."

"Adria," Joel interrupted, and moved to sit beside her on the sofa, his knees brushing against her legs. He laid one of his hands on top of hers. It was suntanned and large, warm and engulfing. "Let's get one thing clear. My life is my own. I want to work with you, but I don't want you to go on this treasure hunt with the thought of salvaging me as well as the treasure. I don't want to be salvaged."

Somewhat overwhelmed by his closeness, she could hardly concentrate on what he was saying. His hand lifted; his fingers caught her chin and tipped it up, his gaze locking with hers. "Do you understand?"

"I'm not trying to salvage you," Adria returned softly, moving her head from his touch. "I thought perhaps you were going to do that yourself." She wished he had not sat so close to her, that he had not touched her. It made clear thinking difficult. They stared at each other for endless seconds before she said, "It's time for me to be getting home. Uncle Solly and Aunt Chessy will be worried."

"I'll walk you back to your car."

"You don't have to." She felt as if she could easily drown in those gray eyes.

"I don't, but I want to. May I?"

"Yes." She smiled. "I'd be glad for the company."

"Do you still want to take the photographs?" Joel asked.

"Photographs?" she asked.

"Of me." The eyes gently mocked her.

"Oh—" She had forgotten. Embarrassment warmed her cheeks. "Of course, but you said something about our trading off. Before I commit myself, I need to know what we're bartering.''

"I'd like to see your hair loose."

Adria felt breathless, as she nodded her head. "How about tomorrow, after we leave the lawyer's office?"

"Make the appointment for later in the day," he suggested. "Let's meet early, say at six, and have a sunrise breakfast on the beach."

"What about the money?" she asked.

"That's my problem," he answered. "Leave it to me. Now, how about breakfast? I'll provide the food—nature, the sunshine."

"It's a date."

As if the sun were already shining in her heart, Adria felt warm and radiant. Although this wasn't a date in the romantic sense of the word, she was looking forward to the prospect of spending some time alone with Joel LeMaster. And she admitted her happiness did not altogether stem from her wanting to take photographs of him. She enjoyed being with him, and wanted to know him better. For the first time in about a year, she looked forward to the next day without worrying about Gilby and Son.

She thought only about Gilby's daughter.

Chapter Five

With the car window lowered and the early morning breeze blowing against her face, Adria hummed with the radio vocalist as she drove to the beach. Although the stars still dimly twinkled, the sun had begun its ascent, a soft gray haze replacing the blackness of night. For a moment, time seemed suspended; serenity cloaked the earth. Nocturnal creatures scurried as they settled for the day, and civilization had not yet begun its hustle and bustle.

An early riser, Adria always loved this time of the day and eagerly awaited the burst of radiant color on the eastern horizon. She also looked forward to her meeting with Joel. In fact, she had been anticipating it since she left him last night. Again she reminded herself that their being together this morning didn't constitute a date in the purest definition of the word, but it was quite close.

Surely the sunrise breakfast could be aptly described as a social event, and the photography session was absolutely pleasure. But, she reluctantly admitted, it was also business. So if she was keeping tally, she would have to consider it half social, half business. There was no hesitance on her part to label the trip to the attorney's office; that was business—all business. Still the entire agenda promised pleasure.

Thinking about Joel, she smiled. Last night when he had suggested they go swimming, a part of her had wanted to. Born and reared in Freeport on the Cape Fear River and not many miles from the Atlantic Ocean, she had learned to swim before she learned to walk. The water was her second home. Today, if Joel suggested a swim, she was prepared. Beneath her jeans and shirt, she wore a bathing suit.

When she stopped for a signal light, she gazed into the distance at the Beachcomber, now a silhouette against the sky. No lights or noise or people to testify to its popularity as a beach lounge. Adria thought about Rose Redding—one of the two women consistently in Joel's life. Joel had explained his relationship to Rose, but still Adria wondered if it was more than what he had mentioned. As a business associate, his personal life was really none of her concern. But she wanted to know, and her curiosity had nothing to do with their working together.

She heard a car horn honk and looked up to see a brilliant green light. Lifting a hand to wave thanks to the driver behind, she turned right and headed for the bungalow farthest down the beach. When she parked in front of Joel's place, he ran down the steps and stopped in front of the Topaz, the headlights acting like a spotlight to illuminate him.

"Over here," he called and pointed. "I already have the Jeep loaded. We'll take it. Your car looks too delicate for a tough mission like this."

Following his directions, Adria parked her car next to the house and got out. "A sunrise breakfast on the beach?" she questioned. "That didn't sound like a tough mission last night. What's happened since we made our plans? Do I now learn that you can't cook?"

"Rest assured, Adria, I not only cook, but I cook quite well. However—" Wearing an unbuttoned cotton shirt over his T-shirt and denim cutoffs, he stood beside the car, peering in the back windows "—I did some heavy thinking during the night and came to a pleasant conclusion. Instead of our staying here on the public beach, soon to be swarming with people, I decided to take you to my favorite beach, which is quite secluded and quiet."

"Where's that?"

"Off the Cape Fear River a few miles above Southport," he said, then described the place.

As she listened, Adria felt a twinge of misgiving and wasn't sure she liked this change of plans. She wanted to avoid impulsive decisions, where Joel was concerned. She was learning how easily she could become seduced by his physical presence. She peered over the car at him, the morning grayness obscuring his features.

She assigned no ulterior motive to his actions and accepted that he felt it was the better choice, but being with him in a public place was one thing; being with him in a secluded place was another. From the moment he walked into the office of Gilby and Son, she had been aware of him, of the charisma he exuded. Last night when she sat so cozily in his house, listening to him spin tales about his nautical exploits and looking into those enigmatic gray eyes, she had again fallen under Joel LeMaster's spell. On the way home she had been unsettled, realizing she could easily become attracted to him.

He had said he wasn't hero material, and at first glance she might be inclined to agree with him. He wasn't handsome in a smooth, suave sense; he was too rugged and individualistic. But he was definitely attractive. That was one of the reasons she wanted to photograph him.

Still, he was not the kind of man to whom she wished to be attracted. She wanted him to model for her; she wanted them to be business acquaintances, but that was as far as she wanted their relationship to develop…certainly for the time being.

Adria had spent her drive home the previous night rationalizing her feelings for Joel, and had discovered the answer. She had a penchant for wanting to save strays and fighting for underdogs—and Joel LeMaster fit both categories. Only this morning as she was packing her gear and loading the car, Aunt Chessy had reminded her of this trait. With a gentle smile the older woman also pointed out that Joel LeMaster was not the kind of stray and underdog Adria usually befriended. Those went to the humane society; this kind went to the heart. While Aunt Chessy accepted that Adria and the crew were going treasure hunting, she did not want Adria losing her heart in the process.

"I'm sure you'll like it," he concluded.

For a moment Adria stared at him, then she remembered. "Yes, I probably will," she said. "It's just—"

"You don't want to go?" He sounded genuinely disappointed.

"Your announcement took me by surprise," she answered. "I just wasn't prepared for it."

"I would have called and asked, but it was so early when I thought about it. I didn't know if a call would disturb your family or not," he apologized, and moved so that the light from the deck lit his features. His brow was furrowed in thought, and he stared at her. The ocean breeze teased his hair, blowing several strands across his face. He reached up and brushed them away, his hand lingering on his forehead. "If you don't want to go, we won't. I just thought it would be nicer."

Sorry she had made an issue of it, irritated because she was overreacting to him, Adria shook her head. "No, it's a great idea and I don't mind going. I just told Donald we'd be at his office by ten, and I told Uncle Solly and the boys I would be here in case they needed to reach me. Can we work this into our schedule?"

Joel's expression cleared. "Sure we can, but it won't give us any time for dallying."

"Have the plans for the photographs changed?"

"Absolutely not." He bounded up the steps, stopping and turning around when he stood on the deck. "I just saw an article about some movie star posing for *Cosmo*. I was wondering if I'm in for an ordeal like his."

"I don't know what you're talking about. What kind of ordeal?"

A mischievous smile tugged the corners of Joel's mouth. "His only covering was a strategically placed towel."

Adria grinned. "Absolutely not! All I'm interested in photographing is your face, Mr. LeMaster, not the rest of your body."

"Wow! What a letdown!"

"We'd better be on our way," Adria said, deliberately changing the subject. Although he was teasing, his words had the ability to titillate her and set her imagination soaring. Her gaze ran the expanse of lean, muscled legs, covered in crisp black hair, that were revealed by the denim cutoffs.

He laughed quietly, then said, "Let me turn out the lights and lock up."

Reluctantly Adria turned her head and opened the back door of the Topaz.

He called out, "I'll do that for you."

"That's okay," she answered. "I'm accustomed to doing it for myself."

"I'm sure you are, and I don't want to infringe in any way on your freedom, but—" the lights turned off and the door locked, he bounded down the steps "—I don't want you to mess up my packing. I have a place for everything and everything in its place. And I'm a nut for orderliness. I don't want anything moved from where it is right now." Pushing her aside, he opened the back door and caught the handle of the black leather case, easily swinging her equipment out. "This all the gear you have?"

"No, that's my camera. The rest of my stuff is in the trunk."

He pulled back, his gaze quickly running over her jeans and shirt. "I hope you came prepared for a swim. In case you haven't, please start thinking about it now."

Adria smiled. "I'm ready."

"Great! You're going to love this spot, Adria. Sunrise is spectacular to behold anywhere, but at my place it's even more so."

As Joel talked more about their destination, he unpacked her car. In a matter of minutes, Adria's cameras and scuba gear were loaded into the back of the Jeep, her car was locked up, and she was seated beside Joel.

"How did you happen to find this place?" she asked, as they drove up the beach, headed for the main thoroughfare.

"A friend of mine," he answered. "He's been wanting to sell the property to me for quite a while, and I've seriously been considering buying it. So much so that I already consider it 'my' place."

"I hope he knows we're going to be using his property this morning for breakfast. I'd hate to have our meal interrupted by gunfire and someone ordering us off posted property."

"He never knows when I'll show up," Joel answered, "but he doesn't mind. He's told me I can visit any time I want to. And you don't have to worry about forceful eviction. He doesn't believe in violence."

The headlights of the Jeep beamed through the morning grayness as Joel headed south. He turned the radio on, soft music filling the interior, and Adria relaxed.

"Have you had any second thoughts about our deal?" he asked.

"Lots of them," Adria admitted, resting the back of her head against the upholstery and staring out the side window at the trees, which were black silhouettes against the sky. Low across the horizon, a ribbon of soft color heralded the arrival of dawn and a new day.

"This doesn't mean a change of mind?"

She heard the concern in his voice and rolled her head over to look at him. "No. How about you? Can you live with the changes we discussed last night?"

He spared her a quick glance before he returned his attention to the narrow road that snaked through the forest. "Yes. And to set your mind at ease, I have the money. My parents loaned it to me. I want to be sure I've answered all questions to your satisfaction and have put your doubts to rest."

"You've taken care of the ones that concerned me the most, those that had to do with Vanessa Langston's death and the *San Pablo* excavation," she replied. "If others arise, believe me, I'll ask you about them. How soon before we leave?"

"The way I see it, at the latest, we'll be underway by the fifteenth."

"Earlier probably," Adria said. "I'm ready as soon as I get the check and we sign the contract."

"Are you excited?"

"I think apprehensive is a better word to describe my feelings." She sighed. "This is really scary for me, Joel."

"Thinking about your father and brother?"

She nodded.

"Did you ever accompany them on any of their treasure hunts?"

"A couple of times during the summer, when school was out," she answered. "Daddy didn't really get into treasure hunting, to the exclusion of all else, until I was in my early teens. It never held the fascination for me that it held for him. I guess I saw him die a little each time he went on a hunt and returned with an empty boat and purse. Disappointment piled on top of disappointment turned into deep depression. Then he suffered a fatal heart attack."

"I'm sorry."

She was, too, but that didn't bring her father or brother back. Joel's words, though thoughtful and sincere, didn't fill the emptiness in her heart that her family's deaths had left. Nothing could bring them back. She had gotten through the initial trauma of their deaths, and could go for long periods without suffering bouts of loneliness. But always there would be that little something to trigger a special memory. Sometimes she would catch herself thinking about something and call Danny's name because she wanted to share the thought with him. Then she would realize her brother was gone, and his name would trail into silence.

Adria missed her family the most on holidays. Once the house had been filled with their laughter and anticipation. Selecting the turkey for Thanksgiving dinner. Buying and hiding gifts until Christmas. Cutting down and decorating the tree. Attending church together on Christmas Eve. She still did all these things, but now the family was only three—Aunt Chessy, Uncle Solly and herself.

Negotiating a sharp curve, Joel said, "Although I accentuated the monetary value of the *Golden Fleece* last week when I first talked with you, I'm not on this hunt purely for the money."

"I know that," Adria replied, her eyes now on the road ahead of them. "If you were only a treasure hunter and your only reason for this find was the money, I wouldn't be here with you. Your being a dedicated archaeologist, rather than a greedy man out to get all he can from the sea without sharing the treasure with the world, is what persuaded me to throw in with you."

"Today you're complimenting me, yet last night you accused me of running from life."

"Maybe I spoke too hastily," Adria said. "Time will tell. However, it doesn't matter whether you ran from life or not. You are a marine archaeologist. You respect the sea and your find, and you want to preserve the artifacts for the world. I can live with that."

They drove a while in silence before Joel asked, "You live with Solly and his wife?"

She nodded, and although Joel hadn't asked, she began to talk about her foster family. "Uncle Solly went to work for Daddy years before I was born, and Aunt Chessy was our housekeeper. After Mama died, Aunt Chessy was the nearest thing to a mother I had. I can't imagine life without them. They're all I have left. When I thought life wasn't worth living anymore, Uncle Solly and Aunt Chessy proved to me that it was." She swallowed the knot in her throat. "Without them, I would have no business or home. The Gilbys would be only a name in Freeport's history—which might not be so bad."

"Heritages and legacy sometimes get heavy, don't they?"

"If you're talking about my saving Gilby and Son and my home, the answer is yes. Sometimes I think about letting Corbett have it all, packing my bags and leaving."

"But you can't, and won't," Joel said. "Because you realize that in doing that you would be turning your back on more than a faltering business and old house. You'd feel as if you were running away from yourself. You have roots in Freeport that are deeper than those of the trees that surround your house."

"You're right. How did you know?"

"Archaeologist in me," he replied lightly, his gaze catching and holding hers for a second before he returned his attention to driving, "and a good judge of character. Even if you were to sell out, Adria, you wouldn't sell out to Corbett."

"No?"

"You have integrity," Joel explained. "Corbett doesn't."

"You seem to know a lot about me, Joel. Tell me something about yourself." Adria thought about the photographs at his home, and wished she had taken a little more time to study them. It wasn't until she arrived home last night after their discussion that she had begun thinking about the impact Joel LeMaster was having on her personal life. She truly wanted to know who he was and where he came from.

"Didn't you learn enough about me in those articles you read?"

"I learned about you, the archaeologist and diver, in relation to the *San Pablo* excavation, but I'm interested in learning about you, the man."

Joel laughed quietly. "Does this mean you're getting interested in my body?"

Adria laughed with him, but his quiet laughter and provocative teasing caused her heart to beat a little faster. "I never denied being interested in your body. I've wanted to photograph you from the first moment I laid eyes on you."

The smile lingered on his lips, but his eyes were quite serious. "Your interest is totally photographic?"

"Until—" her mouth suddenly went dry "—I learn more about the soul and intellect."

"If you discover that I'm more than just a treasure hunter, will you have a different opinion of me?"

"I'm sure I will," she replied, then added impishly, "however, I don't promise that it will be for the better or the worse."

"It'll be for the better," he promised. "I'm really a lovable fellow. I have to be. I'm the youngest of three boys, and I do mean youngest—as in baby of the family."

Suppressing a grin, Adria glanced at Joel. Habit caused him to use the word "boys" to describe himself and his brothers, but they were hardly "boys." She couldn't remember the photographs in detail, but all the males were mature. Certainly he was no boy.

"All of my family is scattered around the world," he said.

"You must miss them."

"I do," Joel answered, "even though my oldest brother is fourteen years my senior, and the next one is twelve years older, we're a close family. We're all planning to meet this year at Christmas, which—if we can—will be a miracle." He glanced over at her. "My parents are young seventies, and they haven't retired yet. Right now they're on a dig in Brazil—"

"They're archaeologists?" Adria exclaimed.

"They are, and they're insisting all of us join them there for Christmas. We're insisting they meet us in Florida."

"Who do you think will win?" Adria asked, suddenly interested in his family. As he talked, her opinion of him definitely was changing, and as he had promised, it was for the better.

"Probably my parents. But the scales are loaded in their favor. Allen, my oldest brother, and his family are living in Rio de Janeiro."

"Another archaeologist?"

"No, he's a doctor/missionary who teaches at one of the medical universities there. My other brother, Robert, is an officer in the Marine Corps, and I'm never quite sure where he is. Right now I think he's on a float somewhere. At least, the last time I heard from him, that's where he was. What do you want to bet that by Christmas time he'll be stationed in Brazil, and I'll be the only one close to home."

Adria laughed with him. "Home is where?"

"Florida."

She listened, while he talked about his childhood. He loved his family, and although his mother and father were dedicated archaeologists, they were devoted parents. By the time Joel was a teenager, he had traveled throughout South America and the Middle East. As a small tot, he had always been fascinated with history and with water—but not with heat and dust—and determined to follow in his parents' footsteps he became a marine archaeologist.

"Naturally because of my brothers' marriages, our family has grown. Allen has been happily married for about twenty-five years and has given me three nieces, ranging from the early to mid-twenties, and one nephew, who is eighteen. One of my nieces is married and has two small children, a daughter and a son. Robert, on the other hand, has been happily, then unhappily married twice, also resulting in about twenty-five married years. By his first wife, he has a grown daughter and a son whom we generally see sometime during Christmas. When they were smaller, they spent their summer vacations with my parents. Bob recently completed his college degree, and Sandy has just entered, so that limits their visits. By his second wife, Robert has a thirteen-year-old son, Lane. After his second divorce, Robert decided marriage wasn't for him. However, friends keep encouraging him to try again. They contend that the third time should be a charm." He glanced over at her and grinned. "And, of course, I'm single."

While she had been eager to learn about Joel's family, Adria was even more eager to learn more about him. "Have you ever been married?" she asked.

"No, Vanessa was the closest I came to the altar. How about you?"

"I seriously dated a guy through my first two years of college, but the relationship fizzled out. We went our separate ways." She shifted, drawing one of her legs up on the seat.

"There's no one in your life presently?"

"By no one, do you mean a steady boyfriend?" When he nodded, she said, "No. During the past year, all my time and energy have been channeled into the business. I'm not even sure what a social life is anymore."

Last night Joel had told her that Tassja and Rose were business acquaintances; he had reassured her that Tassja was nothing more. She had not felt the same assurance about Rose. And what about all those women Charlie, the Friendly Bartender, had told her about?

"Are you going with anyone seriously?"

"No."

The answer came without hesitation, and Adria was content with it. Smiling to herself, she rolled the back of her head against the upholstery and gazed out the window. Again they lapsed into silence, radio music softly filling the interior of the Jeep. Joel turned off the highway onto a narrower road and drove for several miles.

"We're almost there," he announced. "And none too soon. Looks like the sun is eager to be up and going."

"Me, too," Adria said.

Shortly the pavement became a dirt road, and dust swirled behind them as they drove through the thick forest. Adria sat back and enjoyed the ride, the wind blowing against her face. She loved the country, the solitude and peace that it offered. She inhaled deeply, breathing in the pure spring air, the faint fragrance of flowers, among them honeysuckles, dogwoods and azaleas. She looked forward to her morning with Joel.

CLAD IN HIS BATHING SUIT, Joel sat on a patch of thick grass on the bank, one leg drawn up to his body, his chin resting on his knee, the other leg stretched out. He stared at the woman who swam in the river. Her strokes were clean, smooth and strong. She made swimming seem effortless. She had a rapport with the water, a kinship he looked for and expected in swimmers and divers but seldom found.

Her hands slipped around the large tree trunk that had fallen into the edge of the river. She pulled herself up, balanced momentarily on her palms and looked into his face, her lips slowly curving into a smile. She levered herself onto the trunk, then tilted her head, letting the water sluice down her back.

"I hope breakfast is ready," she said.

"It is. I was waiting for you."

He eased his leg down and watched her as she rose, then walked the length of the log to the bank where he sat, balancing herself with outstretched arms. The first thing he had noticed about Adria Gilby when he had walked into the office of Gilby and Son was her eyes. Their color was extraordinary, in itself, but her ability to communicate with them was unparalleled, in his experience.

He let his gaze leisurely travel her height. She was a beautiful woman, tall and slender, with firm breasts and long legs. Having been reared on the coast of Florida, he was accustomed to seeing women in bathing suits, and the sight of a partially nude body did not often stir his senses. Rather than being the exception, it was the norm. But the sight of Adria in the white one-piece did stir him. She was absolutely provocative.

She reached back, caught her braid and flipped it over her shoulder, the white bathing suit a perfect foil for her glistening brown hair. Stepping off the log, she walked to the blanket spread beneath the canopy of oak trees that lined the river bank.

"How did I do?" She sat down.

"How did you do what?" he parried.

"Don't play games with me, Joel." She smiled. "The excuse you used to bring me here was the photograph—the reason was to test me."

Adria was also an unusually astute woman. Last night he had accused her of being brutally honest, but as he was getting to know her better, he realized that it was honesty, simple and direct. He admired this trait in her. He had long grown tired of subterfuge.

"You're right," he admitted and turned onto his stomach, stretching out. He broke a blade of grass and pulled it between his fingers. "And you're good. Can you handle your camera underwater as well as you handle yourself?"

"I'm good," she answered. "Every time I go down, I learn something. I'm careful, but not to the point of being unable to respond quickly to an emergency. Generally, I don't panic."

She pulled the tiny rubber band off the end of her braid and her fingers deftly untwisted her hair. Soon luxurious waves were falling down her back, sunbeams piercing through the canopy of leaves to touch and highlight it.

Her hair looked like a thick satin curtain, and Joel wanted to touch it. "Will you verify that your divers are as good as you?"

"They're better," Adria replied. "Ford Lowell—the man you met the day you came to the office—and Hub Chambers have been diving together all their lives. Both of them accompanied Daddy and Danny on every trip they made, no matter what the quarry. Ford and Hub are one of the best diving teams you'd ever find, and Uncle Solly is a top safety-boat attendant."

She unzipped her bag and pulled out a brush, running it through her hair in long, sweeping strokes, first over the right shoulder, then the left. She closed her eyes and held her head back, gently rotating her head from side to side. Joel looked at the length of her arched neck, down to her collarbone and further to the swell of her breasts revealed in the cut of her suit. Her skin, slightly tanned, was soft and smooth.

"I love the sun," she murmured, lifting her head and flexing her shoulders but gazing across the river rather than at him. After she returned the brush to her bag, she pulled out a white swimming jacket which she slipped on.

"Your hair is beautiful," he said.

"I need to get it trimmed." She flipped onto her stomach, balancing her upper body on her elbows, strands of hair falling over both shoulders to frame her face. "I've been so busy this past year, and it's so easy to braid my hair every morning that I wasn't aware of exactly how long it was until now."

"I like long hair."

"On me, or on all women?" she asked.

"Is this a damned-if-you-do and damned-if-you-don't question?" he asked.

Adria grinned. "I noticed that both the women who are the most consistent in your life have very short hair."

"Ahh," he drawled, "you are testing me, to see if I can give the right answer."

She nodded. "You might describe this as walking on burning embers without blistering your feet or on egg-shells without cracking them."

"I think a woman should wear her hair the way it suits her personality best. Even if your hair was short, I'm sure you'd have a style that was a reflection of you. But I prefer it long."

"Quite well done," Adria said.

Joel rolled over. "And speaking of quite well done, I think that's the way we'll find our breakfast." He held his hand down to her, and her fingers wrapped around his as he pulled her to her feet.

When they sat around the portable stove, Joel handed Adria a bowl into which he ladled several spoons of breakfast cereal.

She eyed it suspiciously for a few seconds before she asked, "How long have you been into this kind of food?"

"For quite a few years," he answered, and immediately took a bite. After he had chewed and swallowed, he said, "Go ahead and eat some. You'll find it's delicious, as well as nutritious. It's oats, bulgur grain, raisins and cinnamon."

Her forehead furrowed.

"If you don't like it, I'll promise to stop at your favorite restaurant on the way home and buy you what you like." When she grinned and her eyes began to sparkle, Joel said, "What makes me think I have a fast-food connoisseur on my hands?"

"AUNT CHESSY, just cook what you cook best," Adria said into the telephone receiver. Clad in jeans and shirt, her hair once again braided, she let her gaze swing around Donald Spear's office. Joel was on his way over with the certified check, and Donald was in the next room giving his secretary instructions on the drawing up of the papers. "I know I told you Joel is a vegetarian guru, but if he eats at our house, he'll eat what we cook and love it. Anything you fix will have to taste better than what I ate for breakfast this morning. He said it was oats and bulgur. I'm not sure if that's spelled with a *b* or a *v*. However, it tasted like the latter."

Chessy's husky laughter flowed through the line. "And what time do I expect the two of you for dinner?" she asked.

"How about seven? And thanks, Aunt Chessy, you're one in a million." Adria hung up the receiver and turned, almost colliding with Joel's broad chest, now covered with a casual blue-and-gray plaid shirt. Her gaze lowered and she saw that he had changed out of cutoffs into jeans.

"So I'm a vegetarian guru?"

She lifted her face, to stare into two laughing gray eyes. She grinned. "You called me a fast-food connoisseur first."

"Connoisseur has a more positive ring to it than guru."

"What's that old proverb about eavesdroppers?" she asked.

"Not me," Joel declared. "The receptionist said Donald was expecting me and directed me to the office. And I didn't arrive a moment too soon. What's this about my breakfast tasting vulgar?"

She laughed and said, "Well, you shouldn't have sneaked up on me."

The inner office door opened and Donald, a tall, thin man whose nondescript brown suit draped his body rather than fit it, walked into the room. Although he was only in his forties, he looked older. For one thing, his short hair was prematurely gray, his thin features, sharp and gaunt. For another, his facial expression was always dour, a smile adding to his sullenness rather than erasing it. His eyes were deeply set. Adria had frequently captured him in photographs—one of them winning her a merit.

He laid a sheaf of papers on the desk and extended his hand. "Donald Spear," he said, angling his head and rolling his eyes which peered above the top of his round wire-framed glasses. "I presume you're Joel LeMaster."

After they shook hands, he settled himself into the large leather chair behind his desk, then reached up and pushed his glasses farther up on his nose. "I'll deposit the check Joel has given me, Adria, and set up your account today. But the papers won't be ready to sign until tomorrow. This will give *you*—" He paused, looking from Adria to Joel and back to Adria. "This will give each of you, some time to reconsider before you sign on the dotted line. Naturally, before you do that, I'll expect both of you to read the documents carefully. I'm due in court in the morning and I want to be here when you sign these, to answer any questions. I want no misunderstandings between you."

Adria suppressed a grin. Donald had been irritated about her going on the treasure hunt, from the beginning, and did nothing to hide his feelings and everything to persuade her to change her mind. This was one of the advantages—perhaps disadvantages—of a small town—everyone felt as if they were the other's keeper.

After Donald leaned forward to pull a tissue from the dispenser, he took off his glasses and began to clean the lenses. Again he looked from one to the other. "Do you mind coming by the office tomorrow afternoon, say about two o'clock?"

The appointment made, Adria and Joel exited from the building and walked to their cars, parked side by side in front of the three-story building—one of the most modern edifices in Freeport.

"If you don't know the way to the house, follow me," Adria said.

"Do I need to change into something more formal?"

"Not for our house. During the week, we eat in the kitchen. We're really old-fashioned southerners, Joel." Suppressing her grin, she teased, "Before I went to the university, we ate breakfast, dinner and supper. Upon receiving an education, I learned that we eat breakfast, lunch and dinner."

He leaned inside the Jeep and picked up a pair of shades from the dash. As he slid them over his eyes, he asked, "What meal are we having tonight?"

Adria did not immediately answer. The shades added a piratical touch that thoroughly fired her photographic imagination. As clichéd as the image was, she envisioned a bright red bandanna tied about his head, black hair escaping the confines to curl about his face and neck, and a black patch over one of those sparkling gray eyes. An unbuttoned white shirt with billowing sleeves was tucked into black breeches, his chest uncovered. A North Carolinian buccaneer. Possibly another merit . . . if he would do it.

"I said—"

Jogged out of her fantasies, she answered hastily, "Supper."

The price of the first photograph had been wanting to see her hair hanging freely. What would be the price of the second?

AVALON, ON THE OUTSKIRTS of the town, was a beautiful three-story colonial home nestled among huge oak trees, moss draped from their limbs. Scattered about were several magnolia trees, filled with fragrant white blooms. The sun, sinking in the western sky, still shone brightly, penetrating the thick foliage, to throw a mottled brilliance over the drive and house. Joel followed Adria to the back of the house to park.

By the time he slid out of the Jeep, Adria was standing beside him. "This used to be the carriage house," she said and grinned. "I guess it still is. Only the carriages have changed."

He walked closer to the entrance, Adria behind. In addition to housing the cars, the building was also used for storage, boxes neatly stacked on shelves that lined the walls. The clean side windows allowed the sunlight to spill into the room. In a well-lit area to the back, an old table and several chairs were clustered together. Stacked nearby were cans of turpentine and furniture-stripping mixtures, empty pails of varying sizes, and a pile of rags. Next to it was a woodworking area with bench and saws.

"Hobby land," Adria said. "Aunt Chessy loves to refinish old furniture, and sells some of it for pin money. Uncle Solly is a pretty good cabinetmaker. You'll see his handiwork inside the house."

"Where's your niche in this land?" he asked.

She pointed to an inner door, deeper in the building. "My darkroom," she announced. "Now we better be getting in. Aunt Chessy's going to be all fired up to meet you."

Joel followed Adria across the flagstone walk to the house. When they entered the kitchen, a tall, big-boned woman in a pink dress was standing in front of a counter. She turned, her gaze locking on him instantly, carefully looking him over.

"Aunt Chessy," Adria said, "this is Joel—our soon-to-be partner."

Chessy set the bowl down and wiped her hands on a hand towel. "Well, Joel, I'm glad to meet you."

"Hello, Mrs. Smith."

Chessy shook her head and laughed, a deep, husky laugh that filled the room with warmth and friendliness. "Please call me Chessy," she said. "And Solly is just plain Solly. None of us stand on titles or ceremony around here. We're just one big family."

"Thanks," Joel said.

"Can I help you with supper?" Adria asked.

"No, I have it under control," Chessy answered. "Why don't you get Joel and yourself a drink and the two of you go into the den and talk until I call you?"

"Really, Mrs.—I mean, Chessy," Joel said, "we'd be glad to help you. The old saying is two heads are better than one, so six hands in the kitchen must be better than two."

Chessy, now standing in front of the stove, lifted a long-handled wooden spoon. "Don't guess you heard the one about too many spoons in the soup. That's the one I believe in. Believe me, if I need or want help, I'm not above asking."

Adria walked to the refrigerator and opened the door. "Soft drinks, wine, beer, lemonade and tea. Which will it be?"

"Beer, please."

Pouring herself a glass of wine, Adria led the way to another room. Several large French doors opened and led onto the lawn, now ablaze with the bright blooms of azaleas, dogwood and honeysuckles. Because this room was used as the den, the furniture was contemporary. The accessories added the colonial touch.

"This used to be the downstairs music room," she announced, "but we use it for the den. The state historical society has been urging us to open Avalon for tours."

Joel meandered to the open doors and gazed at the lawn. "Are you thinking about it?"

"Sometimes, yes, but most of the time, no. Certainly not as long as we live here." She joined him at the doors. "Isn't this beautiful? I can't imagine a person wanting to live anywhere but in North Carolina in the springtime."

"It is pretty," he agreed.

"Let me show you the house," she said. "The view from the upstairs balcony is fantastic."

Standing on the third-story balcony, the afternoon breeze blowing against his face, Joel gazed into the distance, the sun reflecting off the surface of the Cape Fear River to make it look like a field of sparkling diamonds. The fragrance of the river and the flowers wafted up to him, filling him with a sense of well-being.

His gaze strayed to Adria who sat, with eyes closed, in the rocker, holding loosely in her lap the empty wineglass. Tendrils of short brown hair curled around her face, and dark lashes formed a crescent on her smooth cheeks. As if she sensed his scrutiny, she lifted her lids, and now he stared into those fathomless blue eyes.

"It's out of this world, isn't it?" she asked, and he knew she was referring to the view.

He nodded. He moved to where she sat and reached out, doing what he had wanted to do for so long. He caught one of the silken curls and twined it around his finger, then brushed it back from her face, his hands lightly brushing against her smooth, warm skin. He felt her blood pulsate beneath his hand. For a moment time was suspended, and the world was made up of only the two of them.

Joel took the glass from her hand and set it on the balcony railing, then he took her hands in his and pulled her to her feet. "Adria—" he murmured, his face lowering, his mouth touching hers in a kiss of discovery. When he would have deepened the kiss, Adria pulled away.

Softly she said, "It's time to go down to dinner," her words bringing them back to the real world.

Joel stared into her blue eyes. He totally disagreed with Adria. His only desire was to hold her tightly in his arms and truly kiss her. Still he respected her desires. He nodded.

Chapter Six

Up earlier than usual on Tuesday morning, Adria arrived at the salvage yard before anyone else, including Solly. She parked the Topaz in the reserved space, slid out and quickly ascended the steps to unlock the door. Humming, she moved around the office, pulling the blinds and preparing morning coffee for herself and the crew. As soon as the chores were done, she sat at her desk and pulled the overflowing in basket toward herself. Being away from the office yesterday had taken its toll, she thought, and picked up a handful of papers, but she couldn't concentrate.

She dropped them on the desk and walked into the kitchenette to fill a plastic bottle so she could water the plants. Her day and evening with Joel had been wonderful. She lifted her fingers and lightly touched her mouth. She still felt the pressure of his lips on hers when he had kissed her on the balcony last night. As his lips had firmed on hers, she had been tempted to let it deepen. It had been a long time since she had been this attracted to a man, but she mustn't forget her common sense.

She and Joel were going to be working together, and somewhere down the line, a wise person had once said business and pleasure do not mix. So far it had. Her gaze went to her camera case on top of the file cabinet. She had taken many shots of Joel; hopefully one of them would win her another merit. The plants watered, she returned to her desk and leaned back in her chair. She closed her eyes, capturing in her imagination the pose she had loved best—the pose that might bring her a coveted merit.

Dressed in his unbuttoned cotton shirt and denim cut-offs, he sat pensively, one leg bent and drawn up to his chest, his chin resting on his knee. Branches from a dogwood tree in full bloom hung low to shade him from the sun, as he gazed across the peaceful waters of the Cape Fear River.

She wasn't sure, yet, what the title would be, but several names had passed through her mind. The Hermit...the Recluse...the Loner. Sure, the titles had been used time and again for books, songs, paintings and photographs, but any one of them captured the spirit of the pose. She never reined in her creativity; this was only the beginning. By the time she was through with the project maybe she would have a better name, one more innovative and unique to the man and the pose.

However, the more she learned about Joel, the more she realized she didn't know him. When he was discussing the *San Pablo,* he seemed hard and indifferent, but she had begun to believe that deep down he was vulnerable, simply hiding behind a facade of cool indifference. But she couldn't be sure, because Joel never really opened up. In the short time she had been acquainted with him, a part of him seemed to be withdrawn and hidden away.

Her gaze returned to the mail on the desk. She wished it would disappear, but knowing it wouldn't, she gathered it up.

Half an hour later and the mail sorted, she was pouring herself a cup of coffee when she heard a knock and a man call out.

"Adria, it's me. Can I come in?"

Hanson Godair! "Of course," she answered. "The door's open."

An obese older man, about an inch taller than Adria, entered the office. A round, ruddy face framed dark brown eyes. He took off a sweat-stained royal blue baseball cap and stuffed it into the back pocket of his khaki-colored overalls. He ran the other hand through flattened brown hair.

"Hanson, what a surprise!" Adria said. "You're the last person I would have expected to see this morning."

His mouth twisted into a crooked, friendly grin. "I thought about calling you, but decided I wanted to speak to you in person. So I got up early and drove over here."

"Coffee?" she asked, and when he nodded, she filled a second cup and handed it to him. "What's wrong?"

"I'm sorry about Corbett underbidding you. I wish there was something I could do about it."

"Thanks for caring, Hanson." She shrugged, displaying a nonchalance she was far from feeling. "But it comes with the territory."

Hanson's callused hand dwarfed the coffee mug that he lifted to his mouth. He swallowed several times, then lowered the mug. "Not really. This is infringing on territory. Corbett's out to get yours. All of it, Adria, no matter what he's got to do to get it. Me and your Pa, we worked to get where we are, and we helped one another, when it was necessary. I don't intend to let nobody take it away from us."

"Is Corbett that obvious?"

Hanson nodded. "What does he want with all these jobs? Lord, the man has more contracts than he knows what to do with now. He don't need these little ones. Fact of the matter, he's losing money on 'em." Hanson smiled and set the cup on the edge of Adria's desk. "But I didn't come all the way over here to talk about Corbett. I came to talk business. I—uh—I had to dock one of my ships for repair, and my job load is too heavy without it. I kinda wondered—well, that is, I'd be mighty obliged if you would help me with one of my contracts."

Adria felt the tears prick her eyes. She didn't doubt Hanson Godair had a ship in dock for repair; she did doubt that he couldn't wait for the repaired ship to fulfill his contract. But he operated by the salvager's code. He offered no charity, only a job for pay. He was truly a friend.

"I'll admit it's not one of my biggest jobs, Adria, but it's got to be started immediately. As I said, I'm not sure that I can do it. I really need your help."

Adria heard the pleading in his voice, the apology, the hurt and caring.

Realizing he was waiting for her to speak, she said, "Forgive me, Hanson. I can hardly talk because I'm overcome with gratitude. I—I don't know what to say, except thank you, and any job is better than none. Please, tell me about it."

The uncertainty was gone from his voice when he spoke. "We'll be doing some offshore construction work for the Akeroyd Company. The way I see it, it'll best be done in two phases. I can handle the second phase, if it's absolutely necessary. It's the first one that I'm concerned about."

"How about switching—" Adria began, but Hanson waved her protest aside.

"Can't be done," he declared. "The order of the jobs can't be switched, because one depends on the other. Hear me out and see if you don't agree." He launched into an explanation.

As he talked, Adria moved to her desk and sat down. The task was easy enough; her men could handle it without any problems. It promised payment, but she had already verbally committed to going with Joel. Dear Lord, if only she had waited two more days.

"The first phase will require the *Silver Colt*," Hanson continued, "and only a few of your men. That'll leave the *Black Beauty* open for bigger jobs on your own. Phase Two, I'm not sure about. Fact of the matter, I'm a little worried about it. There's about three ways it can be done." Succinctly Hanson outlined the alternatives, Adria agreeing with him.

She hadn't felt so lighthearted since she learned Corbett had taken the bids out from under her. At least, with this contract, she could keep the creditors at bay a little longer. Finally she asked, "Are you asking me to do the entire job or just the first phase?"

"Actually the entire job if you can...and will. Can you do it?" Without waiting for her to answer, he went on, "I'm not worried about your ability to do it, Adria, but I'm wondering if you're going to have the ship and experienced men to do it with?"

This had also worried Adria, but she couldn't turn down Hanson's job. She absolutely would not. When angels appeared in disguises and handed out miracles she believed in taking them. Somehow she would make things work out.

"I can do it."

"What about the piling?"

"I can hire some extras."

Hanson thought a minute, then nodded. "As far as the equipment, I have some for sale. It's used, but it's still got a lot of life and service left in it. I sorta thought you and I could come to an agreement about it. You see, I'm buying me some new gear, and—"

When he finished, Adria rose and walked to where the man stood. She held out her hand, gripping his firmly. "Hanson Godair, I wonder if you're an angel in disguise."

He laughed, and his grip tightened but did not crush her fingers. "Nope, I promise you I'm not. This here is no charity offering, Adria. I came to you because of the quality of your work. My name's on the contract, and I'm the one who will be responsible for the work done, no matter who I subcontract the job to. I gotta choose the best."

Long after Hanson Godair had gone, his words kept running through Adria's mind. She walked to the window and stared into the empty salvage yard. Hanson's offer had brought with it a chance for her to purchase some of the equipment she desperately needed in order to bid for bigger jobs to keep her in business and out of Corbett's clutches. It also gave her an opportunity to back out of the treasure hunt with Joel LeMaster. The thought should have brought her pleasure, but it did not. She turned, her gaze focusing on the telephone. All she had to do was pick up the receiver, dial the Beachcomber and leave a message telling him she had changed her mind.

Yes, she should call Joel.

She moved to her desk, her fingers curling around the ivory-colored receiver. She lifted it and began to dial, then replaced it. No, that was the coward's way out. She would tell him in person. She owed him that much.

THE DOOR OF THE BUNGALOW opened and Adria stared into Joel's surprised face. "I would have called to let you know about the visit," she said, "but you don't have a phone, and Charlie wasn't willing to send a messenger to let you know I was coming.''

"Your being here is enough to make me reconsider getting one," he said. "Had you been ten minutes later, you would have missed me. I had some errands to run before we were to meet at the attorney's office.'' He opened the door wider. "Come on in."

"Go ahead and run your errands," Adria said. All her talk about bravery was empty. "You and I can talk later."

"They can wait until another day," he told her. "You wouldn't have driven out here, if the visit hadn't been important. So come on in out of the heat and tell me about it."

She followed him into the house. Wearing a sports shirt, jeans and deck shoes, he sat on a bar stool and looked at her, waiting for her to speak.

"Hanson Godair stopped by the office this morning. He's offered me a contract," she began, then rushed on to tell Joel why Hanson had offered her the job. "I took it. I couldn't do anything else, Joel.''

"No, you wouldn't have, Adria." He pushed off the stool and walked over to the curio cabinet to pick up one of the tankards and ran his finger over the delicate etchings. Without looking at her he said, "Now that you have this contract, I suppose you want to back out of the treasure hunt?''

Here was the perfect opening, her opportunity to slide out of her agreement with him. "No," she answered, almost as surprised by her answer as Joel was.

But she shouldn't have been. During her drive from the office to the beach, she had argued with herself. Reason dictated that she abandon the hunt; a gut feeling pressed her to take the risk. But until this moment she had pushed the risk-taking urge aside. She had decided to take Hanson's contract and walk away from Joel LeMaster. But now she realized she had not come to face Joel LeMaster, but herself. Her answer was to herself, as well as to Joel.

He returned the tankard to the shelf and turned to stare at her. "You didn't drive over here to tell me about a contract that doesn't affect me."

"You're right. I was—" She drew in a deep breath. "I was going to take Godair's offer and forget the *Golden Fleece*."

"You may have taken the offer," Joel said, "but you would have never forgotten the *Golden Fleece*."

"Again you're right. So I'm going to do both. I'll have to assign a crew to the *Silver Colt,* part of the crew I planned to use on the treasure hunt."

"Solly, Ford Lowell or that other diver you mentioned?"

"Hub Chambers. No, if you want them, Solly, Ford and Hub will come with us. All three have the experience you need, for treasure salvaging. Your contract is first, so you'll have the first choice."

Joel walked to stand in front of her, his hands closing around her shoulders. Although the touch was firm, it warmed her. While the gray eyes were friendly, they were also wary. "Adria, Donald held those papers up—deliberately, I might add—so that you'd have time to reconsider. If you want out, now's the time. I know you're not absolutely sold on it."

Here was her second opportunity, and again reason urged her to get out. She was not like her father and brother; she was not a treasure diver. Her main interest was the well-being of the company. However, she said, "Solly and the crew are."

If she continued with the treasure hunt, she had told herself many times this morning, she was doing it for Solly and the boys. But in her heart of hearts she knew that wasn't the truth. She had a way out, but her not taking it proved that *she* wanted to go on the treasure hunt.

"We're not talking about Solly and the crew," Joel said, "but about you. What do you want, Adria?"

"As I said earlier, I thought about getting out," she confessed, paused, then added, "but I want to go with you. I want to be a part of the hunt for the *Golden Fleece*. It's a risk I'm willing to take."

"But with Hanson's offer, your risks have been lowered and your mind set at ease."

"For the moment."

A slow smile curved Joel's lips, and he gently kneaded her shoulders. "There is some adventuring spirit in you, Adria Gilby."

More than Adria was willing to admit. Common sense told her to put distance between herself and Joel Le-Master. His smile and those beautiful gray eyes would be her undoing yet.

"Yes," she admitted and moved out of his clasp, "I suppose there is. It must be in the Gilby genes."

He returned to the breakfast bar, picking up his mail. "If this is all of your confession, I'd better run these errands—one, in particular. If not, I'll be without water and electricity. Of course, I won't be needing either for a while, but think of the hassle I'd have to go through when I returned, if I were in arrears with my payments." The gray eyes twinkled. "Would you like to spend an exciting hour or so with me paying bills, or do you want to meet me at the attorney's office?"

"I'd love to go with you," Adria said, "but I've got to get back to the office. When I'm gone, none of the clerical work gets done, and I'm already a day behind, as it is."

During the year she had been running the business, she had not taken a day off, had not even been tempted to take one. Yesterday was her first truancy. How easily she could have played hooky with Joel today. She fell in step with him, and they moved to the front door.

"Have you developed your film yet?" he asked.

"I've already sent the colored roll off. It should be ready by next Monday. I'll develop the black-and-white ones myself tonight."

At the door, he stopped walking and turned to look down into her face. "I suppose you know about the special exhibit of cameras on loan from Japan at the museum in Wilmington?"

"Yes, I watched a documentary about it on television last night. It's fascinating, the way the Japanese have traced the history of photography through cameras."

"May I take you to see it after we sign the contract this afternoon?"

"Yes."

He opened the door, and she followed him onto the deck, lightly sprinting down to the bottom step as he locked the door.

When he stood by her, she said, "While we're in Wilmington, could we attend the plantation antique auction?"

"I thought that was Chessy's hobby?" A smile softened the corners of his mouth.

"Well, I'm a tagalong. We're looking for several pieces of furniture, in particular," she added, the two of them slowly moving to the Topaz. "Pieces that are identical to those that were once a part of Avalon. Getting them is part of my restoration goal for the house."

"How long have you been doing this?"

She unlocked and opened the door on the driver's side of her car. "I've been going to antique auctions as long as I can remember. Aunt Chessy loves them and always took me with her. I began the restoration when we found a fainting lounge that matched two of our spot chairs. Later, Aunt Chessy and I were going through some old photographs and found one of my great-great-great-grandmothers sitting on a lounge identical to the one we had purchased. I guess you can say this is a hobby that Uncle Solly, Aunt Chessy and I share. We refinish and upholster the furniture ourselves."

"Will Solly and Chessy meet us at the auction?"

"Not tonight." Sliding into the car, she lowered her window before she shut the door and switched on the ignition. "I'm on my own. The two of them are going to a monthly senior citizens' dinner sponsored by the church, and as Uncle Solly says, 'It's for mature people. Young kiddos like you aren't invited.'"

"I'll see you at Donald's office at two," Joel said.

"I HAD NO IDEA this would happen," Joel apologized for the second time since they had signed the contract and walked out of Donald's office. He pushed open the door of the Spear's Building and he and Adria walked onto the sidewalk of downtown Freeport. "The likelihood of Robert's showing up at Camp LeJeune right now is about one in a million. If he was going to be here longer, I wouldn't go meet him tonight. But he's in Intelligence, and it's catch as catch can. Sometimes we don't even know where he is. Other times we think he's at the base in San Diego only to receive a call from Europe."

"Really, I understand," Adria said, reaching into her shirt pocket for her sunglasses to shield her eyes from the afternoon glare. "These things happen. We'll go to the museum another night. It'll be here. Your brother won't, and family is important.''

Joel didn't want to wait until another night to be with Adria. Last night he had stayed awake for a long time thinking about her and the effect she was having on him. He liked it, and wanted to be with her now and tonight. He had been looking forward to their evening together. He hadn't realized how two-dimensional his life had become until he met her. In just a few short days, she had opened doors to emotions he had forgotten he possessed.

They stopped by the Jeep first, since it was parked closer to the building than her car. ''I know this doesn't sound much like a date,'' he said, ''but would you consider driving to the base with me? I'd like to have your company.''

''Would your brother mind your bringing someone along?'' Adria asked.

Joel shook his head. ''Especially not when he discovers that he ruined such a pleasant evening for me.''

Her face burst into a smile, and she nodded. ''I'd love to go with you. What time is he expecting you?''

''More or less when I get there. I told him I'd leave after we finished up at the lawyer's office. As soon as I find a telephone, I'll give him a call to let him know I'm on my way. Camp LeJeune is right outside Jacksonville, and I figure we'll stop for dinner on the way. Right?''

She nodded. ''Where are we going to meet him?''

He grinned. ''At the base.''

Teasingly Adria made a face. ''Exactly *where* on the base?''

''Visitors' center. Once we get there, I'm to call him, and he'll meet us.''

''This sounds rather clandestine.''

"In a sense everything Robert does seems to be like that. Through the years, I've come to accept the secretive part of his work."

She nodded and glanced over at the yellow Topaz. "I need to go by the house first."

"Good. If you don't mind, I'll call from there."

Adria stood for a second, then said, "I'm not sure I want you to call him from my house."

Puzzled, Joel stared at her. "I was going to use my calling card," he said.

"Oh, I'm not worried about the cost." She brushed his words aside. "You know in the spy movies, they always bug the innocent person's house and that person ends up getting blown to bits in an explosion or something like that." Her eyes twinkled, and she grinned mischievously.

"I don't think we have to worry about that in this case. Besides, I'm here to protect you."

Laughing, she moved to her car, calling over her shoulder, "I feel better already. I never knew when I first met you that you were a knight in shining armor coming to rescue the damsel in distress."

"I'm not so sure the metaphor fits," Joel retorted. "I will protect you, but I don't quite cast myself in the role of knight. Even if I were, my armor would be rusted not shining."

Unlocking her car, she opened the door and gazed over the roof at him. "I think not."

Joel said nothing as she slid under the wheel of the Topaz and closed the door. He, then, climbed into the Jeep. After turning on the ignition and fastening his safety belt, he unzipped the small leather portfolio that lay on the seat and slipped his copy of the contract into one of the side pockets.

His deal with Adria was signed, sealed and delivered. He was going after the *Golden Fleece*. Rather *they* were, and they were going to find it. He knew it; he felt it deep within himself. In the past when he had a hunch this strong, it had paid off, and this one would, too. His only concern was having to use commercial divers, but they were his only option.

He pushed aside his worries and pulled out behind Adria to follow her to Avalon. As they had done last night they parked in front of the carriage house. Climbing out of the Jeep, he heard Adria speaking.

"Aunt Chessy, that's beautiful. I would never have guessed it was cherry wood."

"Ten coats of paint will cover anything. It never surprises me anymore what people will do." Chessy tossed the cleaning cloth into an empty pail and stood, with hands on her hips, staring at the antique chair she had stripped. Then she turned to look at Adria. "How come you're home so early?"

"I'm going to Camp LeJeune with Joel to see his brother."

Chessy's gaze moved past Adria to Joel. "Now?"

"As soon as I change clothes," Adria answered.

"Pretty warm," Chessy said and walked out of the carriage house. "Would y'all like to have something cold to drink?"

"Joel might. Not me." Adria skipped across the flagstones, up the steps and across the veranda into the house.

"Well, Joel," the older woman said as they walked at a more leisurely pace into the house, "what's your pleasure? I have some soft drinks, beer, tea and homemade lemonade."

"Lemonade sounds refreshing," Joel answered.

"Come on into the kitchen," Chessy invited. "We'll sit in there and wait for Adria."

"May I use your phone?" Joel asked.

"Sure can. We have one in the kitchen, but why don't you use the one in the study. That way you can have a little privacy." She pointed. "You know where it is?"

He nodded and walked out of the room into the hallway, turning right at the first door. The study was fully restored, the mahogany floor-to-ceiling shelves polished to a high sheen and full of books. On the west wall were two windows, the burgundy drapes drawn to either side, the shades raised midway. Afternoon sunlight filtered into the room through sheer ecru curtains. Two wingback chairs were in front of the fireplace.

In the middle of the room was a large desk with a matching chair, upholstered in brown leather. A black candlestick telephone sat on the desk next to a lamp with double globes. Using his calling card, Joel dialed the base number and waited while his brother was paged. Finally he heard the familiar voice flow through the line.

After greetings and pleasantries were exchanged, Robert asked, "Does this call mean you're leaving Freeport now?"

"Give me about three hours," Joel said. "I'm bringing my new partner with me and we're stopping for dinner on the way."

"The woman you were telling me about earlier?"

"The same."

"I hope she's as pretty as you described. These old eyes sure could stand to feast themselves on some soft feminine beauty for a change."

"She's prettier than I described," Joel answered. "But wait and make your own judgment."

"Joel, thanks for changing your plans and coming on such short notice," Robert said, an air of urgency in his voice. "I'm sorry I messed up your evening, but I don't know when I'll be stateside again. I'm not even sure about Christmas, and I do need to talk with you. Really I do."

"Don't worry, Rob," Joel assured him, and wanted to ask Robert what was so urgent about their meeting, but he didn't. He had learned, through the years, that his older brother explained whenever the occasion demanded and not a second before. "Everything's under control. We'll see you in a little while."

After Joel replaced the receiver, he walked over to one of the shelves and looked at the books.

"Here you are," Adria said.

He turned to see her standing in the doorway, sunlight spilling around her. Her hair was pulled into a ponytail, its rich waves flowing down her back. The long-waisted white dress had a scooped neck and short sleeves, a beautiful contrast to her dark hair and tanned skin. The cotton knit flowed with the lines of her body to accent her slender figure and height. A tiny gold anklet gleamed on her right leg, just above the strap of her red sandals.

"You look lovely."

"Thanks." She smiled, her eyes never leaving his.

"I like your hair like that."

"I hoped you would. Aunt Chessy has your lemonade in the kitchen."

"Oh . . . yes." He had become so involved in Adria that he had forgotten about his drink. How easy it was for the two of them to create a world of their own. "You aren't having anything with me?"

"I will now," she answered. "I didn't want to keep you waiting."

"Even if you had—" he cupped his hand beneath her elbow, liking the feel of her skin against his, and guided her through the study into the kitchen "—it would have been worth it."

As they walked into the old-fashioned room, Chessy was crocheting and rocking in front of the fireplace, the opening covered with an Oriental silk screen. Like the other rooms in the house, this one boasted several large windows, the shades and curtains drawn to allow plenty of light.

"Your drink's on the table, Joel," Chessy said.

"Thank you." He walked to the round oak table to pick up the glass brimming with cubes of ice and lemonade, moisture beading and running down the side.

"Adria, did you call Solly to let him know that you weren't returning to the office today, and to remind him that he'd have to lock up?" Chessy asked, as Adria opened the door to the refrigerator and reached for a can of Diet 7-Up.

She glanced at her foster aunt and smiled. "Sure did. And he said to tell you he'll be home early and not to forget your date tonight."

"He's more likely to forget than me. If it hadn't been for me remembering, I wouldn't have got any anniversary gifts for the past thirty-six years." She dropped her hands into her lap. "When are y'all gonna leave in search of the *Golden Fleece?*"

"Before the end of the week, hopefully," Joel answered, then took several swallows of the lemonade.

"And only God knows how long y'all will be there looking," she murmured, slowly rocking back and forth, staring straight ahead.

"You could come with us," Joel suggested. "We need a good cook."

"Young man, I don't put my feet on any boat." Chessy turned to stare at him, the sparkle in her eyes taking the sting out of her words. "I'm not a fisherman, a salvor or a treasure hunter. This here house is my territory, and I take real good care of it. I'm always here waiting."

He drained the glass and set it down on the coaster. After he had complimented her on the lemonade, he said, "Just remember, in case you change your mind, you've already passed the cooking test. I'm ready to sign you on."

Chessy laughed. "You two go on and get out of here. I'd like to clean up my kitchen before I leave tonight."

"Are you ready?" Joel asked Adria. When she nodded and set her empty can on the kitchen counter, he moved to where she stood, caught her hand and twined his fingers through hers. "You don't have to worry about Adria, Aunt Chessy. I'll take good care of her."

Chessy stood and smiled, her gaze running over Adria's face. "I don't guess we have to worry," she said softly and stepped closer to Adria, "but something inside us, something called love, makes us do it anyway. Now the two of you have a good time, you hear me." She lifted a hand and touched Adria's face.

Adria leaned forward and kissed the older woman on the cheek. "You and Uncle Solly have a good time, too."

Still holding hands, Joel and Adria walked out of the house to the Jeep. He guided her to the driver's side and when she slid in and slipped all the way over, he grinned.

"I wish you didn't have to sit that far from me. It's not as if this is our first time together."

"No, but it's our first formal date."

Adria was one of the most fascinating women Joel had ever met. A smile softly molded her lips, and her ponytail hung over one shoulder, the brown hair gleaming in the afternoon sunlight. Her blue eyes sparkled with a challenge.

"When I first met you, Adria, you said you were a jack-of-all-trades and wore a hat for each. Which hat are you wearing now?"

The smile deepened, and Adria held a hand to the back of her head. Affecting a deep southern drawl, she said, "My best Scarlet O'Hara leghorn."

WHEN THE OFFICIAL VEHICLE pulled into the parking lot, Joel and Adria were leaning against the Jeep waiting. The car stopped, and out of the back door a tall man in military uniform emerged. For a second, Joel and the stranger stared at each other. Then they rushed forward and hugged.

Robert pulled back to look at Joel. "Little Bro, I'm so glad you could make it. I've had one he—" he looked up to see Adria still leaning against the Jeep "—one heck of a time finding you. The Marine Corps does a fine job of keeping my agenda hidden from everyone, including me, but they don't hold a candle to the excellent job you do for yourself."

"Nature of my business," Joel answered.

"I can understand that," Robert said, then, "Let me get rid of the car, and we'll go somewhere to talk."

Joel returned to the Jeep, and Robert to the olive-drab sedan. He reached into the back and pulled out a briefcase, and stood for several minutes speaking in low tones with the driver. Finally the car drove off, and he walked to where Joel and Adria stood.

"Sorry, Joel. Sometimes I'm not my own man. I have five hours before I have to report back here."

Joel nodded. "Robert, I'd like you to meet my new partner, Adria Gilby."

"Hello, Robert."

Her hand was engulfed in his for a firm handshake. "Adria, it's a pleasure to meet you. Thanks for letting me mess up your date with Joel."

"You changed its focus," Adria said, "but certainly didn't mess it up. I love the ride from Freeport to Camp LeJeune in the springtime."

"Well, Rob," Joel asked, "where shall we go? Springtime, anytime, a parking lot is about the same."

"A friend of mine has a house in town, and he's in San Diego on special duty." He reached into his pockets. "I have the key. Let's go over there where we can relax."

"Do you have directions," Joel asked, "or do we make another phone call and wait for someone to meet us?"

"I know the way," Robert answered and opened the back door to the Jeep.

Adria thought it odd that Robert had the key to a friend's house, but she guessed this was part of the secrecy Joel had talked about on the drive to Camp LeJeune. Recently she had watched an old movie that starred Gregory Peck and Anthony Quinn. She remembered the briefcase containing the secret documents had been chained and locked to Peck's wrist. Although she knew this was rather farfetched for today, she did glance down at Robert's wrist. When she raised her head, Joel was looking at her, a grin tugging the corners of his mouth. She felt warmth flushing her cheeks and hoped her thoughts had not been transparent enough for him to read.

As Joel pulled into the traffic and turned left, he asked, "Can you tell me anything about your trip?"

"Nothing. Right at the next signal light, then go about two miles to the new housing tract." He gave Joel the street address. "The house we're looking for should be a redbrick two-story on the left side of the street in the middle of the block.''

Adria listened as Joel and Robert talked, the conversation centering on the family. The children were doing fine. Sandy was finishing up at the university, earning a degree in computer science; Bob had just passed his CPA and was promoted within the firm where he worked. And Lane was the typical thirteen-year-old. Something in Robert's tone alerted Adria that Lane LeMaster was anything but typical; yet neither Joel nor Robert said more. The conversation then turned to their parents and older brother.

When they reached the house, Robert unlocked the door and ushered them into the den. Depositing the attaché case on the breakfast bar, he went to the refrigerator.

''Beer, colas and wine,'' he announced. ''What's your preference?''

''Nothing for me,'' Joel answered.

''Nor me,'' Adria replied, and walked over to the sliding glass patio doors to gaze at the backyard, landscaped with blooming flowers of all varieties. Wanting to investigate them closer and also wanting to give the brothers time to themselves, she said, ''I think I'll go out and look around.''

When the door slid behind her, both of the men watched her slowly meander around the yard. His beer in hand, Robert sat down in the large chair.

''She's pretty, Joel.''

''Yes, she is, and she's also intelligent.'' Joel dragged his gaze from Adria and looked at his brother. His face was gaunt and the skin beneath his eyes dark. ''Is something wrong, Rob?''

Robert lifted the bottle to his lips and took a long drink. ''This is my last mission, Joel. I'm going to get out.''

''Of Intelligence?''

"No, the Corps."

Joel never let his surprise show. "When did you make this decision?"

Robert brushed a hand over his furrowed brow and through his short hair. "Ellen called me about two weeks ago. She's having some problems with Lane and wants me to take him for a while."

"When?"

"First of June. That's when he'll finish school." Robert stood and paced the room. "He's a brilliant child, especially when it comes to computers, but he's using his creativity to get into trouble. Somehow or other, he got into some of the teachers' testing files. He didn't do anything with the information, but distraught school officials called Ellen, telling her what had happened and swearing that they had caught him before he could do anything. You know how Ellen is. She fell apart and blames me for what's happening."

"You can't accept all the blame, Rob," Joel said.

"The hell, I can't!" his brother exclaimed. "Don't you think I'd like to point at my ex-wives and say they're the reason why my marriages failed and that Ellen is responsible for Lane's problems? I would, Joel. I'd like someone to blame besides myself. But in all honesty, I can't. Marriage and parenthood are a twosome, and I'm as guilty of failure as either of those women is."

"You're being too hard on yourself, Rob," Joel said. "You always have been. I'll have to agree that you were partly to blame for the breakup of your marriages, but you can't shoulder all the blame for Lane. He has to carry some—if not most—of the blame himself."

"If I'd been home to be a father to him, as I was for Sandy and Bobby," Rob said, "Lane would be different today."

"You don't have to give up the Corps to do that," Joel pointed out. "Just get out of Intelligence. Rob, this is the only life you know. What will you do if you get out?"

"I'm not sure," Rob said, "but by the time I return from this mission, I'll have it figured out. I just know that I have to give some prime time to Lane. The kid's too bright to let run loose."

"Have you considered a military academy for him?"

Robert nodded. "Ellen and I discussed it, but she swears Lane could never adjust to that kind of life. I'll have to use this summer getting to know Lane and finding out what he really wants out of life."

"I wish there was some way I could help you," Joel said, truly sympathizing with his brother, "but I can't. This is a decision you have to make on your own, Rob." Joel rose and walked to the door, watching Adria as she leaned back in one of the patio chairs with her eyes closed. He was grateful to her for giving him and Robert time to themselves and promised to make it up to her later.

"It's going to take me a little time to process my papers," Rob said, "and I'm not quite sure how long this mission will take. You said you wished there was some way you could help me."

Joel turned a questioning face to his brother.

"Will you pick up Lane for me and keep him for a while?"

Joel stared at Robert. "I'm leaving in a few days to hunt for the *Golden Fleece*."

"I wouldn't ask, if it weren't important. I need to get Lane away from the crowd he runs with quick. And he likes you, Joel." Rob walked to where his brother stood, laid a hand on his shoulder and squeezed.

"I can't postpone the hunt," Joel said. "I'm already pressed for time. Westbrook is dogging my heels. I'm always afraid that he'll be just minutes ahead of me."

"Take Lane with you," Robert suggested. "He'd enjoy it, Joel."

"This is no joyride, Rob," Joel exclaimed. "What if Allen suggested you take one of his children on a mission with you?"

"It's not the same," his brother argued. "You won't have to keep him long, Joel. I promise."

"Robert, I can't do it. I can't take the responsibility for having a child on an excavation with me. My God, have you forgotten what happened to Vanessa?"

"Joel, you're not signing Lane on to be a diver, and it's not going to be for long."

"But you can't guarantee that," Joel countered.

"You've got to help me. This is my son." Robert brushed his hands over his forehead. "Joel, the only way I'll be any good on this assignment is to know that you have Lane."

Joel studied the drawn, haggard face, the prematurely wrinkled forehead. The gray eyes were shadowed with pain and worry, and this was one worry Joel could alleviate for his brother. He sighed.

"Can Ellen get him to Freeport?"

"Yes."

"I'll call and make arrangements for her to bring him," Joel said. "Also I'm going to talk with Lane and let him know he'll be working with me as my helper until you arrive to get him."

"Thanks," Robert said.

Joel nodded, thinking about the complications he had just added to his life. He could only wonder at Adria's reaction to his news. "That's what brothers are for."

"I'm going to call Ellen now," Robert said and walked into the kitchen, where he set his empty beer bottle on the breakfast bar.

"Rob," Joel said, as his brother's hand closed around the telephone receiver, "there's more that's bothering you, isn't there? This thing with Lane is serious certainly, but it's not enough to have you this worried."

Robert dropped his hand from the telephone and gazed at Joel for a long while before he nodded his head. "Ellen is seeing someone else. She's thinking about marrying him."

"Why should that bother you?" Joel asked. "You and she have been divorced for two years now."

Robert opened the refrigerator and pulled out a second beer. After he opened the bottle, he took several long swallows. Finally his eyes riveted on his brother. "I still love her, Joel. I didn't realize how much until we met several weeks ago to discuss Lane. I don't want to lose her."

"Rob, you didn't lose her—you turned her loose two years ago. I think maybe your ego is badly bruised and you're overreacting because she's interested in another man."

"I knew I loved and wanted her back in my life before I found out about the other guy," Rob said. "I didn't know about him until I called Lane earlier today."

"Your getting out of the service has more to do with Ellen than with Lane?" Joel asked.

"No, no matter what happens between Ellen and me, I'm going to get out. I owe this to Lane." He lifted the bottle to his lips and drank deeply.

"Have you told Ellen how you feel about her?"

Rob moved restlessly around the room. "Yes. The last time I saw her, I told her I loved and missed her. I wanted us to get back together and give it a second try. She admitted she still loved me, but she didn't know if she wanted to try marriage again. We hadn't made it work the first time, and she wasn't sure she wanted to subject herself to the same misery again. She still can't accept my work, Joel."

"Rob, if you feel this way about Ellen, if you're willing to make this sacrifice for her, tell her now when you call. Let her know what you feel, and what you're willing to do to make the marriage work."

Robert nodded and again picked up the receiver, dialing the number. Joel walked toward the patio doors, but Robert called him back.

Cupping his hand over the receiver, he said, "Don't leave. We'll talk to Lane first, then I'll talk to Ellen." He removed his hand. "Lane, this is Dad. I told you everything would work out all right. I've talked to your Uncle Joel, and he wants you to stay with him. Here. You can talk to him yourself."

Joel took the telephone. "Hello, Lane."

"Hello," a petulant voice said.

"Well, Lane, what do you think about coming to stay with me for a few weeks this summer until your dad gets through with his assignment?"

"Stay where?" the thirteen-year-old asked, with tentative excitement.

"Actually, I'm going to be looking for sunken treasure," Joel said.

"Real treasure?" He was interested for sure.

"That's right. A ship, or rather a fleet of ships, sunk in the late 1500s."

"Where?"

Joel laughed. "That's classified information."

"How am I going to find you, if I don't know where you are?"

"Your mother will bring you to my bungalow at Freeport and I'll meet you there. I really want you to be with me, Lane, but you have to understand that we'll be doing some important work, and you'll be a part of the crew. Also you're going to have to be closemouthed about our project. Don't discuss it with anyone but your mother."

"Wow! This sounds great. I like being part of the crew," Lane murmured. "That's not bad, Uncle Joel."

"You'll be paid, of course," Joel continued, "but you'll have to understand that I'm not only your uncle but I'm also your boss. You have to respect my authority."

There was a long period of silence, then Lane laughed shakily. "Mom's been talking with you, hasn't she?"

"No," Joel answered, "your father told me about the computer episode, but that's not what prompted my talking to you the way I am. Hunting for sunken treasure can be a great deal of fun. It's certainly adventurous, but it's also dangerous. One of the first rules any of us has to learn is to respect authority."

"Okay," Lane answered, then asked, "Are you working with a computer?"

"Sure am, and with sonar equipment."

"Uncle Joel—" the young voice throbbed with excitement "—will I be allowed to work with either of them?"

"Yes, if you're as knowledgeable about them as your father says you are."

Lane laughed, the sound full of happiness. "I'm probably better than he says. I love computers and they love me."

"Then you, Lane LeMaster, are the man I need to complete my crew. I know enough about computers to get by, but now I'm going to get an expert."

Again laughter flowed through the line; then Lane said, "Maybe I'm not an expert, Uncle Joel, but I know a lot about them, and I'm willing to learn more."

"That's the kind of attitude I like. You and I are going to get along just fine. Now, I'm going to let you talk to your father. He'll give your mother my address and a phone number where she can reach me. Remember what I said: Mum is the word."

"I'll remember, Uncle Joel."

"I'll be seeing you in about three weeks."

Joel handed the receiver to Robert, who said to his son, "Lane, call your mom to the phone for me."

Picking up the pencil and pad on the counter, Joel started to write down the number of the Beachcomber, but thought better of it. Neither Ellen nor Lane knew the importance of secrecy for this quest. Still he needed to give them an address and phone number where he could be reached. Adria. Quickly he jotted down her home address and phone number. Aunt Chessy could be trusted.

He said to Robert, "Give Ellen this number and address. It's Adria's, and while she's gone her Aunt Chessy will be there to take messages. I don't want either Ellen or Lane calling me at the Beachcomber. No one is to know where I am or what I'm doing."

Robert nodded and Joel walked away to stand at the patio doors. He stared at Adria and wondered how he was going to break the news to her that he had hired his thirteen-year-old nephew to be part of his crew.

Chapter Seven

Knowing what he must do, Joel opened the doors, walked across the patio and stood looking down at Adria.

"Hi," she murmured, never opening her eyes. Her lashes were a dark crescent on her smooth cheeks, and her lips curled into a lazy smile. "I'm glad you joined me. It's beautiful out here this time of evening."

Joel sat on the side of the lounge chair next to her. "How do you know?" he teased. "You aren't even looking at it."

Slowly the lids lifted, the movement altogether provocative as they revealed the warm, dreamy blue eyes. "I'm absorbing it with all my senses. Now you can enjoy it with me."

His gaze caught and held hers. "Is that the only reason you're glad I joined you?"

"No—" she took a breath, her breasts rising and falling; soft color tinged her cheeks "—I was lonely. I missed you."

He reached out to clasp her hand, their fingers twining together, her flesh warm and soft in his. "Me, too."

He held their hands up and looked at hers. Her fingers were slender, the skin smooth, the nails neatly clipped. He moved his thumb, the pad coming to rest on her wrist where the pulse thumped wildly. Because of him? he wondered. He hoped.

"Did you . . . and Robert have a nice visit?" she asked.

Did he imagine the catch in her voice? He thought not. He wanted Adria to be as affected by him as he was by her. "Yes," he said. "Thanks for letting us talk alone."

"You're welcome," she said. "I figured the two of you had some heavy talking to do—otherwise, he wouldn't have asked you to make such a long drive in one evening. And I didn't mind being out here. Actually I prefer to be outside in weather like this. Spring has to be the most wonderful time of year. Everything in full bloom—beautiful to look at, to touch and to smell."

Still holding her hand, tracing designs on her wrist, Joel slid fully into the chair, stretched out and crossed his legs at the ankles. He leaned against the cushioned back until he was almost reclining and let his gaze move from the branches of one tree to another. They were native trees saved when the house was built and almost formed a canopy over the entire back lawn. The leaves gently rustled in the evening breeze.

"Listen to it," Adria said. "Nature's symphony. It's so wonderful, Joel. Nothing can compare."

Although the sun set much later now, day was surely turning into night. "Except maybe the sound of the water gently splashing against the side of a ship, the stars glistening in a night blue sky, and the moon a huge silver orb. Just you and the universe."

Adria laughed softly. "I guess that runs a close second."

They lapsed into silence, as Joel mentally rehearsed how he was going to tell her about his decision to bring Lane with them. Nothing seemed quite right. Anything he said would break the magic of the moment, and he was reluctant to do that.

It was something special that he had shared only with Adria, which was odd, considering he had been in love with Vanessa . . . or at least, he had thought at the time he was in love with her. Now that he thought about it, he realized their relationship had never developed beyond the physical. His and Adria's had; that's what made it magical and special. Simply holding hands with her filled him with pleasure.

Still, she had to know about Lane. He wanted to tell her before Robert did. It was something she should learn from him, not from his brother.

"Adria," he finally said, "Rob's having some trouble with Lane."

"I wondered about that, when we were driving here." She turned her head to look at him. "What kind?"

Briefly Joel explained, then said, "Ellen—Robert's ex-wife is having difficulties being a single parent."

"It can't be easy."

"She feels like Lane needs to be with his father."

"That's going to be hard to arrange, with him dashing in and out of the country on these classified assignments."

"This is his last one," Joel said. "He's going to get out of the service."

"That's a serious decision, but I suppose he's thought it through."

So far the discussion was not making his confession any easier. Joel decided his best tactic was to plunge right in. "I've agreed to keep Lane with me until Rob completes this assignment." When Adria only stared at him blankly, he said, "I don't want Robert worrying about Lane while he's gone."

"I can understand," she said. "How long will you be keeping him?"

"I'm not sure."

"What about the hunt for the *Golden Fleece?*"

"I'm going to take Lane with us."

Adria sat up, her hand slipping out of Joel's clasp. She stared at him in disbelief. "You've agreed to bring this child with us on an excavation of great magnitude and you don't even know how long you're going to keep him?"

"Adria, there was nothing else I could do. Lane is my nephew."

"I agree that your options were limited," she said. "I don't mind your taking care of your nephew, but this isn't a pleasure cruise we're taking, Joel. This is work."

"I know. That's what I told Lane. I hired him to be part of the crew."

Adria's jaw went slack. "You were worried about using my men, who are certified as divers, and you've hired a thirteen-year-old child."

"It's not quite as cut-and-dried as you make it sound," Joel pointed out. "He's not going to be diving. He'll be doing odd jobs. He's very good with computers, and we're going to need someone who knows how to operate one."

"I thought you did."

"I do, but my knowledge is limited. Also I was going to get someone to be my backup. It's a hindrance if you're the only one who is specialized in a field on an excavation of this magnitude. Now I'll let Lane be my backup."

"A thirteen-year-old child!" Adria exclaimed.

"If he has the knowledge, his age doesn't matter. I'll be there to guide him. Lane is going, Adria. I'm going to keep my promise to Robert, but Lane isn't going to spend the summer doing nothing. He's going to work. He's going to be part of the crew."

She stood and gazed down into his face. "The ink is barely dry on the contract, and already you're exerting your authority."

Joel rose and stepped toward her, but she turned her back to him. He placed his hands on her shoulders. She held herself rigid. "Adria, I didn't mean that the way it sounded. I should have discussed this with you before I made a decision, but I didn't feel as if I had an option. Rob's in trouble and he needs me. I'm not in the habit of taking children on finds with me."

He gently kneaded her shoulders. Finally she sighed, and the tension eased out of her body. "I'm not as upset about your taking Lane on the trip with us as I am about your not talking to me about it first. I guess I'm extra sensitive. It's not easy to give up your ship and your crew."

"I know."

"In the future, Joel, please do me the courtesy of talking things over first. Maybe I don't have a say-so, but I do have an opinion to share with you."

"I will," he promised. "I guess I've been on my own for so long, I've forgotten how to share."

She turned, and he caught her in his arms, holding her close. "This is something we'll learn together."

When Vanessa broke their engagement, he had been hurt. At the time, he thought he was heartbroken; now he knew he had suffered from a deflated ego. Vanessa's death was heartfelt because it was tragic for someone to die that young.

He had only known Adria a short time, and while he was physically attracted to her, she had made inroads into his affection and was quickly moving into his heart. If something were to happen to her, his life would be affected indelibly.

She laid her face against his chest. He lowered his head and rested it on top of her head, her hair like silk against his cheek. Through the fabric of his jeans, he felt the evening wind wrap the material of her skirt around his legs. Holding Adria in his arms could become a pleasant habit, he thought, a lifelong habit.

The patio door opened and Robert walked out of the house. Adria pulled away but not out of Joel's embrace.

"Well, it's settled," Robert said. "Lane will be arriving at Adria's house on the second Sunday in June. Ellen is going to bring him herself. I gave her Adria's phone number and address, as you instructed."

When Adria looked up at him, Joel said, "I knew your Aunt Chessy would be circumspect. I wasn't sure about the people who answer the phone at the Beachcomber."

Adria nodded.

Joel said to Robert, "You didn't talk long."

"No, our conversation was short and sweet. Her boyfriend was there and she couldn't talk long. She has the house in Cherry Point up for sale." Robert's tone was as clipped as the statement. He stepped off the patio onto the carpet grass and walked across the lawn.

Joel had never seen his brother in such anguish. Of course, after Robert had graduated from college and joined the Corps, Joel hadn't seen much of him.

In a low voice, Adria said, "He's still in love with her, isn't he?"

"Yes, and I think she's in love with him. She just couldn't come to grips with his job. She worried herself sick when he went on one of those missions, when none of us knew where he was or when he was coming home."

Robert turned and called out, "By the way, while I was talking to Ellen, another call beeped in. My departure has been delayed for another couple of hours. The driver will pick me up here, when it's time to go." He slowly walked toward them. "I know the trip to Freeport is a long one, two hours, at least, and it's late. The trip would be easier to make in the morning, after a night's rest. If you want, you can stay over. The house is yours to use."

Adria gaped at him, and Joel grinned, imagining the thoughts that were passing through her mind. Robert looked from Adria to Joel, then seemed to realize the conclusion Adria had drawn. He grinned.

"It has four bedrooms," he added, then shrugged. "Do whatever you want. It was only a suggestion."

"It's appreciated," Adria said. "We'll think about it."

"While the two of you are thinking it over, I'm going back inside and get me another beer."

"Rob—" Joel dropped his arm from Adria's shoulder and stepped toward his brother; he caught his arm "—don't you think you've had enough for tonight?"

In the light that spilled from the den onto the patio, the two men stood staring at each other. They were brothers; yet physically they were different. Robert, with the Corps haircut, the uniform, and the clipped speech pattern, appeared to be contained and disciplined. Joel, on the other hand, was the opposite. He was several inches shorter than his brother, but his wiry physique gave the illusion of added height. His hair was fuller and longer, curling over the collar of his shirt. While his shirt and jeans were nice and fit him well, showing his physique to an advantage, they were softer and less regimented, as was his whole appearance.

Finally Robert jerked away from Joel. In a low, firm voice—a tone similar to that Joel had used when he told Adria that Lane was going on the hunt with them—he said, "Little Bro, I don't need a keeper. I can take care of myself.'' He pushed open one of the sliding-glass doors and walked into the house.

Those were almost the same words that Joel had spoken to her the night she met him at the Beachcomber. They were brothers, and although they didn't resemble each other physically, she wondered if they thought and reacted alike. From what Joel had told her about his brother and from what she had learned about Joel, neither of them trusted other people. It seemed that both were cut from the same fabric. Her gaze swung to the breakfast bar and to the two empty beer bottles. Adria admitted that two beers was not excessive drinking, but her mind kept running back to the articles she had read about Joel. The writers had emphasized his drinking; they had accused him of drowning his sorrows in the bottle.

She wondered if this was what Robert was doing. How much alike were the brothers? Did both try to resolve their problems and skepticism with a bottle?

No, of course not, a tiny voice deep within her answered reassuringly. You've been around Joel for several weeks now, and he hasn't shown a tendency toward inebriation. He's too strong physically and emotionally for that kind of weakness.

''Damn!'' Joel muttered under his breath, and she returned her attention to him. He stared after his brother, his hands balled into fists, hanging to his side. Concern was evident in his expression.

''Joel,'' she said, and he slowly turned his head to look at her, ''if you'd like to stay with Robert until he leaves, we will. I'll call Aunt Chessy and let her know that we'll be staying the night, so she won't worry.''

''Thanks,'' Joel murmured. ''Ordinarily I wouldn't ask a date to do this, but I'm worried about Robert. I've never seen him act like this before. Things must really be piling up on top of him—his mission, Lane, and Ellen and her involvement with this other man.''

''Was he this upset when he and his first wife divorced?''

''No divorce is pleasant,'' Joel answered, ''but he and Sandy seemed to have drifted out of the marriage as easily as they had drifted into it. His relationship with Ellen had been different from the beginning. I guess she was really the love of his life. Somehow, he seemed to think they would get back together one of these days and was totally unprepared for her having a serious relationship with another man.''

''Some people don't know how to take care of love once they find it,'' Adria said. ''Because they believe they don't deserve love and fear losing it, they unconsciously do things that cause them to lose it.''

''Are you the philosopher now?'' Joel teased, and Adria remembered her accusation the night she met him at the bungalow.

She grinned and shrugged as Joel opened the patio doors and they entered the house. ''Nope, just repeating a psychologist. It's one of the few things I remember from my sophomore psychology class. But if you think about it, it makes sense.''

''I'm not so sure about that.'' He shut and locked the door.

''I really believe it, Joel,'' she said.

''We'll discuss this at a more opportune time,'' he suggested. ''Maybe you can convince me.''

''It's a deal.''

''What's a deal?'' Robert asked.

Setting the coffee maker on the counter, he rummaged through the overhead cabinets, then bent to go through the lower ones.

"Philosophy," Joel answered.

"Finally," Robert muttered and straightened up with a bag of filters in his hand. Turning to the refrigerator, he opened the freezer and held up a can of decaffeinated coffee. "Thought I'd fix some of this. Have you decided what you're going to do?"

Joel nodded. "Thanks for the offer of the house. Adria and I are going to take you up on it. That way I'll get to spend several more hours with you."

Robert grinned, and his eyes sparkled, looking quite a bit like his younger brother's. "I'm glad, although I think you're staying because you want to save me from myself."

Both stared at the coffee maker.

"And I'm going to call Aunt Chessy to let her know that I won't be home tonight," Adria said. "Where's another phone?"

"Master bedroom," Robert replied and pointed to a door that led from the den. "Two more are upstairs. Take your pick."

"The one in there will do fine." Moving into the large room, Adria sat on the edge of the king-size bed and dialed the number. Several rings later, Chessy answered.

"Sorry to call so late," Adria said.

"Is something wrong?" Chessy interrupted.

"No, Joel's brother isn't leaving for several more hours and we're going to spend the night here . . . at the home of one of Robert's friends . . . and drive home in the morning. We didn't want to be on the road this late at night."

After a significant pause, Chessy said, "That's a wise decision. I'm glad you called to let me know."

At this moment, Adria appreciated Aunt Chessy more than ever before. The older woman was fighting a battle, but she did not give vent to her curiosity or berate Adria for making her choice. Chessy respected Adria's right to choose and trusted her to choose wisely.

"Will you tell Uncle Solly to open up the office for me in the morning and to gather the crew? Joel and I will leave here about eight and drive directly to the office."

"I'll pass your message on," Chessy promised, then added softly, "Sweet dreams, baby."

"Sweet dreams, Aunt Chessy."

After Adria replaced the receiver, she lay back on the bed and thought how fortunate she was to have someone like Solly and Chessy for her family. They loved and cared for her, but didn't smother her. As she lay there, getting more and more relaxed, her gaze meandered around the room, pretty, new and *unlived* in. The contemporary decor was dominated by gray, mauve and burgundy accessories. The entire house seemed to have a showroom quality about it, almost as if it had been designed to be looked at but not to be lived in. Again Adria pondered about Robert and this house; she wondered about his relationship with the owners.

"Everything okay?"

Adria looked across the room to see Joel standing in the doorway. She pushed her questions aside.

"Fine. I told Aunt Chessy to expect us at the office about eleven in the morning. That way, you can sit up as late as you want with Robert, and we can sleep in. We don't have to be in a rush to get back."

The gray eyes met and held hers; the glance, one of gratitude, was so intimate Adria felt a tremor of excitement run through her. She had been attracted to Joel from the first moment she had seen him, although she had dismissed her attraction as mere photographic interest. Now she could not hide behind such an inaccuracy. Plain and simple, she was attracted to Joel LeMaster, and the more she learned about him, the more attracted to him she became.

"Do you want anything to drink?" Joel asked and walked further into the room.

"Yes."

"We have a pot of decaffeinated coffee."

Adria sat up. She was not prepared to share a bedroom with him, no matter how innocent the sharing was. His presence further accentuated the aura of intimacy his gaze had initiated.

"No coffee," she replied. "Do they have any decaffeinated diet drinks?"

At the side of the bed now, Joel nodded and caught her hand.

She felt the warmth and strength of his clasp. It was reassuring. "7-Up?" she asked.

Again he nodded and tugged gently, pulling her to her feet. Their fingers twined, they walked into the den. Adria sat on the sofa; Joel walked into the kitchen. Holding the remote control, Robert sat in one of the large recliners and flipped from station to station.

"You believe you're close to finding the *Golden Fleece?*" he asked.

"Closer than I've ever been," Joel answered.

"But you think Westbrook is right behind you?"

"If not ahead." Joel opened the refrigerator, took out two cans of diet soda and set them on the counter. Then he opened the cabinet doors in search of glasses. As he filled them with ice, he said, "He's out there, Robert. Forever a shadow over my life. He's not happy with taking the *San Pablo* from me. He wants the *Golden Fleece*. He seems to know what I'm thinking at the same time I'm thinking it."

"Don't worry about him, Little Bro. You're going to find your ship before he does." Finally settling for a basketball game, Robert laid the remote control on the arm of the chair. Then he picked up his cup and took several swallows of coffee. "If I get back in time, Joel, I'll join you. It's been a long time since I've been on a dig."

"I'd love to have you." Joel carried the glasses of soda into the living room and handed one to Adria. The other he placed on the coffee table as he sat down beside her. "However, Mom let me know that you're due to visit them."

"I am," Robert replied, "but I'm not ready to see the Preacher yet."

Joel laughed and glanced over at Adria. "Sometimes we call my older brother Preacher, but it's not done in a derogatory way. Allen's not the kind of person to point a finger of blame or to preach to us."

"Not intentionally," Robert replied, "but his entire life points to blame. Married to the same woman for nearly thirty years. Never a doubt about his vocation. No trouble with any of his kids. At times, I'd swear Allen is perfect."

"Mavis disagrees with you there," Joel said. "Although she loves him, she'd be the first to admit that Allen is no saint. Mom and Dad wouldn't be far behind."

"I'll never forget that time, Joel, when we were on that dig in the Middle East with Mom and Dad." Robert looked at Adria, a special smile on his face as he lost himself in memories. "Allen and I struck out, exploring by ourselves. We knew better. It was foreign terrain, and Allen wasn't that strong physically. About two miles from camp we were lost. The desert looked exactly alike in all directions, and we wandered, getting farther and farther away. If it hadn't been for Allen, I wouldn't be alive today."

Joel swallowed the soda, then lowered the glass. "To hear Allen tell the story, you were the one who did the rescuing."

"I had the physical endurance," Robert admitted, "and carried him the last mile, but he was the one who finally determined which way we were going to go and kept saying 'you can do it, Rob.' If he hadn't been so sure we were walking in the right direction, if he hadn't been so sure I could do it—" Robert broke off, shaking his head. "I don't know, Joel. To this day I'm really not sure if I could have done it without Allen."

"You could and would have," Joel quietly affirmed.

"As much as Joel likes to explore, I'm surprised he wasn't with you," Adria said.

"He was too little at the time," Robert said and laughed. "As soon as he was able to toddle, however, he went with us. Lord, but you were a pesky little kid, Joel. You thought you ought to be with Allen and me whatever we were doing. At times you made the dating game a misery." He paused a moment, as if in reflection, then laughed and said, "Do you remember the time you decided you were going to help Mom with the cataloging, even though she repeatedly told you not to touch anything?"

"Do I," Joel answered. "Mom never lets me forget it, and even if she would, the rest of you wouldn't."

Adria squirmed back into the sofa, sipping her drink, as she listened to the two men recount cherished incidents from their childhood. As they laughed and talked, Adria realized how closely knit the family was. Also they had a mutual respect for one another. After Joel had spoken to Robert about having a third beer, Robert had chosen to drink decaffeinated coffee.

"By the way, Joel," he said, "if I have the opportunity to join you, I need to know where you're going to be."

"I don't have a specific location right now, or a telephone number. Call Adria's house. I'll check in there every day for my messages." He looked at Adria and grinned. "This will probably drive your Aunt Chessy crazy."

"If I haven't done that by now," Adria replied, "I don't think you can."

"The way you love to play these cloak-and-dagger games, Little Bro, it's a wonder you're not in Intelligence."

Adria pondered what Robert meant by cloak-and-dagger games.

As if Joel read her mind, he said, "Robert, you have a knack for overexaggeration. I'm just being cautious. I don't want someone else to get credit for my find. I'm the one who ferreted out the information, and I intend to get credit for the discovery of the *Golden Fleece*."

"Westbrook," Rob murmured, and Joel nodded, briefly bringing his brother up to date on his research.

Adria, listening to Joel talk, heard a flinty resolve in his voice as he spoke. His countenance even became closed and guarded. He took on the characteristics of the man who walked into her office Friday evening three weeks ago.

The conversation was like a puzzle. Not being privy to all the pieces, she couldn't put it together to get an idea of the entire picture. But she was getting small portions that led her to believe the *San Pablo* was not a forgotten event in Joel's past or a mere memory in his present. Westbrook and the excavation of the *San Pablo* were playing a definite role in his quest for the *Golden Fleece*.

Setting the empty glass on the coffee table, she rose. The day had finally taken its toll. "As interesting as the company and conversation are, I must say good-night. I can't keep my eyes open any longer. Which bedroom shall I use, Robert?"

"Since Joel and I will be up talking, why not take one of the upstairs rooms. It'll be quieter." He rose. "I'll show you."

Adria followed him into the hallway and up the stairs to another large bedroom that emphasized her earlier impression that this was a showcase house, not a home. Although beautifully decorated in a brilliant white, the room had no lived-in quality. French doors with sheer curtains led to a balcony that overlooked the back lawn. The accessories offered splashes of color in black, burgundy and various shades of pink.

Curiosity got the best of Adria. She turned to Robert who stood close to the door beside Joel. "Does anyone really live in this house?"

"They do," Robert answered, the corners of his mouth crinkling as he smiled. "They just bought the house and had it decorated. While Dexter is on TDY in Pendleton, his wife flew to Maine to visit with her parents. When I told Dex that I planned to call Joel, he offered me the use of his house."

"Does his wife know that you're entertaining here?"

"Probably, but Polly won't mind."

"With a house like this, I'd mind. From the way the house is decorated, I get the impression that Dex and Polly don't have any children."

The smiled deepened, and Robert shook his head. "Not yet, but give them time and they will." He looked around the room. "Then we'll see some changes around here, won't we?"

She nodded and walked to the nightstand and switched on a lamp.

"Good night, Adria. I'm glad you came and I got to meet you."

"I am, too. I hope to see you again soon, perhaps at the find."

"Hopefully," Robert said. "Now I'll leave you two to say good night."

When Robert was gone, Joel caught Adria in his arms. "I've spent all afternoon apologizing to you, and here I am doing it again. This hasn't been a typical date, has it?"

"No." Adria rubbed her cheek against his shirt, feeling the hardness and warmth of his chest beneath it. She listened to the steady beat of his heart and inhaled the faint fragrance of his after-shave. "But you're not the typical person, either, Joel LeMaster."

"Is that good or bad?"

Her palms resting against his chest, Adria pulled back and gazed sleepy-eyed up at him. She grinned. "I'm not sure yet if it's good or bad, but at least it's not boring or predictable."

"I'm glad."

"Me, too."

Joel lowered his head and softly touched his mouth to hers in an infinitely sweet kiss. A kiss that told her soon he would be asking for more. A kiss that promised so much and awakened a reciprocal desire in her. He raised his head, and said, "I'll see you in the morning."

"Yes," she whispered.

Reluctantly he released her from his embrace and walked to the door. He turned to see her sitting on the side of the bed. "Shall I turn off the overhead light?"

"Please."

He touched the switch, and soon the room was lit by the soft, muted light of the bedside lamp. Joel, making no effort to leave, stared at Adria. Those gray eyes were now soft and romantic; they looked as she had imagined them to look the day he read the inscription from the ring: *My love is forever.*

A shiver of anticipation ran through Adria's body. She called softly, "Sweet dreams."

His lips curved into a full smile, and when he spoke, his voice was low and husky. "Sweet dreams to you."

JOEL ROLLED OVER IN THE BED, blinked several times, then raised his head and looked around the strange room. When he remembered where he was, he pushed himself up on an elbow and ran his other hand through his tousled hair.

Although he was exhausted by the time he had gotten to bed last night, he had been unable to sleep. Visions of Adria sitting on the bed filled his mind. Again and again he mentally heard the nuances of her voice when she spoke; he remembered her smile and the gentle laughter; he recalled the feel of her hands on him, the feel of her soft, full lips beneath his.

He heard soft music coming from beyond the door, and the aroma of coffee drifted through the room. He had set the timer so that the coffee maker would automatically perk this morning at six. He wasn't sure who set the radio. Pushing back the cover, he went into the bathroom. When he came out later, a towel wrapped around his midsection, he smelled bacon. He hadn't automatically prepared breakfast. Then he heard a rap on the door.

"Rise and shine, sleepyhead," Adria called. "Coffee's perked and breakfast's on the table."

"Are you always this chipper so early in the morning?" Joel called out.

"I'm a morning person," she answered, "which works quite well in our family. Uncle Solly and Aunt Chessy like to sleep in. Are you about ready?"

"Give me ten minutes," he said.

"No longer than fifteen," she responded pleasantly. "We're on a tight schedule, if we plan to get to Freeport by eleven."

Hurriedly dressing and combing his hair, he stripped the sheets from the bed, picked up his washcloth and towel and carried them into the den. Adria was working in the kitchen area.

"Have you located the utility room?" he asked.

"Over there." She pointed. "I have the dials set for a short wash and double rinse and the detergent measured. As soon as we get through eating, we can toss the dish towels in and wash everything. Before we leave, we'll return everything to its proper place, and no one will know we've been here. We'll leave this showcase looking exactly like it did when we arrived."

"And we stayed overnight so we could have a leisurely trip back home," Joel teasingly grumbled.

"The trip will be," Adria told him, as he walked into the utility room and loaded his soiled linen into the washing machine. She raised her voice to be heard. "It's just the couple of hours before we leave that are going to be filled with activity."

When Joel returned to the kitchen, Adria was pouring coffee into the two cups on the table. "You're quite domesticated," he said.

"You sound surprised." She returned the pot to the warmer. "Did you think because Aunt Chessy's been with us all these years that I escaped my fair share of household duties? Well, I didn't. Now how about breakfast?"

Joel's gaze moved appreciatively over the table laden with food. "It looks delicious." He pulled a chair from the table and sat down. "I didn't realize how hungry I was until I smelled the coffee. Now that I smell the food, I'm famished."

During the meal, Joel outlined his agenda for the day, the first thing being his meeting with the crew, then his inspection of the *Black Beauty.* As soon as he had a feel for the ship, he wanted to bring his computer aboard. After they had eaten, Joel helped Adria clear the table. Together they washed and dried the dishes and returned them to the cabinet.

After she carried the dish towels into the linen room and started the washing machine, she called out, "Where are you going to leave the house key?"

"At the visitors' center."

She returned to the kitchen. "Where we'll be met by someone else who will—"

Her words trailed into silence as Joel nodded his head, and the two of them laughed.

THE DRIVE FROM JACKSONVILLE to Freeport ended all too soon for Adria. She truly enjoyed being with Joel. His visit with Robert had spurred his memories, and he spent the trip talking about his childhood. As he parked the Jeep in front of her office, she opened the door but didn't get out.

Since she had met Joel, her priorities were changing. Even now, she was in no hurry to end the carefree hours they had spent together. Selfishly, she wanted more time with him alone. She watched him reach into the backseat to pick up his attaché case.

Looking at her, he asked, "Ready?"

"Yes and no," she answered. "I'm ready for us to start looking for the *Golden Fleece,* but I wish we could spend the day together, just the two of us."

"Me, too."

"Thanks for asking me to go to Camp LeJeune with you, Joel. I enjoyed meeting your brother and the time we spent together. This has been one of the best dates of my life."

"If this has been one of your best experiences—" Joel reached out to clasp her hand, and as he had done the night before, his thumb traced designs lightly on her wrist sending waves of pleasure through her body "—you're in for a great surprise. I have even better times planned for us."

He leaned toward her at the same time that she moved toward him, their lips touching in a kiss that Adria wanted never to end. She wanted to press the length of her body against his and to feel his strong arms wrapped around her.

All too soon he lifted his mouth from hers and murmured, "That's just a promise of what's to come. Given the proper time and place, I can do better—much better."

Her voice husky, she said, "We'll have to make sure we have the proper time and place."

"We will."

Both of them slid out of the Jeep, and Joel walked around to the passenger's side.

"'Bout time y'all got here."

Adria looked up to see Solly leaning out the office window. "We're earlier than I said we'd be."

"True," he drawled, "but when you got a crew bent on treasure hunting all gathered in one room, early would be too late."

"That sounds like music to my ears."

WHEN JOEL ENTERED THE ROOM, he looked at the men sitting in a semi-circle in front of Adria's desk. All eyes focused on him. Without a word being spoken, he could feel the excitement; anticipation crackled in the air. Because Solly was standing behind Adria's desk, using it like a podium, she moved through the men to a vacant chair. Joel closed the door and leaned against it.

"Well, fellows," Solly said, "I don't reckon Adria needs an introduction, and even if she did she's not waiting around for one. She's finding herself a chair."

After a soft rumble of laughter, Adria said, "You're right. I know both Solomon Smith and Joel LeMaster. Solly is going to turn this over to Joel to say a few words. When he does, I want to be seated. Believe me, Joel is long-winded. When he gives his spiel, I want to make sure I have a chair."

More laughter followed—more than the remark warranted—but Joel, knowing it was a release of tension, welcomed it. Adria sat next to Ford Lowell.

"First of all, let me make the introductions," Solly said, and pointed to a man probably in his mid-forties. He was tall and thin, dressed in gray overalls. "This here is Lester Bandy, diesel mechanic and diver."

The man nodded at Joel.

"He's the quiet one of the bunch," Solly continued. "Next to him is Hub Chambers, a cartographer, diver and prankster."

The group, including Chambers, laughed. Hub lifted a hand, pulling his plaid sports shirt tight across his massive chest, and raked it through thick red hair liberally streaked with gray. "Just like to have a little fun now and then, fellows. Think what this trip would be like without me."

"If you keep putting on weight, we may be making future trips without you." A man in his mid-twenties sitting behind Chambers reached up and clapped him playfully on the shoulder.

"That's Dennis Forman," Solly said, "electronics whiz and diver."

"And sometimes company fool," Chambers said, again eliciting laughter from the crew.

An older version of Dennis stood. "I'm Elder Forman, mechanic and diver." He pointed to a young man who sat beside him. "This here is my nephew, Gary Burroughs. He's into computers."

"And a diver?" Joel asked.

Gary shook his head, then pushed his glasses higher on the bridge of his nose. "Only a computer analyst," he answered. I've never been on a treasure hunt, but I'd like to go. I was hoping you'd have need of a computer expert."

Joel pondered. This would mean three of them who understood computers. True, Gary was no diver, but if he were to come along, it would free Joel to perform other administrative duties and Gary would be Lane's immediate supervisor.

"Know anything about sonar equipment?"

Gary nodded.

"You do swim?"

Again Gary nodded.

"Great!" Joel exclaimed. "I can use you."

"And Ford Lowell, welder and diver, you already know," Solly said and beckoned to Joel. "Long-winded or not, men, this here is the person we've been waiting for."

Solly sat down and Joel set his attaché case on the top of the desk. His gaze swung around the semicircle, stopping when his eyes encountered Adria's. Her lips curved into a smile, and she winked at him. The room was quiet; treasure fever was driving anticipatory tension higher and higher.

Joel sat on the edge of the desk. "Well, gentlemen, Adria and I signed the contract yesterday and officially we're going on a treasure hunt." He waited for the whistling and huzzahs to quiet. "We'll be using the *Black Beauty,* and Adria Gilby is the captain. According to our agreement, I will be in command of the entire expedition—the ship and the search and the recovery. From this moment on, you're working for me. I understand that all of you are experienced treasure divers, that is, with the exception of Burroughs, and have worked in the past with Solly and Adria."

Again his gaze traveled from man to man. "As you were instructed from the beginning—" He paused. "At least, I hope you were . . . the less talk about our expedition, the better it'll be for all concerned. When we've found our ship and the mother lode, I'll make an official announcement for the wire services."

Again the crew nodded.

"Good. Now let's move to the next point. This is a treasure hunt—archaeologically and numismatically speaking—but more than that, it's an archaeological excavation. There is only one *Golden Fleece* in the world, and when we find it—and *we are going to find it*—we are going to dismember it slowly and lovingly, so that we can carefully record all the artifacts and preserve an extraordinary historical treasure. The entire time that you are working with the recovery, you must remember that this is a precious time capsule. If properly excavated and recovered, the ship and its contents will tell us much about the culture of the people at the time of the ship's sinking. I'm as interested in this as I am in bringing up the mother lode. When we positively identify our galleon, I will be calling in more professionals to complete our team and to help us with the arduous task of excavating the shipwreck."

"Speaking of the mother lode, do you have the manifests to let us know how much it is?" Chambers asked.

"No, I don't have the manifests. However, I have some information garnered from journals that gives me an idea of how much we can expect if we find it."

"As much as Solly says?" Lowell asked.

"How much did Solly say?" Joel asked. When the man answered, Joel said, "According to my research there should be more, several hundred million more. Now, let me explain the terms of employment. To be specific, how much you'll earn if we don't find anything and how much you'll earn if we find something."

The men listened quietly as Joel talked. Afterward they asked questions until they were satisfied. They expressed some dissatisfaction when Joel told them that he was going to administer a diving test, but he didn't waver in his resolve.

"I know all of you are certified, have mega-hours of diving experience and are trustworthy. Adria has vouched for you, but still I want to see what you can do. I have to be convinced that you can do it."

"From what you've been saying, this is a big job. So what you're doing seems right fair to me. When I'm down there, I want to know I'm protected," Ford Lowell said.

Hub Chambers nodded his head in agreement, then asked, "Where are we going to find this little beauty?"

"You'll know when we get there, not before."

"I've been on a lot of treasure hunts," Solly said, "and on some of 'em we found a little treasure, but this is the first time I've been connected with an excavation. How is this going to affect us treasure divers?"

"This time the treasure is twofold," Joel said. "As I said before, we'll be recovering historical artifacts—including as much of the ship itself as we can—along with the precious gems and metals. Our primary purpose is to find the treasure, at all costs. We'll work according to an archaeological plan of systematic underwater mapping. Everything we find in regard to the *Golden Fleece* will be identified, tagged and cataloged.''

"Sounds to me like we'll be more archaeologists than treasure hunters," Chambers drawled, group laughter following.

"This will be handled as an excavation," Joel announced.

"You talked about calling in more professionals," Lowell said, and Joel nodded his head. "How many?"

"At least five. Another marine archaeologist who's experienced in setting up airlifts and mapping the structure, an anthropologist, a conservator whose experience will improve our documentation process, a ship historian and a shipbuilder."

Several of the men turned to Lowell and grinned. Dennis Forman poked him in the back. "Tell him, Ford."

"Tell me what?" Joel asked.

"He's a shipbuilder," Dennis answered. "Real good at it. He belongs to all kinds of organizations and museums."

"Good. We've now reduced the number of professionals I need to four. I'm hoping that several of them will double as divers. If they do, they can help develop recovering procedures to ensure that the artifacts aren't damaged in handling, and they'll train you in these procedures."

Joel spoke with a conviction he lacked. During the past ten years marine archaeology had become an accepted field of anthropology, and more archaeologists were working with shipwrecks, but they worked only within the professional and/or academic circle. Certainly they did not join forces with a group of commercial salvors. To do so was professional suicide.

It was different for Joel. He had had no choice but to cast his lot with treasure divers, when fate had unceremoniously pushed him out of the academic world with its rigid professional attitudes. His biggest tasks lay ahead of him. First, he had to convince other experienced archaeologists and conservators to withstand academic peer pressure and to develop a solid working relationship with these commercial salvors. Second, he had to teach the commercial salvors respect for maritime heritage, archaeological wisdom and planning. He wasn't sure which task would be more difficult. While academicians had their faults, the majority were not consumed with treasure fever as commercial divers were. For the true archaeologist, the treasure was the maritime find; usually for the diver, it was precious gems and metals.

"I'll be the archaeological director and will help Burroughs computerize the entire operation," he said, then concluded, "Let me remind you again—while this is a treasure hunt, it is an excavation."

The room was quiet, as Joel looked from one man to the next. Finally Chambers said, "Sounds good to me. When are we leaving?"

"I want to leave this afternoon or tonight at the latest, but that depends on you. First, I want to see you guys in action. Then I'm going to check out the ship and get my equipment loaded aboard. If all of you pass my test, we're ready to go. If not, I'll be looking for other divers. Any more questions?" He looked around, then said, "None. Good. Let's go."

Adria stood and said, "I don't have a question, Joel, but I think you ought to inform the crew about our youngest team member."

Joel stared at her for a few minutes, then nodded. He had gotten so caught up in his introduction, then his dilemma, that he had forgotten about Lane. Succinctly he described his nephew and gave his reason for including him on the hunt. Deciding the best way to work with these men was to respect their opinions, he said, "If you have anything to say, now's the time."

For a moment there was silence; then Elder Forman rose and hitched his thumbs under his suspenders. "I'm glad you feel this way about your family. Family is important. You can tell that by the three of us—" he waved his hand to his son and nephew "—going on this trip. However, we're going on a treasure hunt, and as I see it, this ain't no pleasure cruise. We don't have time for anybody who can't pull his share of the work."

"He'll do his share," Joel promised. "I'm thinking about assigning him to Gary. The two of them can work with the computers, and that will free me to do more supervising. Gary, do you have a problem with that?"

Gary shook his head, and the crew murmured their agreement.

Elder continued, "As long as the boy knows he's got to take orders like the rest of us, I reckon I'm willing to give it a try. How about you, fellows?"

Some nodded; others voiced their assent.

"Okay," Joel said, relieved. "That's it for now." Across the room, Adria smiled at him and nodded.

Chapter Eight

The last of his packing done and the Jeep loaded, Joel stood in the door of the bungalow taking one last look to make sure he hadn't forgotten anything. Locking up the house, he headed to the Beachcomber to pick up his messages and to let Rose know he would gone for a few days.

He welcomed the air-conditioned interior. Outside the humidity was high, and the temperature had already begun to soar. Sliding onto the stool at the bar, he said, "Hi, Charlie. How about a beer?"

The burly man shuffled to where Joel sat. "Sure thing."

"Is Rose around?"

"Isn't she always?" a feminine voice said from behind.

Joel swiveled around to see Rose walking toward him. She wore a pair of designer jeans, a pale yellow sweater and high-heeled shoes. As usual, her makeup was dramatic, and today so was her jewelry—long gold earrings brushed against her shoulders, and a varied assortment of metal bracelets jangled on her arms.

"I'm glad you decided to grace us with your presence. Your popularity is growing, and we can hardly keep up with it." She pointed a finger, the nail gleaming with bold color, toward the telephone and the pile of pink message slips next to it. "We're thinking about having a separate line with an answering machine put in for you, so Charlie can tend the bar again.''

"I apologize," Joel said, taking the slips when Charlie handed them to him.

"No need to." Rose waved a hand through the air. "I'm the one who made the suggestion in the first place."

"I've been thinking about getting a telephone installed." Joel took a swallow of beer as he shuffled through the messages.

Rose smiled. "Not on my account. I'm not really griping about the messages. I guess I feel sort of neglected lately."

Rose's statement completely took Joel by surprise. Setting the bottle down, he looked at her. "Why?"

She slid onto the stool next to him and said to Charlie, "Will you hand me my cigarettes, please?" Then she spoke to Joel. "This is the first time you've been gone without letting me know you were leaving and when you'd be back. It's her, isn't it?"

"Her?"

"That woman who came to the Beachcomber last Friday night."

Ironically, this was the second time today, the second time in less than an hour, that he had been questioned about Adria. The first time had been by Chad Wilson. Joel was still puzzled by Chad's impromptu visit to the bungalow less than an hour ago. For someone whom Joel only knew in passing, the college student seemed too inquisitive, especially about his upcoming trip and about the "foxy woman" he'd seen with Joel in the Beachcomber last Sunday night.

Laughing, Chad had said, "If you're going away with her, I can't blame you for being so secretive."

Joel was always on edge when someone began to question him about his business, even when the questioning appeared to be innocent and was done by a summer resident like Wilson.

Maybe he was getting paranoid! Joel thought. Since the *San Pablo* incident, however, he had been a skeptic, assigning ulterior motives to most people's actions, especially until they proved themselves, something Chad Wilson had not yet done.

"You're involved with her, aren't you?"

Nonplussed, he stared at Rose for a second before he spoke. Jealousy was not a motive he could easily assign to her. Yet she was behaving like a jealous woman, which was odd since they had never been more than friends.

"Rosie, aren't you taking this a little too personal?" Exactly what he had thought when Chad had shown undue interest in his packing and forthcoming trip.

"I didn't mean to be," she said. "I just get worried about you, Joel. I didn't know what had happened." She gazed at him earnestly, her eyes sparkling with unshed tears.

"I can take care of myself," he said softly. "Okay?"

"I'm not so sure you can." She lowered her head, looking at her hands as she thumped a cigarette out of the package and lit it. After inhaling deeply and exhaling, she said, "Joel, we've been real close for the past few years, and no matter what happened on the *San Pablo* excavation, I believed in you. I stood by you when no one else did."

Rose's behavior and the disjointed conversation puzzled Joel. "Rose, if you have something to say, say it."

"Did you lie at the inquest when you said you didn't break into Westbrook's office and pilfer through his papers?"

"If you have to ask me that, you don't deserve an answer." Joel's tone was sharper than he had intended, but his perplexity was quickly turning into irritation; he couldn't imagine why she would bring this up now—so many years after the fact.

She drummed her bright red nails against the bar, and bright eyes, framed with thick black liner and mascara and blue shadow, stared curiously at him. "Westbrook came to the Beachcomber last night."

Now Joel was beginning to understand. He had always known that Westbrook was dogging him, but for the man to come this close to his home was a surprise; in fact, it was unnerving. "To find me?" he asked.

Her gaze never wavering from his, she took another deep draw on the cigarette and exhaled. "Indirectly. He tracked me down and wondered if I knew where you could be found."

"How did he know you were here?"

"From Connie, the girl I was rooming with when you called me about the cataloging job. I told her where I was going, and when he contacted her, she told him."

"What did he want with me?"

"He said you stole some valuable papers from him when you left the foundation, research papers that may prove invaluable to your finding a sunken treasure aboard a ship he called the *Golden Fleece*. A find that rightfully belongs to the American Nautical Archaeology Foundation, he claims. He wanted to warn you that the foundation is after you, Joel. They aren't going to let you have claim to this find."

Inwardly Joel flinched. Thinking Westbrook was one step behind him was easier to handle than his knowing it. Joel wondered how much Westbrook or the foundation really knew about the *Golden Fleece*. With this visit, however, he knew that now the foundation was making claim for the discovery of the ships and they were accusing him of stealing his own documents—documents that had nothing to do with his work at either the university or the foundation.

"Rosie, I didn't lie at the inquest, and I don't know why he's insisting I stole papers from him or the foundation. I didn't."

Through a haze of smoke, Rose looked at him. "Is there a ship called the *Golden Fleece?*"

Rose was one of the few people whom Joel considered a friend, but even with friends he remained a staunch skeptic. The only person in whom he had confided about the *Golden Fleece* was Adria, and he had not told her everything. Since their conversation yesterday, it had niggled at him, but not enough for him to tell her yet. He believed in the proper timing, and this wasn't it.

"Westbrook is the one making the claims, and since I never stole his papers I'm not sure what he's talking about. If you want to know about the *Golden Fleece,* you'll have to ask him. I'm still unclear about the purpose of his visit. Surely he didn't travel all the way up here to accuse me of thievery."

"He wants to meet with you, Joel, to talk. He thinks maybe the two of you are working toward the same goal. He wants you to work with him and the foundation."

Joel hiked a brow. "He's offering me my old job back?"

Rose shook her head. "He said that as much as he wants to, the foundation won't let him. So he's willing to go against them and hire you on as a treasure diver, giving you a larger cut of the find than they usually pay their divers."

Joel emitted a soft, bitter snort. "Yes, Woody would like that," he drawled, not sure what Westbrook was up to, but distrusting the man enough to question anything he did or said. "Woody Westbrook and I have not, and will never work toward the same goal." He took several more swallows of his beer. "When he gets in touch with you again—"

"What makes you think he will?" she interrupted.

"I know Woody," he answered. "Tell him you're not my business agent and if he wants to hire me for a job to wait to discuss it until he's speaking to me. But for the record, since I'm going to make sure he doesn't speak to me, I'm not interested."

"Joel—" Rose moved closer to him "—I'm sorry about this. I had no idea Connie would tell anyone I had moved here."

"I know. Sometimes I underestimate Woody, and that's a fault. Despite the man's low self-esteem, he's fairly bright. As my friend, you were a lead he couldn't bypass."

"Woody heard rumors that you were hunting a ship."

Joel laughed softly. "As the locals jokingly say, Rose, that didn't take too many 'smarts' on his part. I've been hunting ships all my life."

"Hunting one, in particular," Rose said. "Adria Gilby is a salvor with a business in Freeport."

"So you've done your homework, I see."

"After Woody left I began to wonder what you were up to, so I checked on her. That's another reason why I'm worried, Joel. I don't trust Westbrook. No telling what he'll do."

"To set your mind at ease, did you find out that Adria Gilby has an aversion to treasure hunting?"

Rose nodded her head and reached out to lay her hand on Joel's lower arm. "Joel, I don't care about Westbrook, and I don't believe him for a second. I simply delivered his message. I do care about you."

"Thanks." He laid his hand over hers and squeezed.

"I'm not asking for any particulars, because I know your rules, but if you're onto something," she continued, "I want to be included. Please, don't leave me out."

"I won't," he promised. "I came by to let you know that I'd be out of town for the week. I'll be in on Saturday to get my messages. Oh, by the way, Chad Wilson—you know that college student who's spending the summer here on the beach—"

Rose nodded.

"He dropped by the bungalow a few minutes ago and wanted some help with artifacts he's found while diving. I didn't have the time to look at them. If he should ask for your help, will you steer him in the right direction? If they're worth anything, he wants to sell them for his college tuition."

"I sure will. Chad's a good guy."

"Yeah, maybe." Joel again thought about Chad's puzzling visit.

"Well, I guess I better get back to work," Rose said. "I suppose you'll want to make your telephone calls before you leave."

"I'll do that later." Sliding off the stool, he stuffed the message slips into his pocket.

He was at the door when Rose called, "Charlie and I are having a clambake the second Sunday in June. You want to join us?"

He turned. "I'd love to, Rose, but I'll have to take a rain check this time. I'm expecting company." He paused, then added, "My thirteen-year-old nephew. I promised to baby-sit him this summer."

"Baby-sit," Rose murmured dryly. "Your summer sounds exciting."

Joel's thoughts went to Adria, something they were doing with great regularity lately. She brought the warmth and brightness of spring into his life. He had been separated from her for only a few hours, yet it felt like days. He already missed her and looked forward to being with her again. It had been quite a while since he felt this way about a woman, and he was thoroughly enjoying the feeling.

"Yes," he murmured, more to himself than to Rose, "my summer does promise to be exciting."

"THESE ARE GOOD." Chessy pushed her glasses up on her nose as she looked over Adria's black-and-white collection of five-by-seven photographs that lay across the table in the dark room. "Of course, it would be difficult to take a bad one of Joel. He's a mighty handsome young man. I imagine all the young girls have a hankering for him."

Adria, double-checking to make sure her equipment was unplugged and protected while she was away, turned her back to the older woman. "Are you asking me if I'm one of the young girls who has a hankering for him?"

Chessy picked up one of the photographs. "Yes."

"I am." Adria opened a drawer of the counter and pulled out a brown portfolio. Standing beside her foster aunt, she picked up the photographs one by one, studying each one before she slipped them between the protective sheets of clear plastic.

She was excited because she was a part of the quest for the *Golden Fleece,* but she was more excited because she was going to be with Joel. As she became better acquainted with him, she realized that he was truly dedicated to preserving maritime heritage; he was an archaeologist, not a treasure diver.

She held the last picture and her favorite, the one of him sitting on the shore beneath the shade of the dogwood trees. He seemed to be a man happy with his solitude. The only phrase she could think of at the moment to describe the photograph was *The Loner*. But even that was not the right description of him. A loner generally was alone because he chose to be, because he preferred to be. Joel had not chosen to be. When he no longer fit into what his professional associates considered their proper social and cultural niche, they had set him adrift.

The Outcast. The Misfit.

Those were words that rightly described Joel LeMaster. She slid the photograph between its protective covering and wished she could protect him as easily as she did his photograph. Something within her wanted to reach out to Joel LeMaster; she wanted to take him into her arms and reassure him, to touch his heart, to let him know that she cared for him.

Yet Adria was wary of opening herself fully to Joel. His words of warning still rang in her ears. He had told her he didn't wish to be salvaged. Perhaps he wouldn't allow her to touch his heart; perhaps he didn't want her to care. He could keep her from his heart, but he couldn't stop her from caring. That same feeling from deep within, that made her care and made her want to protect him, assured her that Joel LeMaster had hidden his heart in an attempt to protect it from hurt.

She closed the book with a snap, looked at Chessy, and said, "To answer your unspoken question, Joel has a hankering for me—nothing more, that I know of. I'm not sure where we're going from here, but I'd like to have the chance to find out if we can have more than *hankering*."

Chessy gazed at Adria a long while before she nodded her head. "You're old enough to know your own mind, and this is a decision you must make, baby. I trust your wisdom and your judgment."

Adria threw her arms around her foster aunt and hugged her tightly. "Thank you, Aunt Chessy. You always know what to say to make me feel loved." She pulled away and looked into those understanding brown eyes. "You're the most wonderful person in the whole world. I'm going to miss you while I'm gone."

Chessy nodded. "You will be careful, won't you? That ocean can be mighty treacherous."

"I will," Adria promised, knowing full well that her aunt was speaking of Joel, as well as she was of the voyage.

BENEATH A NAVY SKY ablaze with twinkling stars and a luminous moon, Adria stood beside Joel on the deck, a fine mist of ocean spray moistening her face as the *Black Beauty* sailed south for the third day. It had been a long time since she felt so carefree. Her troubles were left far behind, and filled with anticipation, she threw back her head and laughed aloud. Joel put his arm around her shoulder and drew her close to him. Willingly she turned, moving into his embrace and lifting her face to his.

His head lowered, until his lips were only centimeters away from hers. "I've missed you," he said, his lips skimming delightfully along her cheek, up her temple and over her forehead. "I've looked forward to our being by ourselves again. Since we've been on board, I've wondered if that time would ever come."

"Me, too."

"Days and nights of being so close together," he said, "yet so far apart. A few kisses and embraces stolen here and there."

"As you say 'a promise of things to come,' " she murmured.

He laughed quietly. "I think perhaps Solly knows what's happening and has been intentionally keeping us apart. You at one end of the ship, me at the other. Me below-deck, you above."

"I wouldn't doubt that. He's always been protective, where I'm concerned," Adria said.

"Are you enjoying the trip?" he asked.

She nodded. "Knowing that we're almost there is exciting."

"Tomorrow we arrive and set up camp—then the hunt really begins. I know you haven't had a good experience with treasure hunts before, Adria, but you're going to enjoy this one. I'll make a treasure diver out of you yet."

She smiled and ran the palms of her hands up and down his back, loving the feel of his hard muscled body. "In all the rush to get underway, I forgot to tell you the black-and-white photographs are developed. I brought them with me. If you'd like, you can come to my quarters and see them sometime."

"Do they come up to your expectations?" he asked.

"Oh, yes!" She pulled back to look into his night-shadowed face. "They're so good, Joel. I know I'll win a merit. I can hardly wait to get the colored ones back."

"May I see them now?"

Although he was asking to see the photographs, Adria knew—as well as he—that he was asking another more important question. The two of them alone in her cabin would generate an intimacy even greater than that which they had shared the other night in Jacksonville. She had met Joel a few short weeks ago, but she felt as if she had known him for years.

Because she was a photographer she fantasized in order to create a certain mood to fit her model, a mood she tried to capture in picture and relay in her title. Now that Joel was asking to come to her cabin, she wondered how much of her feeling for him was due to her photographic fantasizing. Would the real Joel LeMaster step forward?

He released her from his embrace, but made no effort to move away from her. His dark hair curled profusely around the face that hovered above hers. His white shirt, tucked into tight-fitting jeans, was unbuttoned partway to reveal a wedge of muscled chest covered in dark hair. If only he were wearing a red bandanna, a black patch over one eye and a small gold earring in his left ear! She would have her pirate, her handsome scoundrel of the silver seas!

"I really want to see the photographs," he said, "and if anything else happens, it will be because both of us want it. Right now, I confess, I want it."

His head moved that infinitesimal distance and his lips touched hers, brushing back and forth gently. The touch was light, but Adria trembled from the onslaught of emotions it aroused within her. When his lips settled into a hard, firm kiss, her arms slid around him, her fingers digging into the muscles of his back.

His arms tightened about her and the kiss deepened, pleasure warmly flowing through Adria's body. She was delighted by his touch as his hands stroked her, making her feel as if he were dragging her very soul from her body and claiming it for his own.

When finally he lifted his mouth from hers, they stared into each other's face. The ocean and wind howled around them, but they were lost in their own world. A tranquility permeated both of them; it surrounded them. They didn't speak; they merely clasped hands.

This loving, considerate man, Adria thought, looking into his rugged face, softly illuminated in light spilling out of the bridge, so different from the man she had imagined him to be the first time she saw him, was the real Joel

LeMaster. She really cared for him. She trusted him. Her confession sent a rush of desire through her.

Without uttering a word, she turned, her hand still entwined with his, and led the way to her cabin.

"AREN'T THEY GREAT?" Adria exclaimed.

Standing in the small cabin next to Adria, Joel flipped through the portfolio. "None of them looks too impressive to me," he answered. "Which one are you going to enter into competition?"

When he reached the last page, she thumped it with her index finger. "This one. It's a winner."

He turned to look at her, the cabin light at his back, lighting her face. She wore no makeup; she needed none. Her blue eyes were bright, their color enhanced by her thick, dark lashes. As usual, tendrils of hair escaped the braid to curl around her face.

"Just the photograph?" he asked.

The question was loaded, and each knew it.

"Both," she answered.

They stared at each other for a long while before he said, "I hope you're saying what I'm hearing."

"I am," she whispered, all thought of the photograph and competition slipping from her mind.

At the same time that Joel moved toward her, she moved toward him. He took her into his arms, lowered his head and captured her mouth, tentatively and softly at first. But when she moved so that her body pressed firmly against his from chest to thigh, desire gripped him and his mouth settled firmly on hers. She arched herself to the gentle pressure of his hand at the curve of her hip.

Finally he broke the kiss, and his lips nipped hers, moving around her mouth. In butterfly motion they moved across her cheeks, down to nuzzle the hollow of her throat.

His searching hands pulled the shirt out of her jeans to touch her warm, velvety flesh. Her soft scent wrapped itself around him. She gasped, lifting her hand to still his movements.

"Adria—" even to his ears his voice sounded husky "—I want to make love to you."

"Yes."

Although she had uttered only one word, it was the necessary one. "I'll protect you."

"I know."

He was humbled to know that she trusted him to take care of her. Since Vanessa's death he had engaged in nothing more than casual affairs and was always prepared, but since he had known Adria he had not wanted to make love to anyone else.

She placed light, feathery kisses against his neck and snuggled against him. When her hand slid through the opening of his shirt to touch his body, an exciting tingle skittered across Joel's chest. His heart pounded against his ribs and his hand moved in agonizing sweetness up Adria's arms, over her shoulders and down her back. Again, he placed quick kisses along the hollow of her neck, along the opening of her blouse.

When Joel finally lifted his face, both of them were breathing heavily. He moved to the door and stood for a moment, his hand on the lock, giving Adria time to change her mind. He wanted to make love to her, but their doing so had to be by mutual consent.

"I want to," she said.

He flipped the lock.

In a few steps he covered the distance between them and began to unbutton Adria's blouse. He pushed the material aside and lowered his head to lay his mouth against the creamy skin of her shoulder.

"Adria," he murmured, his hands sliding beneath her blouse to circle the warm flesh of her waist, "I'm so glad I met you. You're the most wonderful thing that has happened to me in the past five years."

"Oh, Joel," she whispered and melted into his embrace.

His head lowered farther, and he pressed his mouth over the tip of a breast covered in lacy underwear; he blew his breath against her, then curled his tongue around the nipple, leaving the lace damp. She trembled and sighed, the soft sound coming from deep in her throat. Her fingers spread through his hair, her caresses fueling Joel's desire even more.

His lips moved over the silky contour of her breast, which swelled above the seductive fluff of silk and lace, back to her mouth. He kissed her again and again, each kiss longer and more drugging. As his hands caressed her, their desire became fevered.

They undressed and lay on the bed, the howl of the wind and ocean closed out of this magical world that belonged only to them. No barrier between them, both protected, they allowed themselves to be swept away with the fervor of their caresses.

"Oh, Adria, I do want you," Joel murmured, pulling her to him.

"I want you," was her soft reply, her words lost in a sigh of sheer pleasure, as he tenderly penetrated her.

Time was of no essence; it had ceased to exist. His primary desire was to give pleasure, then to take his. At first their loving was slow and languorous, but as their passion mounted Joel's thrusts were more powerful, yet always tempered with care and restraint, lest he hurt Adria. She moved in rhythm with him.

She gasped, tensed, then began to tremble uncontrollably in his arms. He buried his face in her shoulder and groaned as he released himself.

They clung together for a second before he rolled over, and they lay quietly in the peaceful afterglow. Adria pressed her head and palm against Joel's chest, and he wrapped his arms around her, both of them going to sleep.

LATER WHEN SHE AWAKENED, it was still dark outside, the stars twinkling, the moon shining. She lifted herself slightly and looked at Joel.

"Hello," he murmured.

"Hello."

"Didn't I tell you there was something special about the sound of the silver sea gently splashing against the side of a ship, and the night sky with its glistening stars and brilliant moon?"

"Um-hum."

"They're magical."

Contented, Adria snuggled even closer to him and stared through the open porthole at the scene he had described. She truly believed it to be magical because it had cast its spell over her. She enjoyed the feel of Joel's fingers as they pushed her damp tendrils of hair, long since released from the confines of the braid, from her face and traced the outline of her ears. Her release had been so intense and fulfilling that it left behind a beautiful glow of satisfaction, which she felt even now.

"Happy?" he asked.

Adria propped herself on an elbow and smiled down at him. "Are you fishing for a compliment?"

His big hands curled around each of her shoulders and he gently kneaded them. "No, I just want to know if I made you happy."

She leaned down and kissed him on the tip of his nose, her hair falling about her shoulders and brushing against her cheeks. "Yes, you're a wonderful lover." Suddenly feeling shy, she asked, "Did I make you happy?"

"Very."

She lay back down, this time her cheek resting on his chest, his arms wrapped around her. She felt the rise and fall of his body as he breathed; again she heard the familiar beat of his heart.

"I have a confession to make," she murmured.

"Oh?"

"I've been interested in your body ever since I first laid eyes on you."

"Is this unqualified interest?" he asked, his hand brushing lightly down her back to rest on her hip, his lips nipping the lobe of her ear.

"Yes," she murmured, sliding up his chest until her lips met his in a passionate kiss.

When she finally lifted her mouth from his, she held herself over him, looking into his face, streaked silver by the moonlight.

"Joel," she said tentatively, "I need to ask you something personal."

"All right."

"Do you still love Vanessa?"

He paused before he said, "Vanessa was spoiled, but she wasn't all bad. I wouldn't have loved her, if she had been. There are qualities about her that I'll always love and admire. But she's not part of my life anymore, only a memory. The hurt and grief are behind me."

Adria lay back down and rubbed her palm up Joel's chest through the crisp black hair. "If she had lived, would the two of you eventually have made up and married?"

"No. Each of us had already begun to grow disenchanted with the other, and her behavior during the excavation reinforced my feelings. Physical attraction, while it's wonderful and fulfilling, is not enough to cement a relationship between two people."

"That's what I learned from Bryan," Adria said.

"Is he the guy you were serious about?"

She nodded, her cheek brushing up and down against his chest. "We met during registration, when both of us were signing up for the same elective class. From the moment we met, we were attracted to each other and began dating. Our interests were the same—both of us were getting degrees in photography, although we were specializing in different fields. I taught him to dive, and we spent weekends doing underwater photography."

"What went wrong?" Joel asked.

"By this time, we were juniors. His grant was running out and his parents didn't have the money to pay his tuition. Since we were talking about marriage, he wanted me to quit the university and go to work to send him through school. He promised that once he had his degree, he would put me through. About that time Aunt Chessy let me know that we were in financial trouble, and I quit school. Instead of putting Bryan through university, I sent the money home to save the business and Avalon. Bryan never understood why I did this. He said I loved Avalon and Gilby's more than him." She paused, then said, "By mutual consent, we began seeing each other less and less."

"Legacies are often heavy burdens to bear, aren't they?" Joel said.

"But if he had loved me enough," Adria contended, "he would have been willing to share it."

"By the same token," Joel said, "he could have claimed that if you had loved him enough, you would have given them up for him."

Adria nodded. "I've thought about that often. It's a good thing the two of us discovered we didn't love each other before we married. It probably saved us a lot of unhappiness."

"Were you hurt when you broke up?"

"A little, but of the two of us, I think Bryan was hurt more. He thought I was selfish and shortsighted, not wanting to send him to school so he would be better prepared to support us after we were married. I realized that I didn't love him enough to make the sacrifices necessary for our future together. My heart belonged to Avalon and Gilby's."

"Is there no room in there for more than Avalon and Gilby's?" Joel asked softly, and ran his hand through her hair.

"There's room for love," she replied. "I want to marry and to have a family."

"What are you looking for in a husband?"

"The usual things that make for a solid foundation. Love, physical attraction, mutual interests and respect. Most of all, honesty and trust."

"Ah, yes," he drawled, his warm breath splaying against Adria's neck to send pleasure through her body, "honesty, to be sure, and trust."

"Whatever else Daddy may have been, he believed in honesty. He said all meaningful relationships were based on honesty and trust."

Again Joel felt a twinge of guilt. He hadn't been dishonest with Adria, but he had not completely confided in her. The guilt was weighing heavily on him, but he kept remembering what happened on the *San Pablo*. The

Golden Fleece belonged to him, and he was going to make sure of that. The fewer who knew all the details about it, the better off he was.

He propped himself up on his elbow, his fingers combing through her hair and drawing it softly away from her face.

"Do you think it's possible for us to have a meaningful relationship?" Adria asked.

"Yes," he murmured, his face coming closer and closer to hers.

"I think so, too."

She lifted her hands to cup his face and to guide his lips to hers, kissing him hungrily. She lowered her hands and ran her palms across his chest to tangle her fingers in the crisp whorls of hair. She struck a nail across one of his nipples and saw that it hardened beneath her touch.

Although their lovemaking this time was slow and sensuous, it was also fiery—and more explosive than before. Intimately they touched each other, caressing and kissing and murmuring endearments until they were once more aflame with desire; until both reached satisfaction.

Joel wrapped his arms around Adria and they laid there together talking quietly until they finally drifted off to sleep.

WHEN ADRIA AWOKE, sunlight poured through the port-hole into the cabin, filling it with warmth and light. Joel was gone, and the only reminder that he had been there was the indentation on the pillow where his head had rested during the night. As she thought of the pleasure they had shared, her entire body tingled. Pushing the sheet aside, she jumped up, quickly washed her face and brushed her teeth. Before she could put on her clothes, she heard a knock.

Then Joel called out, "How about breakfast in bed, sleeping beauty?"

Dashing back to the bunk and under the sheet, she said, "I'm not so sure about the beauty, but I could do with some pampering."

The door opened and he entered, balancing a tray on one hand. The gray eyes sparkled, and a smile curled those sensuous lips. "Then, madam, while aboard the *Black Beauty* you shall be pampered."

Holding the sheet above her breasts, Adria's gaze locked with his. "Only while I'm aboard ship?" she questioned.

He set the tray down on the adjacent table and slid into the bed beside her, his lips angling for hers. After a wonderful good-morning kiss, he pulled back and grinned. "Hmm," he droned, and moistened his lips with his tongue. "Am I tasting Colgate or Crest?"

"How romantic!" Adria teased.

"It is quite romantic," he agreed, a hand tracing imaginary designs on her breasts, which were exposed above the upper hem of the sheet.

Adria sucked in her breath. "I noticed you brought enough food for two. Would you like to join me?"

His eyes glinted suggestively. "Yes, I would."

Again Adria laughed, the sound flowing from the depth of her soul. "For breakfast."

"That, too." He caught her in his arms and kissed her thoroughly, both of them breathless when he finally lifted his head. "I would much rather we stayed locked up in your cabin making love all day, but we can't. We all have to pull our share of the load."

"I know," she murmured and stretched, the sheet falling to her waist.

She reached for her wrap, slipping into it while Joel held it by the shoulders. He moved to the tray and poured their coffee, handing her a cup. He walked over to the porthole and stood.

"Adria, I'm serious about us having a meaningful relationship," he said.

"Me, too."

His brow furrowed, and he lifted a hand to push it through his hair. "I need to talk to you."

Adria's heartbeat slowed; she felt a cloud of fear hover over them. The matter seemed grave, and she could only wonder what he needed to discuss.

"The *Golden Fleece* is mine," he said. "All mine."

After a lengthy pause, Adria said, "So?"

"When I was working on the *San Pablo,* I was a member of the American Nautical Archaeology Foundation, known as the ANAF. And it was at that time that I got my first inkling about the *Golden Fleece.* When I was asked to leave ANAF, I found many of my papers missing from my files and suspected that Woodrow Westbrook had taken them. Knowing that Westbrook is an intelligent and competent archaeologist, I've known that he's also searching for the *Golden Fleece.*"

"That's the reason why you wanted the obscurity my name and ships would provide."

Joel nodded and walked to the tray to refill his cup. "The other day before we set sail I stopped by the Beachcomber and talked with Rose, who told me Westbrook had been there looking for me. He's claiming that I stole the papers from the foundation and that I am using them for my own gain."

"Are you concerned that I'll believe you're a thief?" Adria asked.

He shook his head, then took several swallows of coffee. "I have no reputable source to vouch for me. However, I *think* I can prove my claim," he finally said.

"Westbrook has the university and the foundation on his side. There's a possibility they can tie up the *Golden Fleece* in litigation."

Adria set her cup down and slid off the bed. Moving to where Joel stood, she grasped his arm. "What does this really mean? How will it affect me and my men?"

"If Westbrook and . . . or the foundation press charges stating that I stole classified documents belonging to the foundation, which made the finding of the *Golden Fleece* possible, I could have my license and permit rescinded, pending the investigation."

"And during this time we can't search, because the permit is in your name." She shook her head, her hair flying about her shoulders. "Why didn't you tell me this before, Joel?"

"Before, it was like a dark cloud following behind me. I knew Westbrook was somewhere out there, but it wasn't until several days ago I fully realized he was dogging my heels and that he was accusing me of stealing classified documents from the foundation."

"But you knew the kind of person Westbrook was, and you know that he had access to the same documents you have," she accused.

"Perhaps. Even if he does have the same ones, he hasn't interpreted them correctly, because he hasn't filed a claim yet and he's still following me. I always thought he was trying to beat me to it, but I was wrong. He's hoping I'll lead them to the *Golden Fleece,* so they can jerk it from under me."

"In doing that to you, they do it to me," Adria said. "Basically, Joel, everything I have, with the exception of my savings—which is a reserve for my house mortgage— is tied up in this excavation. And I don't just stand to lose the company— I'll lose Avalon." She released his arm and backed away, staring at him. "Just like Bryan," she whispered. "You didn't really care about me. You didn't think about what I stood to lose. I feel like you've used me."

"No, Adria, it's not like that. I do care about you."

At the moment she pushed aside the niggling thought that she could have backed out of the hunt anytime she wished, that Joel had given her ample opportunity. At first, she had been afraid they wouldn't find the *Golden Fleece;* now she was afraid that if they did find it, this Westbrook and the foundation would take it away from them. Most of all, Adria feared losing her company and her beloved home. If the hunt went sour and didn't prove to be profitable, the crew would have their guaranteed wages. She had seen to that. But she worried about Uncle Solly and Aunt Chessy.

They were too old to start again. This was the time in their lives when they were thinking of retiring, not returning to the job market. She owed them something, after all they had given to her through the years. They had poured their lives into the Gilbys. All of these thoughts rushed through Adria's head and she felt the need to lash out, to release her pent-up tensions. Tears pricked her eyes, but she wouldn't let him see her cry.

"All you care about is finding the *Golden Fleece,* no matter what the cost."

He moved toward her. "No, you're wrong."

"Please leave. I'd like to be alone."

"Adria—" He reached for her, but she backed farther away.

"Please go."

Chapter Nine

That afternoon the *Black Beauty* reached its destination, a tiny island named Isla Esmeralda off the coast of southern Florida. After they dropped anchor in the clear green water of the bay, Joel ordered the crew to disembark and to set up camp.

Adria was glad for the activity: it kept her and Joel separated and allowed her to forget, for a time, the events that had occurred between them earlier in the day. After her tent was erected and her belongings unpacked, she still wanted to be alone to think. Taking into consideration all that Joel had gone through since the discovery of the *San Pablo* she could understand his propensity to keep things to himself and to be distrustful. As long as he felt this way, however, their relationship could not mature.

In a quandary, she reached for her camera and moved out of the tent. Taking photographs eased her mind and allowed her to find solutions to her problems. Isla Esmeralda was a beautiful semitropical paradise, and she wanted to visit the nearby village she had sighted when they sailed in. Walking out of camp, she waved to Solly who was hammering a tent peg into the ground.

"I'm going for a walk," she told him.

He straightened and reached into his back pocket to pull out a large handkerchief and wipe the perspiration from his face. "Don't go too far," he admonished. "You don't know your way around yet."

"No farther than the village," she promised, then laughed. "Uncle Solly, the island is hardly large enough for me to get permanently lost."

"I don't even want you temporarily lost. If you want to save this ol' man some worry, you'll be back before dark." Swinging the hammer over his shoulder, he resumed his work.

"Yes, sir," Adria replied. When he looked up and flashed her a smile, she grinned back.

Enjoying the scenery, she walked slowly down the dirt road into the old-fashioned village of Emerald Cove. She felt as if she had stepped into another era, a time of privateers and Spanish dons and doñas. The people were warm and friendly, and Adria was soon involved with taking photographs of a group of children—two boys and two girls, ranging in ages from five to ten. With the parents' permission, she promised the children ice cream when she was through with the pictures.

"One more, Sarah, and we'll go get our treat," she called to the youngest child who sat on a large barrel in front of the general store, her bare feet hanging down. Sarah reached up with a grubby little hand and swiped a strand of straight black hair from her forehead. Solemn brown eyes stared at Adria.

"Can I have a double-dip?" she asked.

"You certainly may," Adria answered, her sentence punctuated with the click of the camera. She turned to the other three children who flocked around the barrel. "All of you may have two dips of ice cream, because you've been such excellent models."

Among the shouts of happiness, Sarah jumped down from the barrel and the four of them skipped into the drugstore. They took their time making their choices, all the while moving up and down the freezer, peering into the various ice-cream containers. Finally, their choices made, their treats in hand, they thanked Adria and exited from the drugstore. Adria followed, stopping outside the building to watch them walk down the sidewalk. Laughing and talking, they weren't paying attention to where they were going, and Sarah stumbled against a display in front of a store, dropping her ice cream. Immediately the happy commotion stopped, and the other children gathered around the stricken five-year-old to watch the ice cream melt on the hot sidewalk.

"You should have watched where you were going," one of the older boys chided.

Sarah looked up, her gaze going from the boy to Adria. The large brown eyes were filled with tears that spilled down her cheeks. "I was watching." She sniffed and lifted a fist to her eyes.

"Here, Sarah," the boy said, "you can have some of my ice cream. Don't cry."

Adria felt as if her heart was breaking. She moved down the sidewalk until she was kneeling beside Sarah. She placed an arm around the child's shoulders and drew her close to her chest. "I'll tell you what, Sarah," she said, "if you'll let me take some more pictures of you, I'll buy you another cone."

"Oh, yes," Sarah exclaimed, her tears drying up instantly.

From across the street, Joel watched the scene with interest. The child's face brightened visibly, and she slid her hand into Adria's, the two of them returning to the drugstore, the other three trudging behind. When they came out later, Adria was so intent on taking photographs of the children that Joel was sure she had not seen him, and not wanting to disturb her or the children's concentration, he remained where he was to observe.

Then she turned and saw him, her lips curling into a slow smile that filled him with pleasure.

"Sarah—" she pointed to Joel "—run over there and stand with Mr. LeMaster. I want to take your picture with him."

Joel squatted on the ground and took the little girl—ice cream and all—in his arms and settled her on one of his legs. He was looking into her small oval face when he heard the camera click. Then the others joined him, and Adria took more photographs. When the sun dipped low in the western sky the children waved goodbye to her and ran to join their parents, who were closing their shops.

As they stood alone in the street, Joel asked, "Taking more photographs for competition?"

"I may, but I took them because I fell in love with the children and the village. I'm so glad we're here." She snapped her camera case, her gaze returning to Joel. "I can't think of a better place to keep Lane this summer than Emerald Cove. This is going to be good for him."

"I think so, too." Falling in step together, they walked toward the camp. "Were you glad to see me?" he asked.

"Yes."

"Solly was worried about you."

"Is that the reason you came?"

"No, I wanted to be with you."

She smiled. "I'm glad."

"Are you ready to return to camp?" he asked.

"Yes."

"Good. By the time we get there, dinner should be ready."

"The mention of dinner reminds me that I haven't eaten since break—" The smile faded and her voice trailed into silence.

"Since breakfast," Joel completed her sentence for her; again she nodded. "Adria, this is one of the reasons why I came to meet you. I want to apologize for having placed you in this predicament. I knew what I was doing, and I willingly made the sacrifices. I'm so sure we'll find the treasure that I didn't stop to think about the sacrifice I was asking you to make without giving you all the conditions of the hunt."

"I've been thinking about this all day," Adria confessed. "No one forced me to come along with you. When I signed that contract I knew there was a risk involved, and you did allow me plenty of time to get out. Even if you hadn't, Donald did."

"Oh, yes," Joel agreed, "Freeport's best attorney was watching out for his client's best interest."

Adria slipped her hand into his. "Together we'll find the *Glorious Bess* before anyone else gets here or even has an idea what we're doing."

Joel was glad for her vote of confidence and her forgiveness. He said, "I'm sure Westbrook knows what we're doing. If Rose found out who and what you are, Woody has, too."

As they turned the bend in the road, they stopped and stared across the Atlantic Ocean, the brilliant oranges and reds and purples of the setting sun reflected in the sparkling water. He moved to stand behind her, slipping his arms around her waist and resting his cheek on top of her head. She leaned back against him.

"Joel, I've figured out a way we can outwit Westbrook."

"How?" he murmured.

"We can file the claim in my name, and there's no way he can touch or contest it." She turned in his arms and looked into his face. "It will be protected this way, Joel."

How simple her solution sounded, yet Joel found himself shaking his head.

"Why not?" she asked.

"It's my find, Adria, and I want it in my name."

She pulled out of his arms. "You don't trust me, do you?"

"The *San Pablo* was taken away from me, Adria," he answered, unable to answer her directly because he really wasn't sure himself. "I want to make sure I get credit for this one. I promise you, I'm going to do everything in my power to protect your interests. I won't let you lose your company or home."

Adria silently stared at him for a long while before she said, "Earlier today you told me that we could have a meaningful relationship, Joel, but we can't—not until you're willing to trust me, not until we're willing to trust each other."

"I'm trying," he confessed.

"I know, and you're doing better, but you have plenty of room for improvement. Trying isn't good enough. It has to be one way or the other." She stood on tiptoe and planted a kiss on the tip of his nose. "Now, let's hurry. I'm famished."

"Adria, about last night—"

"It was wonderful," she told him, her eyes deepening in color as her thoughts grew more intense, "and I'm glad it happened, but let's wait to see how things go, Joel. Before our relationship develops further, I think we have to get to know each other much better."

During the following days they worked long, hard hours, but Adria was happy. She and Joel were getting better acquainted, and he was losing much of his skepticism. At the beginning of the second week, Joel pinpointed the site, and the camp was filled with excitement. Everyone wanted to dive and of their own volition worked from dawn until midnight most days. Because so many were searching, Adria occupied herself with taking underwater photographs. She wanted a picture of their first artifact. However, as the days passed and nothing was found to indicate the presence of the *Glorious Bess,* excitement began to dampen.

One evening Adria was sitting in front of her tent watching the sunset when Joel walked up and sat on the ground beside her lounge chair.

"Do you want to go into town with me in the morning?" he asked. "I have to file an extension, and I thought I'd talk with Miguel Fuentes, the state field-archaeology agent who granted me my salvage contract."

"You sound worried," Adria said.

"Maybe a little," Joel confessed. "I'm running low on cash, and I don't know how much this new lease is going to cost me."

"I have some money in my savings." She laughed softly. "Uncle Solly and Aunt Chessy call it my rainy-day money. I can loan you that, if you need it."

He reached up, clasped her hand in his and squeezed gently. "Thanks, but I think I'll be okay without it."

"Morale is low, Joel," she said. "They think this is like all the other hunts they have been on—bone-dry."

"They're wrong. The *Glorious Bess* is here. I can smell and taste her. We'll soon have more money than we'll know what to do with."

"That's what Daddy and Danny would say each time they went on a hunt," she murmured, sad memories pushing to the forefront of her mind.

"This time it's true, Adria," Joel promised. "It's here, and we're going to find it."

It was easy for her to believe Joel.

"HOW WAS YOUR MORNING?" Joel asked as he slid into the booth beside Adria at the small seafood restaurant in Emerald Cove the next day.

"Marvelous," she replied. "I've taken photographs all over the marina. I can hardly wait to get back and develop them. How about you?"

"I got the extension."

"Great!" She leaned over and kissed his cheek.

"But—" his countenance fell; he looked tired and haggard "—they granted it for only half the time I requested, and added a rider. I must produce an artifact—a new one—to substantiate my claim within the next two weeks."

Adria's excitement over her photographs died. "Can we do it?"

He smiled tightly. "We have to, Adria. We must find the *Glorious Bess.*"

"We've also got to return to Freeport and pick up Lane, this coming weekend," Adria pointed out. "You hadn't forgotten, had you?"

Joel propped his elbows on the table and rested his head in his hands. "Adria, I can't take the time to go get Lane. I'm going to have to call his mother and beg off." He lifted his face to her. "I can't afford to lose the lease now."

"You can't afford not to get Lane, either," she said softly, staring into his worried eyes. "He needs you, Joel. Besides, you promised Robert, remember." She rubbed her hands across his shoulders.

"When I promised Robert, I was counting on a longer lease."

"Lane is still counting on you, and he's too young to understand why you can't take the time to get him. You charter one of the planes and fly to Freeport to get him," she suggested. "The men and I will stay here and continue searching."

"Leave the site?" Joel murmured, looking at her as if what she asked was impossible.

Adria nodded. "Leave the site under my supervision. Trust me and my divers to continue to search as you've taught us. The minute we find something, I'll call Aunt Chessy and we'll wait for further instructions from you. We understand the concept of rudimentary patterning of artifacts. I promise we won't do anything that would destroy the *Glorious Bess*."

Before Joel could answer, the waitress came and took their order, stopping their conversation. When she left, Adria said, "Well, what's it going to be?"

She waited, her gaze never wavering from his as he stared into her face. She had made many decisions since she had become a treasure seeker with Joel, the major one being to put her complete trust in him by turning her ship and men over to his supervision. Now he had to demonstrate his trust in her.

"I'll do it," he said.

ON FRIDAY MORNING Joel flew out. During the next three days, Adria and her divers worked harder and longer hours. At least, they seemed longer to Adria because she missed Joel. So far, many magnetic and side-scan sonar anomalies had been recorded and evaluated, but they had produced no clues that would lead them to the *Glorious Bess*. They dug holes; still they found nothing. Hope, as well as time, was quickly fleeing. In the distance, small gray clouds began to mass, and the wind picked up speed.

Monday afternoon Adria sat at the table in the middle of the camp and studied Joel's map. Hours later, she looked up to see Sarah Guerra, an older woman whom she assumed to be the child's mother and an older boy approaching.

"Hello, I'm Consuelo Guerra, Sarah's mother. We do not wish to interrupt you," the woman said in stilted English, with a hint of an accent, as they neared the table where Adria worked, "but Sarah and Thomas wanted to visit you. Thomas wanted to meet you and the other divers, and Sarah wanted to thank you for the ice cream the other day."

"That's not necessary, Mrs. Guerra," Adria said. "Sarah earned that by posing for me."

The older woman laughed. "Posing is what she likes to do best." She caught her son by the shoulder and guided him forward. "This is my oldest son, Thomas. He will be thirteen this September."

"Hello, Thomas," Adria said. "I'm glad to meet you."

The boy had short, straight black hair and brown eyes. He flashed Adria a friendly smile. "You are a diver, *señorita.*"

"Yes."

"I am, too," he announced proudly. "My father has taught me to dive since I was very little. I was on the other side of the island diving the other day when you were in town. That's why I did not get to meet you."

"He has been insisting that I let him come," his mother said, "but I knew you were working and would not want to be disturbed."

"I'm glad you're here," Adria said and pulled a chair from the table. "Please sit down, Mrs. Guerra."

"Please call me Consuelo," the older woman said.

"And I'm Adria."

Glad to meet Thomas and to find that he was about Lane's age, Adria visited with the Guerras for a while. She learned that Consuelo Guerra worked for the government as a caretaker of the island guest home—a historic villa located on a mountain overlooking the ocean where visiting dignitaries were housed. Thomas worked part-time as the gardener.

About half an hour later, after Adria had introduced them to the crew working in camp, Consuelo said, "Thank you for your time, but we must be going. It looks as if it is going to rain, and I want to be home before it does. Now, Sarah, you may give Adria the gift."

The little girl, standing beside her mother, stepped forward. Her eyes sparkled and her lips curled into a beautiful smile, as she reached into the pocket of her shorts to pull out a long gold chain. She walked to where Adria sat and placed it on her lap. Then Adria saw the exquisite gold crucifix.

"Oh, Sarah," she murmured, picking up the piece of jewelry and balancing it on her palm. It was old, she could tell, and all of the gems had been lost from their mountings. "I can't take this. It's valuable."

The child's countenance fell, and she looked from Adria to her mother, then back to Adria. "But you must take it," she said. "It's my gift to you, and you can't refuse a gift."

Adria looked over Sarah's head to Consuelo, who nodded and said, "Sarah and I discussed it. The crucifix is hers to do with as she wishes. According to our custom, it is an insult to the giver if a gift is refused. Its value is greatly diminished because the gemstones are missing."

"I love the gift, and I wouldn't dream of insulting Sarah," Adria said, her heart overflowing with love for the child, "but it's so precious. It must be a family heirloom."

"No, it's only a treasured possession," Consuelo assured Adria. "We have many such artifacts around here. Through the years they have washed up on the shores or have been located by divers."

"It is yours," Sarah insisted. "I want you to have it."

"I have never received a gift I love more than this." She slipped the chain over her head, its length allowing the cross to fall below her breasts. "Thank you very much, Sarah."

Long after the Guerras left, Adria sat at her table, holding the crucifix in her hand and looking at it. Afraid she might damage it and that the prongs might snag her clothes, she took it off and carried it to her tent. She would put it aboard the *Black Beauty* later and lock it up.

As she walked out of her tent, she saw a large dust cloud and heard the rumble of an approaching car. She moved further across the clearing and soon a blue-and-white taxi emerged. When it stopped, the back door opened and Joel stepped out, followed by his nephew. By this time the taxi driver was at back of the car, opening the trunk lid and dragging out two large suitcases.

Adria's heart was pounding in her chest as she gazed at Joel. His hair was a mass of black waves burnished by the sun to a high sheen. When he saw her, he smiled and waved.

"Hello," she called, irritated because her traitorous heart was beating wildly at the mere sight of him as he walked up to her.

"Miss me?" he asked.

"Of course," she teased, "we haven't had anyone yelling at us."

"Is that the only reason?" His voice was low and caressing.

"No," she murmured.

"Good to have you back, Joel," Solly called. He rose from the table and walked toward them.

"You're not off the hook. We're going to continue this conversation later, and that's a promise," Joel said softly, and shivers of anticipation ran down Adria's body. Raising his voice, he said, "It's good to be back, Solly. Aunt Chessy sends you her love, and says to find that treasure and get home. She's tired of being alone."

Solly laughed, the deep sound rumbling in his chest. "Don't I know it."

"Is this where you're looking for the treasure?" Lane asked.

"That's right," Solly answered. "Welcome to Isla Esmeralda."

"Adria, Uncle Solly," Joel said, "I'd like you to meet my nephew, Lane LeMaster."

"Hello, Lane," Adria and Solly said together.

Squinting against the sun, the thirteen-year-old lifted his face and looked first at Adria, then at Solly. "Hi."

"We're glad to have you with us," Adria said, astonished at how much he favored Danny. "I'm sure you'll enjoy the island as much as we do."

"Not to mention being a treasure hunter," Solly added.

Lane crossed his arms over his chest and frowned at his uncle. "This doesn't look like it's going to be as exciting as I thought it would be."

"I didn't promise you an exciting summer," Joel said. "I promised you a summer of work, remember. A place to stay until your father can get you."

"Yeah," Lane grumbled, and started toward the center of the camp. "A place to stay because no one really wants to be bothered with me. Dad has his job and Mom has Eddy.''

''Both of your parents want you,'' Joel said rather sharply. ''Your mother is having a well-earned vacation, and your father is completing a job assignment. Your mother's having a new male friend in her life doesn't mean that she doesn't love or want you. She's got enough room in her heart to love you both, and if your father didn't work, you wouldn't be living so well, so don't knock him or her. Okay?''

Lane turned around. ''Okay, Uncle Joel, if you say so.''

''By the way,'' Joel said, ''don't forget your suitcases. I'll carry one—you get the other.''

Grimacing, Lane returned and picked up the piece of luggage. ''Where's our tent?'' he asked, letting everyone know his displeasure.

Joel pointed, and Lane struck out at a fast pace. The three adults followed more slowly.

''I see that we have our work cut out for us,'' Solly murmured. ''He sure reminds me of Danny.''

''I thought so, too,'' Adria answered. ''Not only the dark hair and blue eyes, but his attitude and carriage.''

''Well,'' Solly said, taking the suitcase from Joel, ''I'll go ahead and help Lane settle in. The two of you probably want to have a little time to yourselves. But just a little.'' He pointed to the sky. ''We better get the men in and secure the boats. Looks like a storm is brewing.''

''He's right,'' Joel said, as he surveyed the sky. The winds were high; the heavy black clouds, close. ''Fate seems to be against me, Adria,'' he murmured. ''We've got precious little time and look what happens.''

''Uncle Joel—'' Lane poked his head out of the tent ''—are you going to take me to the *Black Beauty* tonight, so I can start working with the computers?''

"Not tonight," Joel called back. "You can spend the time unpacking your suitcases and getting acquainted with the crew. Once the storm blows in, we'll be confined to our tents."

A thin sliver of lightning ran from the top of the sky to the horizon, a boom of thunder following in its wake.

"Get the men in," Joel ordered, Solly and Adria nodding their agreement.

BY MORNING THE STORM had passed. Without awakening Lane, Joel arose before dawn and made a pot of coffee, leisurely drinking a cup before the day's work began. As he lay on the cot, propped on his elbow, he wondered if he would ever locate any part of the *Golden Fleece*. When he and Adria had signed the contract, he had been a little irritated with her for insisting on the certified check. Then he had been so sure of his find, and he had not wanted to go to his parents for a loan. But he was no longer irritated with Adria. He was glad that she was protected; otherwise, he would have felt guilty for taking her money and giving her false hopes.

As the first rays of sun peeked into the tent, Joel leaned over and shook Lane. "Time to get up, sleepyhead," he said, his thoughts going to another morning when he had awakened Adria.

This treasure hunt was turning out differently than he had expected. Although he was still interested in finding the *Glorious Bess,* he was no longer driven as if the hounds of Hades were fast on his heels.

Lane grunted and turned over. Joel shook him again, harder this time. "Come on. We have work to do. If you're not up in ten minutes and dressed, you'll be left ashore to do kitchen duty."

Those were the magic words. In several quick motions Lane was out from under the cover, stripping out of his pajamas and reaching for his shorts and tank top. Running a hand through sleep-tousled hair, he said, "You're really going to let me work with your computers, Uncle Joel?"

Joel nodded. "You'll be working under Gary Burroughs. I've shown him what I want, and he'll instruct you. And remember what I told you when we were flying down here, Lane. You can't goof off—this is a job, and you're going to have to shoulder a lot of responsibility."

"I will, Uncle Joel," Lane promised. "I will."

Later, when Joel and Lane exited from their tent, Adria joined them. They motored to the *Black Beauty* and were soon aboard, Joel and the other divers donning their scuba gear. Adria stayed with Gary and Lane, watching as they monitored the equipment and putting together the maps.

The day passed slowly as the divers worked below the water, digging hole after hole, all of them dry. One by one the divers surfaced, nothing but cold bodies and aching limbs to show for their hours of diligent search. Joel remained below. If only he could find some ballast, he thought. That would eventually lead them to the ship and to the gold. He knew that he alone still searched, but he couldn't leave now. He was too close. He could feel the tingle of discovery all through his body. He had to find something...anything that would attest to the *Glorious Bess* being in this spot.

He swam around one last time, peering through the rippling water at territory he had looked at for hours, at terrain he had looked at so much he almost had it memorized. Then as he turned, he saw something that wasn't quite right. His heart started beating faster, and his strokes grew stronger. Miraculously exhaustion slipped from his limbs, and he felt a new spurt of energy. He swam nearer the anomaly and brushed the sand away, to expose a piece of wood. He brushed again, reminding himself to be careful. A piece of metal. More brushing. Then he saw the anchor.

He tugged the rope for the basket, his heart thumping loudly in his chest. Closer investigation revealed a well-preserved wooden stock, and inscribed alongside the date "1586" were the foundry and weight marks. The evidence he needed to prove that a ship—perhaps not the *Glorious Bess* but a ship, nonetheless—had sunk in these waters. He had found a ship. Elation flowed through his veins.

By the time he surfaced, morale among the crew was soaring. Adria was there to greet him, giving him a kiss as soon as he stepped aboard the *Black Beauty*. The men gathered around the anchor, looking at and touching it, running their fingers over the date and foundry and weight marks.

As darkness settled gently over them, they headed back to camp. After Lane had bathed he went to Gary's tent, the two of them working together on a new program for cataloging the artifacts as they were recovered.

WHEN ADRIA CAME OUT of the tent the next morning, Solly was sitting at the central table drinking a cup of coffee and staring into the distance. Joel was pouring his.

"We have company," Solly announced, and pointed to a large yacht in the distance.

"How long has it been there?" Joel set down his cup and picked up the binoculars, focusing on the vessel.

"It was there when I got up at six. That was two hours ago. I don't know how much earlier," Solly answered. "Wonder what a yacht is doing in these waters?"

"That's my question," Joel said. "I guess we need to pay them a visit and find out."

"Want me to come along?" Solly asked.

"No," Joel answered, "I need you here to get the work started. I'll take Adria with me, and we'll be back as soon as we can."

Solly nodded.

Joel and Adria climbed into one of the smaller boats and motored out.

"Good morning," Joel yelled when they reached the yacht.

"Good morning," a tall, slender man in his early forties said. "I'm Earl Melford. What can I do for you?"

"Joel LeMaster and Adria Gilby. I have a salvage contract on these waters and wondered why you were anchored here. Are you having trouble?"

"Oh, no," Melford said. "As the old saying goes, I just happened to be passing by and decided to stop for a visit. Will you join me for breakfast?"

"No thanks," Joel said. "We've already eaten."

"Then come aboard and have a cup of coffee."

If they were going to learn anything about him, Adria thought, they were going to have to go aboard. The man didn't seem inclined to leave.

Evidently Joel thought the same thing. He said, "All right."

As soon as they had boarded, they followed Melford through the main salon into a separate dining room. Adria was curious about the man, his ship and his reason for being at Isla Esmeralda. The island was small and off the beaten path; therefore, it didn't boast many tourists.

Soon they were seated around the table and servants unobtrusively moved in and out of the room, serving the food. She glanced through the open French doors into the salon. As usual, the paintings and photographs caught her attention. She wished she were closer so she could see them better.

"Isla Esmeralda isn't a tourist attraction, Melford," Joel said, "so what brings you out here?"

Melford washed his bacon, eggs and toast down with hot black coffee. Shrugging, he allowed his gaze to move slowly over Adria. "Sheer curiosity. You might say I'm an amateur treasure hunter. Or perhaps a better definition would be a hobbyist treasure hunter."

He stopped talking, took several more bites, then dabbed the corners of his mouth with a napkin. "For the past four years I've spent my summers here in Isla Esmeralda searching for treasure," he continued, "but I've always come up empty-handed. When I docked in the marina last night the locals told me about your being out here and hunting for treasure, so I decided to stop by."

Leaning back in her chair Adria sipped her juice and studied the man who sat at the head of the table, eating his breakfast and talking. It didn't seem to matter to him that she and Joel weren't participating; he carried the conversation on very well by himself, even to the point of laughing at his own jokes.

Finished with his breakfast, Melford drank a second cup of coffee. "Have you found anything yet?'

Neither Joel nor Adria answered, and Melford raised his hands in mock apology. "Of course, you wouldn't want to divulge such information—in case there were claim jumpers."

"I'm not afraid of claim jumpers. I have a salvage contract that protects me. You're the one who is at fault, Melford. You have no right to be in these waters," Joel said. "The way I see it, my business is not your business."

Melford laughed softly. "You're quite right. It's not." He lit a cigarette, inhaling deeply and exhaling before he laid the lighter on the table beside his plate. "And I sincerely do apologize if my arrival caused you some alarm. I came for no other reason but curiosity."

Adria sensed the man was lying, but Joel only said, "How long are you staying?"

"I'm not sure," Melford replied. "Some of my men wanted to dive."

Joel shook his head. "Sorry, I can't allow that. As I've said, I have exclusive rights to search in these waters. If your men begin diving, it will interfere with my work."

"Even if they stayed out of your way?"

Joel smiled tightly. "Even so, since it's hard to define the parameters of 'my way'."

"You act as if you've found something," Melford drawled, his eyes narrowing speculatively as they darted from Joel to Adria.

His lingering gaze gave Adria an eerie feeling. His interest in their discovery was more than idle curiosity. Still, neither she nor Joel said anything.

Melford continued in a pensive voice, "That's more than I ever did, but as I said, I'm only an amateur."

Melford picked up the lighter, sliding it through his index finger and thumb, thumping it lightly on the table, flipping it over and sliding it again. The design on it was exquisite, and Adria figured it was made of either gold and silver or gold and platinum, and she opted for the latter, judging from the look of his yacht.

"Would you be interested in more financing?" he finally asked.

Joel ran his finger around the rim of his empty cup. "No."

Adria wondered if the man were psychic, also.

"I hope you know what you're doing," Melford said. "I've worked these waters for the past four years. Before the government will extend a salvage contract, the salvor must prove that the find is worth an extension...or he must have enough money to convince the government agent the contract is worth their time." He inhaled and exhaled again, the smoke forming a gray haze around his face. "You never know what may happen to keep you from working. You know, storms, accidents and so on."

Melford's words themselves were softly spoken, but they were menacing and disturbed Adria greatly. Her gaze moved past her host to the large salon that lay beyond the double doors. Something else disturbed her. The ship...the captain . . . the atmosphere. She couldn't put her finger on it, but something vaguely stirred her memory.

Melford reached into his pocket and extracted a card which he handed to Joel. "If you have a change of mind or finances, Mr. LeMaster, please give me a call. Perhaps we can talk business."

Joel read the card and flipped it onto the table. Rising, he said, "Thanks for the coffee. Adria and I must be on our way. We have a lot of work to do today, so we must get started."

Melford glanced at the card. "I hope you're not making a mistake."

"I'm not."

"You may leave through here." Melford waved his hand toward the double doors that led into the salon.

By the time Joel and Adria reached the *Black Beauty* and began searching for the day, Melford had moved his yacht a safe distance outside the waters where they were working. But he remained in the area for two more days. Joel continually wondered about Melford's visit and his offer of financial help, and finally curiosity got the better of him. Wanting to know who Melford was and what he really wanted, he went into the village and questioned the state field-archaeology agent with whom he negotiated his salvage contract.

Miguel knew Earl Melford, as did most of the residents of Emerald Cove. He was an extremely wealthy man who spent his summers treasure hunting, the past four of them somewhere around Isla Esmeralda. The agent also informed Joel that Melford would be attending the fiesta tonight as the mayor's guest of honor. Miguel then invited Joel to attend, but Joel declined. He had other plans.

That night after Lane was asleep and most of the crew were in town celebrating, Joel slipped out of his tent and walked to the beach. In the distance, silhouetted against the night blue sky, was the yacht.

"It's rather ominous, isn't it?" Adria asked as she walked up to join him.

"It has the men worried, and morale has dropped since we've found nothing else to indicate we've located our ship."

"Do you think that's his purpose in being here?"

"I'm not sure," Joel replied. "I know he's pretty chummy with the officials at Emerald Cove. In fact, Miguel told me he's attending the fiesta tonight as the mayor's guest of honor."

"I guess that's why the ship is rather dark, and if his crew is like ours they're in town celebrating, too."

"I would imagine," Joel said, then asked, "Would you like to go?"

Adria shook her head. "No, I want to stay close to the camp." They walked a little further up the beach, and Adria said, "The other day I had the feeling Melford knew about the *Golden Fleece,* Joel, and that he was baiting us."

Joel nodded. "Tonight I'm going to do my best to find out."

"How?"

"Swim over there and search the yacht. Maybe I'll find something that will give me a clue as to who he is and what he wants from us."

"I'm going with you," she said.

"I'd rather you didn't. You'll be safer here."

"Joel, we're in this together. I'm not going to let you go by yourself."

"One of us can slip aboard easier than two," he pointed out.

"But it might not be so difficult for two, if he and his crew are in town celebrating."

"We're not sure about the crew," Joel reminded her.

"But they probably are. When the cat's away, the mice will play." She paused, then added, "I'm going, Joel."

He didn't argue with her. He nodded his head, and said, "All right, but once we're on the yacht, you'll have to promise to obey my instructions."

She grinned. "Aye, aye, captain."

As soon as they had donned their bathing suits they motored as far as the *Black Beauty* where Joel picked up a flashlight; then they swam the rest of the way, climbing aboard the ship undetected by the skeleton crew and slipping into the darkened master suite. They searched through the desk until Joel found a waterproof packet of papers which he opened and from which he extracted some documents.

"What are they?" Adria whispered, peering over his shoulder.

"My original documents about the *Golden Fleece,*" he said. "The ones that were stolen out of my desk at the university."

"Does this mean that Melford's in cahoots with Westbrook?" she wondered aloud.

"I don't know," Joel answered. "I'm confused. I figured Melford knew we were on to something, but I never expected him to have these documents."

Joel returned the papers to the pouch, and as he bent over to open the bottom drawer of the desk to replace it he knocked something to the floor. When it hit, the thud resounded loudly through the room. Flashing the light around the floor, he found Melford's cigarette lighter. Quickly he returned it to the desk and he and Adria slipped out, hoping they hadn't been discovered.

They hadn't gone far when someone shouted, "Halt!"

"Run," Joel hissed, and both of them tore across the deck.

Adria hit the water as two bullets flew past them, the shots lost in the fireworks that were exploding in the village. She couldn't remember a time when she had been motivated to swim as fast as she did now. By the time they reached the motorboat at the *Black Beauty,* both were exhausted and breathing deeply.

"Those...were...bullets," she gasped between breaths. "They...could...have...killed...us."

"I know." Joel slowly pulled himself into the vessel and slumped in the seat. "They're playing for keeps, Adria, and they want the *Golden Fleece,* no matter how they have to get her."

They waited for a while, to see if the shots awakened anyone. Evidently they hadn't. Nothing unusual stirred aboard the *Black Beauty.* Neither was anyone following them. Joel rowed the boat back to camp.

Walking across the beach back to camp, Adria said, "They're not going to get our ship, Joel. The *Golden Fleece* is ours, and we're going to keep it."

Joel smiled to himself. In the beginning, he had promised the treasures of the *Golden Fleece* to her; now she was promising him.

He stopped and caught her in the circle of his arms. "Adria, I can't keep my hands off you."

"And I don't want you to," she murmured, lifting her face to his, letting him claim her mouth in a fevered kiss.

As it grew more passionate, they slid to the ground. He placed a hand against her shoulder and gently lowered her against the sand. Leaning over her, he kissed her again and again, tasting the cool droplets of water that still clung to her skin. As they kissed, his hands moved down her shoulder, to the full roundness of her breast, his thumb gently caressing the nipple until it firmed beneath his touch. His hand moved further down across her flat, firm belly to her thighs.

Adria moaned softly. Too long they had deprived themselves of each other, and her resolve to stay apart vanished in the fever of their desire.

"Love me, Joel," she whispered.

The second she made her request known, Joel's hands began a loving assault on her body. His fingers slipped the straps of her swimsuit from her shoulders, and he caught her breasts in his hands, holding them, gently caressing them, as he knelt above her, the moon a silver orb at his back. His hands slipped lower to her midriff, as he pushed the suit further down.

"You look like a sea goddess," he told her.

"And you, the sea god himself," she said, lifting her hands to trail them over his bare chest. "Or was he ever so handsome?"

He caught her hands in his and pulled her to her feet. "Shall we go to our silver sea, my love?"

"Yes."

Hand in hand they raced to the lagoon, stipulated by camp rules as Adria's private bathing area, where they were safe from prying eyes. Quickly he divested himself of his swimming trunks, then he lifted her into his arms and walked into the cool water that appeared to be painted silver. He lowered her until they sank into the shallow water.

Chapter Ten

Movement on the narrow cot awakened Adria. She lay there for a moment getting her bearing; then she remembered. She opened her eyes and stared through sleep-glazed eyes at Joel, who sat on the edge of her bed. The soft light of early morning filled the tent.

"What's wrong?" she asked.

His hand combed the hair from her temples, the gentle touch sending waves of pleasure through her. "Nothing, love. I have to leave for propriety's sake."

"Oh, yes," she said and sat up, the sheet falling to her waist. "It doesn't seem possible that it's morning already."

Joel laughed softly, the sound warmly caressing Adria and wrapping her in a cocoon of happiness. "That's because you and I had such a long night, love. Sneaking about on Melford's yacht and being shot at."

She ran her hand across his chest, her fingers tangling in the crisp hair before they found the tiny nubs that hardened beneath her touch. She moved her head, her lips following the same trail her fingers had blazed.

"And making love," she whispered.

"And making love," he repeated. "But now I really have to go."

She pulled her head back and gazed into his face, shadowed in the grayness of early morning. He rose and walked to the entrance, standing for a few seconds to look at her. He blew her a kiss before he walked out.

As soon as he was gone, Adria darted out of bed and dressed. By the time the coffee perked, she was seated at the table beside him, and by lantern light they pored over their large-scale and small-scale maps, where Joel had meticulously marked finds and plotted search runs.

Pushing back from the table and refilling his cup with coffee, he said, "We've come a long way since the brass sundials and astrolabes."

"Uncle Joel!" Lane called out and came running from the beach. "The ship's gone. The ship's gone."

Joel and Adria rose so quickly, their chairs rocked back and forth, almost tumbling over. They raced to where the boy stood. Melford's yacht was gone, and only the *Black Beauty* could be seen.

"This is going to be the day," Joel declared. "Something great is going to happen today."

"Yeah," Adria mumbled under her breath, so that only Joel heard, "we're going to be arrested for breaking and entering."

ONE BY ONE ADRIA CROSSED the days from her calendar, as June turned into July. With Melford's ship gone, morale, despite the lack of further evidence of the *Glorious Bess,* rose and time passed quickly. This particular day was lazy and hot, and Adria, having dived earlier, now lounged in the shade in front of her tent.

"Joel! Adria!" Gary Burroughs shouted from the bank, where he and Lane were setting up a remote sensing survey of the area north of where they were searching.

"Somebody! Everybody! Come here. Lane and I have found something. Oh, my God, we've found something."

Adria was on her feet and running to where Gary and Lane were standing, and Solly was right behind her. Her eyes riveted to the spot he indicated with his index finger, she gazed at the metal that gleamed through the rippling water.

"What is it?" he asked.

By now Joel had pushed to the front and was standing beside them. He bent closer to the water, then straightened and turned to the gathering group. "I can hardly believe this," he announced.

"Believe what?" Ford Lowell elbowed past the others to stand beside Joel.

"With all our equipment, we've found nothing to compare to this," Joel murmured. "Right here, visible for anyone to see is a bronze cannon. It's as if it were supernaturally moved here so we would find it."

"A bronze cannon," Hub Chambers parroted. "What does it mean, boss?"

Joel turned, a grin splitting his face. "It means we've found her, men." He plunged his fist into the air and shouted, "We've found our ship, and it's only a matter of time until we find her treasure."

"Me and Gary found it," Lane shouted to be heard above his uncle. "Me and Gary did it, didn't we?"

"You sure did," Joel said, looking from one to the other, both of them grinning.

"And neither of us is a diver," Lane added with a loud burst of laughter. "We did it from right here."

Drunk with elation, the crew laughed with the boy, and Joel said, "Maybe I don't need divers, after all. I should just hire more men to work with the computers and electronic equipment."

"Yeah," Lane shouted, and danced about.

Morale soared as the crew worked to bring the cannon up. Careful digging the remainder of the week produced another large galleon anchor, the markings identical to the one they had already found. With the magnetometer they picked up several barrel hoops. Then with their vacuum cleaner, they shifted out spikes and small rock ballast.

After having found the cannon and the anchor, the men were disappointed with the spikes and rock ballast, but Joel assured them these finds, although small, were relevant pieces to the puzzle. They were the trail leading them to *Glorious Bess*.

On Friday, three days later, Ford Lowell and Hub Chambers returned to camp, grinning from ear to ear. Proudly they displayed their latest find: a thirty-pound ballast rock.

"Happy Fourth of July," they announced.

"No better way to celebrate," Joel declared. "Our cache of artifacts growing in number and significance. And this ballast rock, men and lady, is going to lead us to the gold. It's only a matter of time."

Of which they had little, Adria thought, trying to curb her growing pessimism.

That evening celebration was in order. Beer and conversation flowed freely. Joel, however, took one of the speed boats and headed for the *Black Beauty,* where he studied earlier magnetometer surveys and work done with the side-scan sonar. They had registered several anomalies that might tie in with this shipwreck scatter. He worked late into the night, and everyone was asleep when he returned to camp.

He wanted to go to Adria. In fact, he started walking toward her tent, but stopped. She needed her rest, and the camp was a little too insular for them to sleep together.

Even when he lay down, sleep evaded him. Putting a hand beneath his head, he stared at the canvas roof and wondered if he had made a mistake. Had he allowed himself to be pushed by an obsession rather than facts? This had to be the final resting place of the *Golden Fleece*. That was his last thought as he drifted into a restless sleep.

The next morning work resumed. Digging that day revealed an iron breech-loading swivel gun, cannon shot, rigging and over-residue of a ship's upper superstructure.

Standing on the deck, Adria looked at the artifacts as they were brought aboard. She was happy with the find, but was still disappointed they had found nothing to indicate that this was indeed the *Glorious Bess*. Time was ticking out for her. The money she earned from the *Colt*, and that which Joel had guaranteed her if they found nothing, would stay the creditors for a little while—but not for long.

While Joel would be happy with any archaeological find, she had to confess that she desperately needed the riches the *Glorious Bess* promised. She wanted more than ballast, barrel hoops and anchors, to show for her work. If she was going to save her company and home, she had to have more.

Indeed, she had now joined the ranks of John and Daniel Gilby; she, too, had become a treasure seeker.

A WEEK LATER, Adria and Joel were diving together. As he searched the ocean bottom for the ship, Adria took photographs. Suddenly he signaled her to come closer, and she zoomed in on him and the area where he was working.

On his tablet he wrote: *The hull of a ship,* then pointed to scattered bits of wood. He knelt over a broken placard and gently wiped the silt away to reveal the word *Moon.* The more they searched the area, the larger they deter-

mined the ship to be. Finally they surfaced and climbed
aboard the *Black Beauty.* Elated with their find, both Joel
and Adria talked at once. They stopped, looked at each
other and laughed; then Adria pointed to Joel.

"You tell them," she said.

Passing around the placard, he said, "Although this
isn't the *Glorious Bess,* and probably not one of the
Golden Fleece ships, it's a major find. I'm going to go
ahead and call in the specialists I told you about when we
first began the excavation. We've got to have people who
know how to recover and preserve artifacts we're bound to
find."

The crew was proud of Joel's artifact, but their elation
had not reached the high level of his. Old ships didn't
mean as much to them as gold and silver and precious
gems.

"Reckon there's any gold on the ship?" Lowell asked.

Joel shrugged his shoulders. "If it's a Spanish ship, in
all probability it will have some treasure on it. If it's not, I
can't say."

That night a subdued crew clustered in small circles,
talking and making plans for the coming day. Joel and
Gary, by lantern light, were studying the latest photographs Adria had taken and the newest sonar readings.
Lane was already in bed.

Adria could understand the crew's lack of enthusiasm.
They were glad Joel had found a ship, but they weren't
looking for ships in general. They wanted a *treasure* ship.
Like her, they wanted the riches the sunken ships promised.

Headlights beamed through the darkness breaking into
Adria's reverie. She sat there watching as they drew closer.
Joel, the first to rise, moved to the edge of the clearing;
Adria followed.

"Are you expecting anyone?" he asked, and she shook her head.

When the car neared, they saw it was a taxi. The driver parked beneath two hanging lanterns, and when the back doors opened two well-dressed strangers climbed out. Oddly enough they reminded Adria of the early cartoon characters Mutt and Jeff. One was tall and slender, the other short and heavyset. The older of the two, the short one, talked with the driver, who nodded, shut off the engine and slid down in the seat, pulling his cap over his eyes as if he was in for a long wait.

"I don't know them. Do you?" Adria asked.

Joel paused only momentarily before he said dryly, "Woodrow Westbrook and Baxter Langston."

"I don't believe it," she said. The men neared, and she felt uneasy. "Melford must have sent for them."

"Hello, Joel," the younger man said, moving in closer, the lamp lanterns fully exposing him. His lips curled in a pasty smile. "I don't suppose you're surprised to see me."

"No, Woody, I'm not," Joel answered. "You've always been a good bloodhound."

Westbrook hiked a blond brow that was the same color as his hair, slicked back from his face with mousse. "What's that supposed to mean?"

"You've never been the master, only the dog."

"And you haven't changed one whit," the older man accused, then chomped down on a cigar that protruded from the corner of his mouth. "You're still as arrogant and rude as ever."

"I don't know about being arrogant and rude," Joel answered, "but I haven't changed and I'm not likely to."

Baxter Langston looked at Westbrook. "I told you it was a mistake to come out here. He's still a fool. There's going to be no dealing with him."

"Now, Bax," Westbrook said soothingly, "let's the three of us sit down somewhere by ourselves and talk. I'm sure we can persuade Joel to cooperate with us." Standing in front of Joel, Westbrook's gaze shifted to Adria. "Are you going to introduce us, Joel? Or are you afraid of losing another fiancée?"

Joel clenched his hands into fists, and his face tightened. Wanting to protect him, Adria moved closer. She could feel the tension that emanated from him.

Westbrook laughed, then said, "Just a joke, LeMaster, don't get upset."

"Adria Gilby, this is Woodrow Westbrook and Baxter Langston."

Westbrook smiled and stepped forward. "Just so there is no mistake, Ms. Gilby, I'm Woody. He's Baxter Langston."

Adria had to force herself to be civil; the men had only been here a few minutes, and already she disliked them. "Hello, Mr. Westbrook."

Langston ignored the greetings altogether. "Is there someplace private where we can talk, LeMaster?"

"Anything you have to say, Adria can hear," Joel said. "She and I are partners."

"I don't care if she's with us or not," Langston exclaimed, "but let's go somewhere where we can sit down. My feet are killing me."

Joel led them to his tent, and when they were seated around the small table, Westbrook spoke. "As spokesman for the American Nautical Archaeology Foundation, I want to let you know what happened on the *San Pablo* is a thing of the past. The board of directors extends its apology and would like to effect a compromise so we can work with you on this find."

Joel leaned back in the chair, a sardonic smile playing on his lips. "As clichéd as the saying may be, Woody, I'm going to use it again. Not only no, but hell, no. The *Golden Fleece* belongs to me, and I'm not willing to share it with anyone, especially not the foundation. What happened on the *San Pablo* excavation is not a thing of the past in my life."

Westbrook squirmed in the chair and cleared his throat. "Don't turn this down out of hand, Joel. You have a lot at stake. The university is willing to accept you back on the faculty. You'd be working with me, and I can promise you—"

Joel laughed, the sound devoid of humor. "We've tried that before, Woody, and I came out on the short end of the stick. Despite what Baxter says, I'm not fool enough to do it a second time."

"Damn it," Langston swore, his fist coming down on the table with such force it shook. "I've had enough of this. The *Golden Fleece* doesn't belong to you. You stole those papers from the foundation when you left. It belongs to the foundation and we want it."

"The papers were stolen from me," Joel corrected, "but I don't think that's the point at this time. It seems that others have heard about the *Golden Fleece* and are here to stake their claim to it, also."

Langston's eyes rounded. "Who?"

"For one, Earl Melford," Joel answered, and looked from one man to the other. "Have you ever heard of him?"

Both of them shook their heads.

"It's not possible that he's working with the two of you?"

Westbrook rose, his voice quivering with anger. "I don't have to sit here and take your insults," he exclaimed. "I came to you because I thought we could help you, but you're just as bullheaded now as you were five years ago.''

"Maybe more so," Joel said. "I've had all these years to practice."

He wagged an index finger at Joel. "If you don't record this as a joint find, sharing credit with me and Baxter, we'll find some way to prove that you stole classified documents from the foundation that made the discovery of the *Golden Fleece* possible."

"You may make the claim," Joel said, "but you'll never be able to prove it, Woody."

Adria was numb. She couldn't believe she was hearing this conversation, and the more she heard, the more fearful she grew that something or someone was going to step in between them and the *Golden Fleece* if they did find it.

"One thing I can do," Westbrook charged, "is have your license and permit rescinded, pending the investigation."

"You can try," Joel responded.

Baxter rose, shook a pudgy fist in Joel's face, and shouted, "LeMaster, I'll do *anything*—do you hear me— anything I have to to keep you from getting credit for the *Golden Fleece*. If the ANAF doesn't succeed in getting your license revoked, I'll pressure them into appealing the case until it can't be appealed anymore. I don't care if we win or not. My purpose is to hold up the work until your money runs out and your permit expires. Then the foundation will step in and pick up where you left off." He sucked in deep gulps of air. "I promise you, you won't get the *Golden Fleece,* and you'll be a broken man."

All the time that Baxter spoke, Westbrook nodded his head. Smiling, he added, "ANAF, under me, has been granted a permit to continue the search of the area after your permit expires."

"So, LeMaster, one way or the other," Baxter interjected, "credit for this excavation will go to me and Woody."

"No, gentlemen," Joel said, his voice extremely soft, "neither of you will get credit for my find. I already have the evidence I need to prove there is a sunken ship here. The credit will go to me and to Adria. This is our find, and we're not willing to share it with either or both of you."

Langston looked at Adria. "I hope you know what kind of man you're associated with, lady. He's responsible for my daughter's death."

"I read the accounts, Mr. Langston," Adria said, exerting great effort to control her anger, "and from the testimony that was presented, I have to believe your daughter must shoulder the responsibility for her death."

Langston gritted his teeth, then said to Joel, "I'll see that you and your career are ruined for good, LeMaster. And mark my words, this is no idle threat. I have the money to do just that, and I will."

DURING THE FOLLOWING DAY, two ships loomed on the horizon: Westbrook's salvage vessel and Melford's yacht. Westbrook's purpose was to make his presence known and to intimidate, but Adria was not sure about Melford.

Although morale should have been at an all-time high, it was low. Not only were the men disappointed with the ship they had discovered and frustrated with having to move as slowly and cautiously excavating as Joel dictated, but every time they looked over their shoulders they saw the two ships and wondered what was happening.

Adria sat on the deck, waiting for the divers to surface, her gaze moving from the yacht to the salvage vessel then back to the drawing of the ship Ford Lowell was working on. Using photographs, measurements and original contract specifications of ships built in England during 1586, he drafted a preliminary reconstruction of the ship they had discovered and nicknamed *Moonbeam*.

Joel surfaced, climbed aboard the salvage vessel and divested himself of his diving gear. His eyes were sparkling, and his voice, animated with excitement. "The entire site is mapped," he announced as Hub Chambers also surfaced. "It's the same kind of ship that Billington would have been sailing, and the precursory investigation reveals that a heavy blow to its side caused it to sink."

Adria rose. "Joel, do you think—"

Joel nodded. "If it is, Adria, it would substantiate my theory that the storm hurled the vessels into one another, and we've found the 'other one.' Still," he added, "nothing in my research connects it with the *Golden Fleece*."

Days passed, and much to everyone's disappointment, no treasure was found. Now Joel and Adria began to wonder if perhaps the stories of great plunder associated with Billington were highly exaggerated by either the teller, the recorder or both.

Several mornings later as they were eating breakfast, an official vehicle pulled into the clearing and parked. A middle-aged man wearing a khaki uniform approached their table.

"Mr. LeMaster," he said, and Joel rose. "I'm Paul Galvano, Isla Esmeralda marine archaeologist. I have recently replaced Miguel Fuentes as the state field-archaeology agent. I believe he was the person with whom you worked, when you applied for your salvage contract for this site."

"Yes, I did work with Miguel," Joel answered and waved to a vacant chair.

The agent sat down, pulled a document from his shirt pocket and laid it on the table. "The American Nautical

Archaeology Foundation has asked that your license and permit be revoked, pending an investigation into charges that you stole classified documents from them when you resigned five years ago. According to them, these documents enabled you to find this vessel which they claim is a part of the *Golden Fleece*."

Joel said nothing.

"However, since they have no conclusive proof that you did steal the papers and since they have waited five years to bring charges against you, we have decided to let you continue to excavate and to log your find. While they conduct their investigation, we are going to move you to a house in town and order you to hold all artifacts in inventory until the case is settled."

"Thank you, Mr. Galvano," Joel said and shook hands with the agent. "When do we start moving?"

"Today. The movers arrive within the hour."

"You've taken care of everything," Joel said dryly.

"We believe so," Galvano said.

Joel pointed to the yacht and Westbrook's salvage vessel. "What about them?"

"They are moving also," Galvano replied. "You have no more worries, Mr. LeMaster. Since you are now in our custody—so to speak—we will be patrolling the waters, keeping your area safe from poachers."

After the agent left, Adria knew Joel was concerned about taking the time from their diving to move their camp into the house. "You and the crew take care of the diving," she said. "I'll take care of the moving."

When Adria had volunteered, the job had not seemed so arduous. But hours later, she wished she had let Joel supervise the move while she dived. Unpacking her suitcases for the first time in weeks, she stood in front of the dresser in an upstairs bedroom in the house the government had provided for them. It was beautiful, and fully furnished. Adria was glad they had moved here. She had quickly learned she was no daughter of nature. A few nights roughing it in a tent were all right, but weeks of living like that had worn her pleasure thin.

She opened the photo album, slowly thumbing through the pages, looking at the first photographs she had taken of Joel.

The telephone rang, and Adria jumped. Then she laughed at herself. Yes, she had been too long away from civilization. Moving across the room, she answered.

"Adria Gilby."

"Ms. Gilby, this is Paul Galvano. Does the house meet with your approval?"

"Oh, yes," she breathed and looked out the window at the green water of Emerald Cove. "It's beautiful."

"Good. Since the house belongs to the government and is often empty for months at a time, we have a caretaker. Her name is Consuelo Guerra. While you're staying there, she will be your housekeeper. Her oldest son, Thomas, is the gardener. They'll be along directly."

"How wonderful," Adria said. "I know both of them."

"I thought you would be pleased," the agent said. "I'll ring off for now, Ms. Gilby."

Adria opened her jewelry box and pulled out the crucifix Sarah had given to her. Not wanting to hurt the child's feelings, she slipped it over her head, flipped her braid out from under it, and stood in front of the mirror looking at its reflection. It was one of the most delicate pieces of jewelry she had ever owned.

After Consuelo and the children arrived, Adria returned to the *Black Beauty,* put on her diving gear and dove into the water, spending the rest of the day photographing the site. Joel motioned for Adria to return to the top, but she wanted to take one last photograph. When she motioned that she saw something, Joel shook his head, his hand indicating they go up.

Adria knew the rules, and she understood Joel's growing frustration when she refused to go topside with him. She couldn't leave. She did see something that might be a clue to the treasure that was reputed to be aboard Billington's ships. She moved closer to the outer periphery of the resistant tubing they had used to map the site; Joel moved by her side. Then he saw the object at which she was pointing and moved forward to retrieve it.

As he bent, his air tank caught on one of the grids and the grid tubing broke, trapping him and tangling their lines so that they were unable to go for help. Adria threw down her camera and began the slow, tedious task of freeing him, but the harder she worked the more entangled in the grid he became.

Tears ran down her cheeks. Because of her stubbornness, because she had refused to obey his orders, she had not only endangered her life but his. If he died, it would be the result of her carelessness, of her neglect—the very trait she had condemned in her father and her brother. At this moment she realized the depth of her love for Joel. Without him, her life would be miserable and lonely.

Finally he caught her hands and clasped them between his; he forced her to look into his eyes. They silently assured her of his love and comforted her. Working together, they finally loosened her line, and using sign language he let her know that he had plenty of oxygen left in his tank, but they needed help if he was going to get free. He motioned for her to go above and get one of the men.

When Adria surfaced, she called to Ford and Hub, the two of them immediately donning their suits, getting an extra oxygen tank and joining her in the rescue. When they had freed Joel, they held the grid in place while he searched the area Adria indicated. When Joel picked up the object, he started waving it through the water, and showed it to them. It was the remaining part of the placard with the letters *G-O-D-D* barely eligible.

On his tablet he wrote: *Moon. Godd.* and *Ess.*

Moon Goddess. Another name for Elizabeth.

"I'M SO SORRY." Adria now lay in Joel's arms, her cheek pressed against his chest. They sat in her secluded spot at the lagoon, where no one would disturb them. "When I saw the placard sitting out of the sand, something made me go for it. It was as if I couldn't stop myself."

"All treasure divers experience that, sweetheart," he murmured. "It's something we must all guard against."

"The lure of the silver sea and its riches," Adria said. "That's what killed Vanessa, Joel."

He laid his cheek on the top of her head. "I know. That's one of the reasons why I must know my divers, Adria. The sea is beautiful and wonderful, but if one abuses her she can be treacherous."

"I don't suppose you'll want me to dive again."

"Five years ago, I would have said no," Joel answered, "but that's a decision you have to make, Adria."

"You could have died because of my stupidity."

Joel laughed softly. "It wasn't quite that bad, but carelessness can result in a fellow diver's death."

She lay there quietly for a long time, then said, "It's wonderful knowing we've discovered one of Billington's ships. *Moon Goddess,* another name for Elizabeth and indeed one of the *Golden Fleece.* Who would have ever thought that, Joel? And just imagine we found it little by little on three different occasions." She reached up and touched the crucifix Sarah had given to her. "I think perhaps Providence was watching over us," she said and held the crucifix away from her chest. "I'm glad I was wearing this."

Joel pulled back to look at it. "Where did you get this?" he asked, and she told him.

"You've had it all this time and didn't tell me?" he exclaimed.

Hurt by his tone, Adria said, "I saw no reason to tell you. It was a gift, given to me by Sarah."

"It's also an artifact, Adria."

"I know that," she said. "Consuelo told me that these wash up on the shore all the time."

"Had you really looked at it, you would have realized how valuable it is."

"I pointed that out to Consuelo," she answered, "but she assured me that its value had depreciated because the gems are gone."

Joel asked again, "You didn't notice anything in particular about it?"

Adria shook her head. He gently removed her from his arms, stood and pulled her to her feet. "If you were to imagine emeralds in this cross, it would be a smaller version of the one I have, Adria. You know, the one I showed you the first day we met."

Vaguely Adria remembered the cross, but she had been more interested in the ring. Hurriedly they returned to the house, calling and waving to Solly who read the newspaper in the living room. Up in Joel's bedroom, he pulled the small chest from beneath his cot and unlocked it. He held his crucifix up for Adria to see, and they were similar, his being the larger of the two and having the emeralds in place.

"Joel," she breathed. "I never thought. I was so caught up with the ring, I totally forgot about the crucifix." She touched the emeralds in the larger one. "Perhaps one was made for a man, the other for a woman. Or one for a child, the other for an adult."

"Billington did fleece the Spanish, and his booty is out there waiting for us. At least eight hundred million dollars worth, lying there patiently waiting for us." He rose. "Let's go tell the men. They'll be glad to hear this, and it'll give them incentive."

The emeralds in Joel's crucifix sparkled in the glow of the overhead light. Like sirens beckoning to the innocent sailors of yore, these gems lured the treasure hunter.

Chapter Eleven

The house, filled with spectators, dignitaries, and reporters, was aflurry with activity. Servants moved in and out of the crowd serving drinks and hors d'oeuvres. Cameras flashed and news reporters shoved their microphones into Joel's face. The late-August discovery of the *Golden Fleece* had made headline news. Reporters from the leading national broadcasting stations had been interviewing and filming most of the afternoon. With an aplomb Adria could only admire, Joel quietly answered their questions about his discovery.

As he told the story again, from the beginning, showing the reporters the crucifix, the ring and the coins, Adria listened with rapt attention, as if it were her first time. She followed his narration through the days of searching and digging, through their disappointments and accomplishments.

Gone was her hermit; in his place was the professor. For the occasion, Joel had donned a pair of black slacks and was wearing a soft ecru pullover shirt. His hair had been cut, the black mass still waving thickly about his face, but gone was the wild, untamed look. Again Adria's hands itched to get her camera to get on film yet another facet of her beloved.

"We don't know the name of the third ship or even what happened to it." Joel smiled into a camera as he answered the question. "But we have located the *Moon Goddess* and the *Virginia*. From the size of the latter and from my research, I'm almost positive this was Billington's flagship."

"Is it usual for marine archaeologists to work with commercial salvors?" another reporter asked.

Joel looked over at Adria, their eyes meeting, communicating, and he smiled—that sweet, special smile that was for her alone. She felt joy warmly surge through her body. Each day she discovered another complexity to this man, and each day she loved him more.

"In the past it was, but many are beginning to work with them as consultants," Joel answered. "Commercial salvors are the ones who have the money to recover these underwater treasures before they dissolve in the seawater that surrounds them."

He motioned for Adria to join him. When she stood beside him, he put an arm around her waist and pulled her closer. "This is Adria Gilby, owner of Gilby and Son Salvage Company. She's my partner and without her and her crew, I couldn't have found the *Golden Fleece*. I owe the success of the excavation to her and her crew."

The reporters now bombarded Adria with questions which she patiently answered, glad when they had finally exhausted the story and she could fade from the limelight. Joel seemed to thrive in it, but not she. She looked around the room at the professionals who were beginning to arrive in answer to Joel's summons, the first of whom was Tassja Zeeman. Luke Bannister and Gary were deep in discussion about the computerized recording of the artifacts. Finding the ships was only the beginning of their excavation; now they had to work to bring up the artifacts and treasure and to do it correctly, preserving as much of the historical data as possible.

Adria was proud of her men who were milling with the crowd, telling the story to all who would listen. They were treasure hunters, but were proud of their part in the excavation and preservation of the *Golden Fleece*. Meticulously they followed Joel's instructions—moving slower and more cautiously than a treasure seeker's greed allowed most times.

Moving away from Joel, Adria walked to the window and gazed across the front lawn. Lane was playing with a group of children, among them Tommy and Sarah. Adria smiled. The summer had been good for him. He was proud of his part in locating the ships. Now he was eagerly awaiting his father's arrival. Robert had wired Aunt Chessy two days ago, letting her know he would be coming to get Lane in two weeks.

The doorbell chimed, the sound barely echoing above the clamor in the house, and Consuelo went to the door. Adria could only gape in astonishment when Rose Red walked in, tossed her brassy blond head around, then zeroed in on Joel and moved straight across the room toward him. As usual, she was dressed with dramatic flair to match her makeup, her long red skirt swirling around her tiny ankles and feet, and red, white and blue bracelets and bangles complementing the sailor blouse. How *nautical* can one get, Adria thought with an inward smile. Rose Red had dressed for the occasion.

"Joel," the visitor called out, and he—as well as the reporters—turned. For that split second Rose Red became the center of attention. "Congratulations, darling." She threw herself against him, her hands curling around his arm, the long, red fingernails gleaming. When she stood on tiptoe to plant a kiss on his cheek, cameras once more flashed all over the room.

Joel, genuinely pleased to see her, smiled but gently disengaged himself. "Hello, Rose. It's good to see you. I didn't expect you so soon."

"I came the minute I received your message. I figured you'd want me here quickly, so when the plane landed I wasted no time on taxis or such. I rented a car," she said, the two of them moving toward Adria. "You've made quite a haul. Newspapers, magazines and television."

"We have. The mother lode is worth about eight to nine hundred million, not to mention the wealth of artifacts we're uncovering," Joel agreed. "We're going to need someone to supervise the cataloging."

"You have your woman."

By now they stood in front of Tassja, who was talking with Paul Galvano and Adria.

"Well, Joel," Tassja said, her cheeks dimpling as she smiled, her dark eyes flashing, "it looks like you're going to have your hands full of 'your women.' Can you handle them as well as you handle your ships?"

"Better," Joel teased in return, laughing with her, but again his smile and his gaze were for Adria and her alone. It declared his love and completely separated and elevated her above every other woman in the room.

"Hello, Adria," Rose said. "You're so quiet, I didn't see you standing there."

Reluctantly Adria broke the mesmeric bonding with Joel, and looked at the woman. She was too happy to take exception to Rose's comment. "Hello."

"You really have quite a layout here," Rose said, waving her hand around.

Joel laughed. "Thanks to Woody and the village of Emerald Cove."

"Woody got this for you?" she asked, raising her brows in astonishment.

"Indirectly," he answered and explained to her and Tassja what had happened prior to his and Adria's moving their headquarters into town. "Since the crew is staying on the *Black Beauty,* we have room here at the house for the two of you. Tassja already has her bedroom. I'll get Consuelo to show you to yours."

"Thanks," Rose said. "I'm really bushed and would like to have an early night. I want to get started with cataloging in the morning. Everything has been labeled, hasn't it?"

"Yes," Joel answered.

"Good. I was afraid with your having worked with commercial salvors that they wouldn't have used proper excavation methods."

Adria did not intend to let this remark slide by unnoticed. "Yes, Rose, my men are salvors and treasure hunters. But in contrast to many of the archaeologists and anthropologists who hide behind the hypocrisy of academia, commercial salvors are honest about their desire to find sunken riches."

Tassja laughed. "Good for you, Adria."

"If someone will show me my room," Rose said, "I think I'll call it a day."

"Come with me," Adria said and leaned over to plant a quick kiss on Joel's lips. "I'll be right back."

When all the company had gone, Adria walked onto her balcony and stood looking at the ocean and listening to the waves as they washed against the shore below. They had found their ships and Billington's Spanish plunder, and it belonged to them. She had enough money to save the business and the house.

Now she wondered what she was going to do. Saving Gilby's had been her goal, but she wasn't sure that she wanted to spend the rest of her life being a commercial salvor.

She walked to the dresser, picked up her photograph album and carried it to her bed. Slowly she turned the pages, looking at the photographs of Joel. She still wanted to enter her favorite pose in competition, but she was no closer to a title than when she had first taken his photograph. In fact, the longer she knew Joel, the more she learned about him, the more undecided she was.

During the three months that she had known him he had changed. Even tonight she saw a different Joel LeMaster. His cynicism had lessened, and he smiled and laughed more frequently and freely.

She heard the soft knock and laid the album aside. Opening the door, she found him standing in the hallway.

"May I come in?" he whispered.

She opened the door wider and stepped aside.

"I couldn't sleep without giving you a personal goodnight."

His arms slipped around her waist, and he drew her close, their lips meeting in a wonderful kiss.

When he lifted his lips from hers, he said, "I'll be glad when all this hoopla is over."

Adria laughed and said, "I don't think so, Dr. LeMaster. You love being in the limelight. It's your leonine nature."

Sweeping her into his arms, he carried her to the bed and laid her down. Scooting in beside her, he said, "You're so right, Ms. Gilby, but I also like the privacy of my lair."

"That's exactly what this house gives us," she murmured, her fingers working the buttons loose on the front of his shirt.

The cool evening breeze wafted through the opened French doors to touch their bodies like a sweet caress.

"I can hardly believe it," she said. "We've found our ship."

Joel flipped over, propping on an elbow and ran his fingers through her hair, which spread across the pillow. "It's *our* ship, all right."

"Do you think Westbrook and the foundation stand a chance of winning their charges?"

"No. They're wasting their time, and so are we talking about him."

Joel lowered his head, his lips touching hers in a kiss that soon turned into heated desire. His hands moved sensuously over her body. After several long, drugging kisses, he lifted his mouth. "Adria, I've missed you so much. I can hardly stand our being together all the time and never having a chance to really be alone."

Adria's hand cupped the back of his head, and she pulled his lips to hers. Then she slipped her hand beneath the waistband of his slacks.

Joel groaned softly and against her mouth he said, "I'd like to stay the night with you."

"I'd like that, too."

"In fact, Ms. Gilby, I'd like to spend the rest of my life with you."

"I—I find that idea most appealing, Dr. LeMaster."

"But one you have to think over?"

"No, I've already thought it over. My decision is made."

As if he feared her answer, he said in a low voice that vibrated with sincerity, "Adria, I love you."

"I love you." She stretched out, running her foot down the back of his leg. "And I can't think of the rest of my life without thinking about your being a part of it."

THE NEXT MORNING when Adria wakened, sunlight
poured in through the open French doors and bathed her
in golden brightness. She stretched luxuriously and smiled
as she remembered their wonderful night together. She had
awakened briefly when Joel got up earlier to go to the find,
but she had dropped back to sleep.

Joel loved and wanted to marry her. Although the sun
was shining brightly outside, her world would have been
sunshiny without it. He brought warmth and happiness to
her life.

Jumping out of bed, she quickly showered and dressed,
eager to be at the site. She wanted to see Joel, but they also
had a great deal of work to do. Finding the ships and the
mother lode was only the beginning.

When she entered the kitchen, Consuelo was pouring a
cup of coffee for Rose. At least, she thought the woman
devoid of makeup and brassy locks was Rose.

"Good morning," the young woman said, then smiled.
"Don't look so shocked. When I work at the Beachcomber, I'm Rose Red. Now I'm Rose Redding. So there's
no need for the costume."

"Sorry," Adria murmured. "I've never seen you without all your makeup, jewelry and wig."

"Now you have," Rose declared and liberally spread
cream cheese over her bagel. "I was waiting for you. Joel
and Tassja left hours ago. Not wanting to wake me, he left
word that you'd take me to the site, so I can see what's
going on."

The way Rose relayed the news that Joel and Tassja had
gone to the site together gave Adria the impression that she
wanted to create doubt in Adria's mind about Joel's fidel-
ity. Adria, however, was not going to play that game. She
and Joel had traveled a long way down the road of trust,

learning that trust in themselves was the beginning of learning to trust others.

"Hi, baby," Solly said as he walked into the kitchen, stopping to drop a quick kiss on Adria's forehead. "If you need me, you'll find me on the patio. I'm going to be interviewing for guards today. Since we're going to be bringing the artifacts here, Joel wants me to tighten up the security. The state will provide some, but that's not enough." After Solly poured himself a cup of coffee, he turned to Rose. "Miss Redding, has anyone shown you where you'll be working?"

She nodded. "The house out back."

"Adria," Consuelo returned to the kitchen, untied her apron and hung it on the back of the door, "I'm taking a group of children to the museum today. Do you think Joel would mind Lane's going with us?"

"I don't think so," Adria answered, "but I'll ask him when I get to the site. What time are you leaving?"

"About two."

"I'll have him here, by then, if he's going." Adria turned to Rose. "I'm ready to leave as soon as you are."

"I'm ready," Rose said. "If you don't mind, we'll go in separate cars. That way neither of us will be dependent on someone to bring us home, and I'd like to get some use out of this one as I've rented it by the week."

Joel and Tassja remained at the *Virginia* that night, but Adria returned at two with Lane. After Consuelo and the children left, Adria stopped by the drugstore to pick up several rolls of film she had taken since she had been on Isla Esmeralda.

She was exceptionally pleased with the ones she had taken of the children. While those she had taken at the marina the day Joel had applied for his extension were good, none of them was spectacular.

When she arrived home, she spread all of them across the bed and began to pick out her favorite. As she played with them, shuffled and reshuffled them around, she thought about Rose Red and Rose Redding. How different the one was from the other.

The telephone rang, and she answered.

"Honey—" Joel's voice flowed through the line "—I'm going to work late tonight. Do you mind keeping an eye on Lane?"

"Not at all," she replied. "Do you need me?"

"Not tonight," he answered. "We're doing all the good we can right now. Probably we'll use you tomorrow."

"What time do you think you'll be home?"

"I'm not sure. We're going to dive until we can't. Go on to bed, sweetheart, and I won't disturb you tonight when I come in. I'll see you in the morning." Before he hung up, he asked, "How is Solly coming with the security guards?"

Adria laughed. "He's doing great. Everywhere I go, I bump into these uniformed men."

Despite her missing Joel, the afternoon and evening passed quickly for Adria. She cataloged her photographs and had dinner with Lane and Uncle Solly. Then she took the children to a video center and rented a movie which they watched until bedtime.

She was soon deeply asleep and dreaming that she was walking in a flower garden. When she reached the roses, she stopped by one that was a vibrant red. It was one of the most beautiful flowers Adria had ever seen and she was compelled to touch it, to lean over and to smell its fragrance. However, it was overpowering and she felt as if she were suffocating. She woke up gasping for breath.

She lay awake for a long in time in the dark, her thoughts again returning to Rose. Suddenly she bolted upright. She remembered what was familiar to her the other night when she was on Melford's ship. Jumping out of bed and hastily putting on her robe, she rushed to the dresser and picked up the packet of film she had taken the day she and Joel were in town. She plundered through the drawers until she found her magnifying glass and held it over one of the pictures.

She thought so.

She looked at the time. Three o'clock. Surely Joel was home. She padded to his bedroom and knocked.

"Who is it?" called a sleepy voice.

"Me."

"Come in." His voice sounded more alert and awake.

When she opened the door, he switched on the bedside lamp and shoved himself up in the bed, fluffing the pillows behind him. Smiling he held his arms out to her.

She ran to him, squirming on the bed, nestling close to him. After several kisses, she said, "Joel, do you remember I told you there was something familiar about Melford's yacht, but I couldn't put my finger on it?"

He nodded.

"Now I remember what it was. He had a photograph of Rose in the salon. I didn't recognize her at the time because I had never seen her without her exaggerated make-up."

"I think you're mistaken."

"I'm not."

She dug into her robe's pocket to extract the photograph and magnifying glass. "Look at this."

He did, then looked back at her. "What's this supposed to prove?"

"Do you recognize the yacht?"

Now Joel looked more closely. "Melford's."

"And the woman on board is Rose. She and Melford are working together."

Joel sighed, and Adria could hear how weary he was. This was an additional worry he didn't want to be saddled with.

"I don't think so. True, there is a woman standing on deck, but the ship is so far in the distance you can't prove it's Rose."

Adria insisted. "Joel, if you'll concentrate with the magnifying glass, you'll see that it's her. Look for Rose Redding, not Rose Red. Tomorrow, I'm going to have this blown up, and you'll be able to see her quite well. She and Melford are in this together. Rose would have known that Westbrook stole your notes, since he made no secret of having them. Somehow she managed to get a copy of the documents, but still did not have enough information to find the site without you. Therefore, she followed you to North Carolina."

"Now, my dear Watson," he said, "your story falls apart. Rose did not follow me. I called her."

"I've thought about that, too," Adria said. "Why shouldn't you have called her? She kept in touch with you, always reminding you that she was your friend, that she wanted to be included on any excavations you knew about or were involved with. Isn't it ironic that once her job was finished she bought a cocktail lounge and stayed at the beach, close to your bungalow? She even agreed to take your messages for you."

Joel raked his hand through his hair. "Adria, you're letting your imagination run wild."

"If I can prove this is Rose in the photograph, will you believe me?" she asked. She ran her fingers up his chest, pushing them through the swirls of hair.

"It would give your story more credence." He took the photograph and magnifying glass from her and laid them on the night stand. "Now, my lovely sleuth, you have awakened me from a deep sleep. What do you propose to do with me?"

"Here." She squirmed farther down on the bed. "Let me show you."

THE NEXT DAY JOEL and Adria left early. He began diving immediately on arriving at the *Black Beauty;* Adria went into her darkroom and worked on blowing up the photograph. She didn't mention it again to Joel until later that night after they had eaten dinner and he was working in the study.

She closed the door and walked to the desk where Joel sat. "Here it is," she said. "There's absolutely no doubt it's Rose."

Joel leaned back in the chair, took the picture from her and stared at it. "I wouldn't have believed it," he said. "I thought Rose was my friend."

"Evidently Melford thinks she's his friend, also."

Joel dropped the photograph into his jacket pocket, pushed away from his desk and walked out of the room. "I'm going to have a talk with her. Maybe she can explain what's going on."

As they walked through the living room, Solly was ensconced in one of the plush overstuffed platform rockers.

"Have you seen Rose?" Joel asked.

Never looking up, the old man said, "She's in the workroom, double-checking the inventory. Said she'd be working late tonight, so not to get worried if we didn't see her for several hours."

Adria and Joel went out the kitchen door to the building in the back. When they arrived, the door was ajar and light filtered through the crack. Joel pushed, and it creaked on its hinges; he heard a moan and a thumping noise. Stepping inside, they found the guard, bound and gagged, lying on the floor.

Joel rushed to the man and knelt down. "Here," he said, and loosened the gag.

"Ms. Redding," the man said, running his tongue around his bruised lips. "A couple of hours ago, she called me into the room to help her move one of the artifacts, and I was hit on the head from behind."

"Adria," Joel instructed, "get Solly out here. Then call the medics and the police."

Between Solly and Joel, they moved the guard to a bedroom to wait for the medics. Consuelo stayed with him, putting compresses on his wound, while Joel and Solly returned to the workroom.

"The most important archaeological and numismatic finds have been stolen," Adria announced when they walked in. "She knew what she was doing, Joel."

"She was a good cataloger," he said, "but I'm not so sure she knew the value of the artifacts. Someone a little more knowledgeable had to have been helping her."

"Melford," Adria said.

"Probably."

While they waited for the police, Joel paced the floor, every so often moving through the tables and touching the artifacts that remained. Then he kicked something and it slid across the room. He walked over, knelt down and picked it up.

Thinking it was an artifact, Adria moved closer and gazed at his extended hand. On his palm lay Earl Melford's cigarette lighter.

"It looks like you were correct," Joel said. "Melford and Rose are in this together."

"This happened two hours ago," Adria said. "They can't be far, Joel. They've probably headed for Melford's yacht."

Joel nodded. "Solly, wait here for the police and medics. Tell them what we think, and let them know we're going to find Melford's yacht."

"Now wait a minute," Solly said. "I don't think Adria ought to be—"

"I'm going, Uncle Solly," she said and ran out of the room behind Joel before Solly had time to say more. "I'll be careful," she called back over her shoulder.

Joel drove directly to the marina, parking his car close to Rose's rental car. "You stay here," he ordered, "so you can direct the police when they arrive. I'm going to slip aboard and find out what's going on."

Although Adria wanted to go, she remembered the incident beneath the sea when she had refused to listen to reason. This time she would think before she reacted. She nodded and watched as he slipped into the marina.

As he closed the gate, she called, "Joel."

He stopped and looked back. She ran to where he stood and leaned over to kiss him.

"Now," she said, "you can go."

JOEL QUIETLY OPENED THE DOOR to find Melford sitting behind his desk, writing.

"Good evening, Captain."

Startled, Melford dropped his pen and stared open-mouthed at his visitor.

"Sorry to slip in unannounced," Joel continued, moving into the room and closing the door, "but I figured that was the best way to get my property back."

Melford's brow furrowed. "I don't know what you're talking about."

"The artifacts from the *Virginia,*" Joel said.

"Are you accusing me of having them?" Melford asked, then shook his head. "You're crazy."

Joel reached into his pocket and took out the enlarged photograph Adria had given him earlier. Long strides carried him quickly across the room, and he laid it on the desk in front of Melford. "Do you deny that you know Rose?"

Melford stared at the picture for a long time before he sighed. "No."

"Are you working with her and Westbrook?"

Again Melford shook his head. "Absolutely not." He picked up his cigarettes and thumped one out with shaking fingers. Then he opened drawer after drawer, digging through them, searching for something.

Joel reached into his pocket the second time and held up the lighter. "Looking for this?"

The cigarette fell out of Melford's slack mouth. "Where did you get it?"

"At my place," Joel answered, then briefly described what had happened.

"Look," Melford said, "I had nothing to do with the theft of your property. Rose and I have been having an affair for the past two years, but I am not working with Westbrook, and I didn't steal any of your artifacts."

"What were you doing at the *Virginia* site?"

Nervously, Melford reached up and massaged the back of his neck. "Baxter Langston hired me to sabotage your excavation, but that was thwarted when the police decided to take you into custody."

"Hello, LeMaster."

Joel spun around to see Westbrook standing in the door, a pistol in his hand. Behind him was Rose who also held a pistol. The side door had opened so quietly that neither Joel nor Melford had been aware they had visitors.

"Move over to stand beside Melford," Westbrook ordered.

"Rose," Melford said, his puzzled glance going full circle from Joel, to Westbrook and to Rose, "what's the meaning of this?"

Westbrook drew her into the room and put his arm around her. "Rose is my sweetheart, Melford, and has been since she attended Florida Coast University and was my student."

Rose smiled. "My apologies to both of you, but a girl must do what a girl must do. Joel, don't you think Woody and I set this up beautifully, using Earl's lighter as bait?"

"Rose," Melford cried and lunged forward, only to be stopped by Joel, "you can't mean this?"

"Oh, yes, darling," she drawled, "I mean it."

"You—you used me?"

"And how," Rose gloated. "We needed a patsy, and you were just right for the job."

Rose moved to a table on the far side of the room and set a large leather bag down. Opening it, she extracted two of the artifacts from the *Virginia*. "I sure hate to leave these beauties behind, Woody," she said, "but we're taking so much for ourselves, we can sacrifice this, and we must." She turned to Melford. "Mel, darling, I hate to tell you this, but you're going to be blamed for the theft. Quite possibly Langston, too, since you work for him. And people are likely to believe he had a part in this." She turned to Woody. "You did say he made threats to Joel, the night he visited their camp?"

Not waiting for Westbrook to answer, Joel asked, "What are you going to do with us?"

"Set it up so that it looks like you and Melford had a confrontation and shot each other," Westbrook replied.

WHEN ADRIA SAW MELFORD'S yacht moving, she knew the time had come to disregard Joel's instructions to wait for the police. Without a second thought for herself, knowing only that the man she loved could be in danger, she stripped off her shoes and socks and dove into the water, swimming to the yacht. Slipping on board, she cautiously made her way to the salon where she overheard Rose and Westbrook talking. She eased closer so she could see into the room through the crack in the door that stood ajar and could make out what they were saying.

"Why not shoot us and get it over with?" Joel asked.

"We want to be closer to our ship," Westbrook answered, "and we need for one of you to write a confessional, of sorts, to give some authenticity to the theft and the shooting. Rose, keep your gun aimed on them, and if either moves an inch, shoot him."

Adria backed up, in order to find a weapon, when her hand brushed against the fire extinguisher. Grasping it securely in one hand, she rushed into the room and sprayed extinguishing foam on Rose. Joel took advantage of the diversion by overpowering Westbrook and knocking him out. Rose, wiping the foam from her face, ran from the room, Melford behind her.

"Oh, no you don't," he shouted.

"Joel," Adria cried and rushed to him, "are you hurt?"

He took her into his arms and held her tightly. "I'm fine."

Outside they heard a male voice coming through a loudspeaker. "This is the Shore Patrol. Your ship is surrounded, and we are boarding. Everyone come to the upper deck with your hands raised."

Joel smiled down into Adria's face. "I'm very fine."

ADRIA, WEARING HER ROBE over her nightgown, her hair hanging loose, stood in Joel's embrace on the balcony of her bedroom at the villa. A gentle summer breeze caressed them as they gazed at the moon, a large silver orb in a sky of midnight blue.

"It doesn't seem possible that it's all over," Adria said.

"Only one phase, darling. Tonight a new one is beginning," Joel murmured, his lips nipping the top of her ear. He gently turned her around so that he could look at her. "Adria, I love you and want you to marry me."

"Yes," she whispered, and she melted into his embrace, lifting her face for his kisses.

Later, much later, he led her into the bedroom and switched on the lamp, soft light diffusing the darkness. He slipped his hand into his pocket and pulled out a ring. "I could have bought you another one, and I will later. But I wanted to use this one to formalize our engagement," he said, and held up the English ring he had shown her the first time they had met.

"Oh, Joel," she murmured and held out her left hand.

When he slipped the ring onto her ring finger, he looked into her eyes and said, "My love is forever, my darling."

As she had done the first time, Adria experienced a breathless moment of silent wonder; a poignant moment of gentleness. This time she was not disappointed when she looked into Joel's eyes. They were soft and gray and full of love.

"My love is forever," she repeated.

Joel swept her into his arms, and as he carried her to the bed, she gazed at the beard-stubbled cheeks and the unruly black curls that teased the collar of his shirt. She knew what she would title the photograph of him that she would enter into competition: *Silver Sea Buccaneer.*

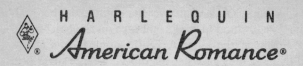

HARLEQUIN
American Romance®

THE ROMANCE THAT STARTED IT ALL!

For Diane Bauer and Nick Granatelli, the walk down the aisle was a rocky road....

Don't miss the romantic prequel to WITH THIS RING—

I THEE WED
BY ANNE McALLISTER

Harlequin American Romance #387

Let Anne McAllister take you to Cambridge, Massachusetts, to the night when an innocent blind date brought a reluctant Diane Bauer and Nick Granatelli together. For Diane, a smoldering attraction like theirs had only one fate, one future—marriage. The hard part, she learned, was convincing her intended....

Watch for Anne McAllister's I THEE WED, available *now* from Harlequin American Romance.

ITW

Take 4 bestselling love stories FREE

Plus get a FREE surprise gift!

HARLEQUIN
American Romance®

RELIVE THE MEMORIES....

All the way from turn-of-the-century Ellis Island to the future of the nineties...A CENTURY OF AMERICAN ROMANCE takes you on a nostalgic journey through the twentieth century.

This May, watch for the final title of A CENTURY OF AMERICAN ROMANCE—#389 A>LOVERBOY, Judith Arnold's light-hearted look at love in 1998!

Don't miss a day of A CENTURY OF AMERICAN ROMANCE

A CENTURY OF
AMERICAN ROMANCE
1990s

The women...the men...the passions...the memories...

If you missed title #381 HONORBOUND (1970's) or #385 MY ONLY ONE (1991's), and would like to order them, send your name, address, zip or postal code, along with a check or money order for $3.25 plus 75¢ postage and handling ($1.00 in Canada) *for each book ordered,* payable to Harlequin Reader Service to:

In the U.S.
3010 Walden Ave.
P.O. Box 1325
Buffalo, NY 14269-1325

In Canada
P.O. Box 609
Fort Erie, Ontario
L2A 5X3

Please specify book title(s) with your order. Canadian residents add applicable federal and provincial taxes.

CA-90

Everyone loves a spring wedding, and this April,
Harlequin cordially invites you to read the most
romantic wedding book of the year.

With This Ring

**ONE WEDDING—FOUR LOVE STORIES
FROM OUR MOST DISTINGUISHED
HARLEQUIN AUTHORS:**

BETHANY CAMPBELL
BARBARA DELINSKY
BOBBY HUTCHINSON
ANN McALLISTER

*The church is booked, the reception arranged and the
invitations mailed. All Diane Bauer and Nick Granatelli
have to do is walk down the aisle. Little do they realize that
the most cherished day of their lives will spark so many
romantic notions. . . .*

Available wherever Harlequin books are sold.

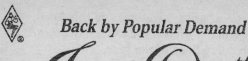